WATTERS · LEYH · BRYANT · MADRIGAL

LUMBERJANES™

HORTICULTURAL HORIZONS

Published by

BOOM! BOX™

BOOM! BOX™

LUMBERJANES Volume Eighteen, May 2021. Published by BOOM! Box, a division of Boom Entertainment, Inc. Lumberjanes is ™ & © 2021 Shannon Watters, Grace Ellis, Noelle Stevenson & Brooklyn Allen. Originally published in single magazine form as LUMBERJANES No. 69-72. ™ & © 2019-2020 Shannon Watters, Grace Ellis, Noelle Stevenson & Brooklyn Allen. All rights reserved. BOOM! Box™ and the BOOM! Box logo are trademarks of Boom Entertainment, Inc., registered in various countries and categories. All characters, events, and institutions depicted herein are fictional. Any similarity between any of the names, characters, persons, events, and/or institutions in this publication to actual names, characters, and persons, whether living or dead, events, and/or institutions is unintended and purely coincidental. BOOM! Box does not read or accept unsolicited submissions of ideas, stories, or artwork.

BOOM! Studios, 5670 Wilshire Boulevard, Suite 400, Los Angeles, CA 90036-5679. Printed in China. First Printing.

ISBN: 978-1-68415-698-6, eISBN: 978-1-64668-242-3

THIS LUMBERJANES FIELD MANUAL BELONGS TO:

NAME:_____

TROOP:_____

DATE INVESTED:_____

FIELD MANUAL TABLE OF CONTENTS

LUMBERJANES FIELD MANUAL

For the Advanced Program

Tenth Edition • June 1985

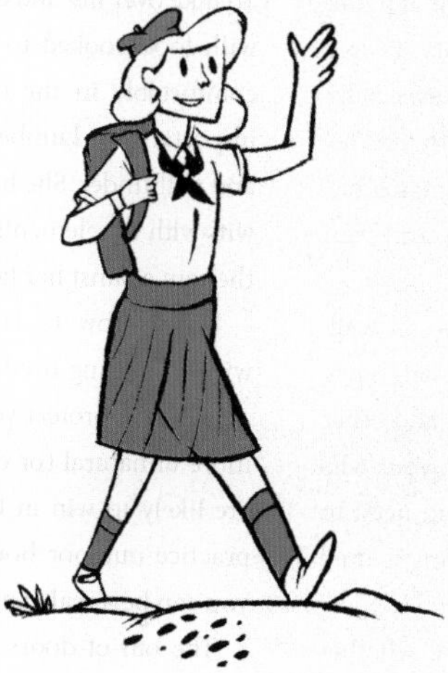

Prepared for the

Miss Qiunzella Thiskwin Penniquiqul Thistle Crumpet's

CAMP FOR [redacted] HARDCORE LADY-TYPES

"Friendship to the Max!"

A MESSAGE FROM THE LUMBERJANES HIGH COUNCIL

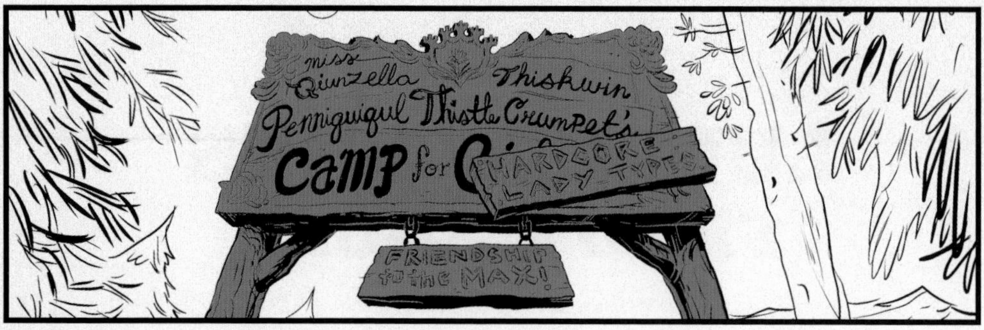
Miss Quinzella Thiskwin Penniquiqul Thistle Crumpet's
Camp for
HARDCORE LADY TYPES
FRIENDSHIP to the MAX!

Well begun is half done. This is something parents and teachers said to us when we were small and protesting cleaning up our room, or practicing the piano, or doing our homework. There are always a number of things to do, and jobs we are responsible for, and it can sometimes be difficult to just begin. There is so much more that needs doing than just getting moving, and when you're standing at the starting line with the list of tasks stretched out in front of you, the distance feels long, and the work feels arduous. You might think of it like a race, and there is such a long way to go before you reach your goal. But it's easy to forget that when you are running a race, and you're standing at the starting line, waiting for the signal to finally take off and run, much of the hardest work is already behind you. You still need to run that distance, whether it's two miles or twenty-six, and the path may not always be smooth, but so much of the training and conditioning is actually already finished, at least for now. It has gotten you to the point that you were ready to actually begin, and to run to the best of your ability.

There is so much that we learn by doing, and by doing badly. And this is also a form of preparation. Think of a baby, taking their first toddles. They're bound to fall, but in falling, they improve and learn. It can be discouraging, but sometimes it's best to push through the difficult parts, taking breaks to rest and recover when needed. There will always be times when the words won't flow, or you struggle to run just a few blocks, or cast on a few stitches, or draw a straight line. But you can learn and be ready to do better next time. Like trudging up a hill before you can go sledding down, the work you put in is often proportionate to the fun you get out.

THE LUMBERJANES PLEDGE

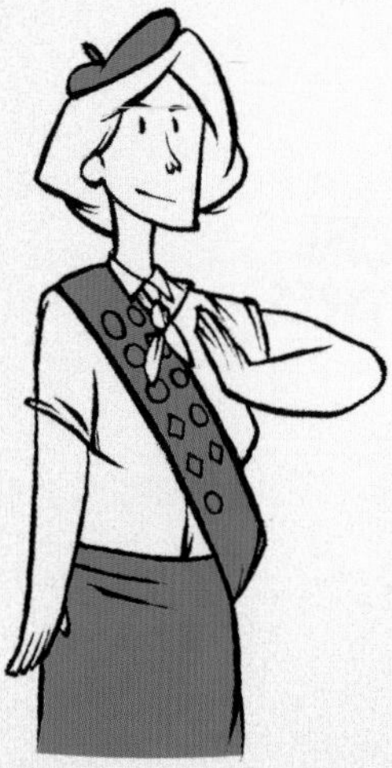

I solemnly swear to do my best
Every day, and in all that I do,
To be brave and strong,
To be truthful and compassionate,
To be interesting and interested,
To pay attention and question
The world around me,
To think of others first,
To always help and protect my friends,
[redacted]
And to make the world a better place
For Lumberjane scouts
And for everyone else.

THEN THERE'S A LINE ABOUT GOD, OR WHATEVER

HORTICULTURAL HORIZONS

Written by
Shannon Watters & Kat Leyh

Illustrated by
Kanesha C. Bryant & Julia Madrigal

Colors by
Maarta Laiho

Letters by
Aubrey Aiese

Cover by
Kat Leyh

Series Designer
Grace Park

Collection Designer
Chelsea Roberts

Editor
Sophie Philips-Roberts

Executive Editor
Jeanine Schaefer

*Special thanks to **Kelsey Pate** for giving the Lumberjanes their name.*

Created by
Shannon Watters, Grace Ellis, Noelle Stevenson & Brooklyn Allen

LUMBERJANES FIELD MANUAL

CHAPTER SIXTY-NINE

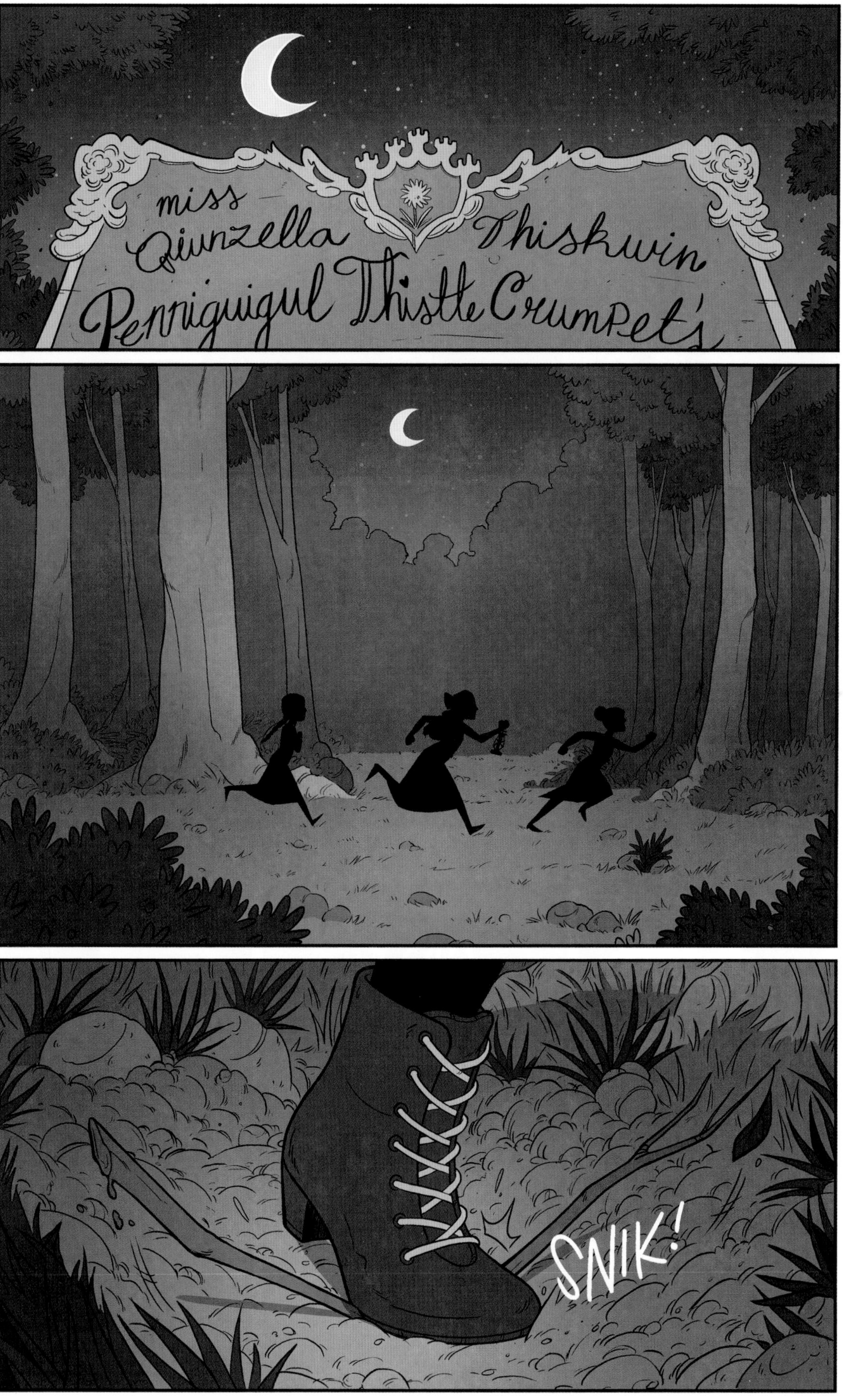
miss Qiunzella Thiskwin
Penniguigul Thistle Crumpet's
SNIK!

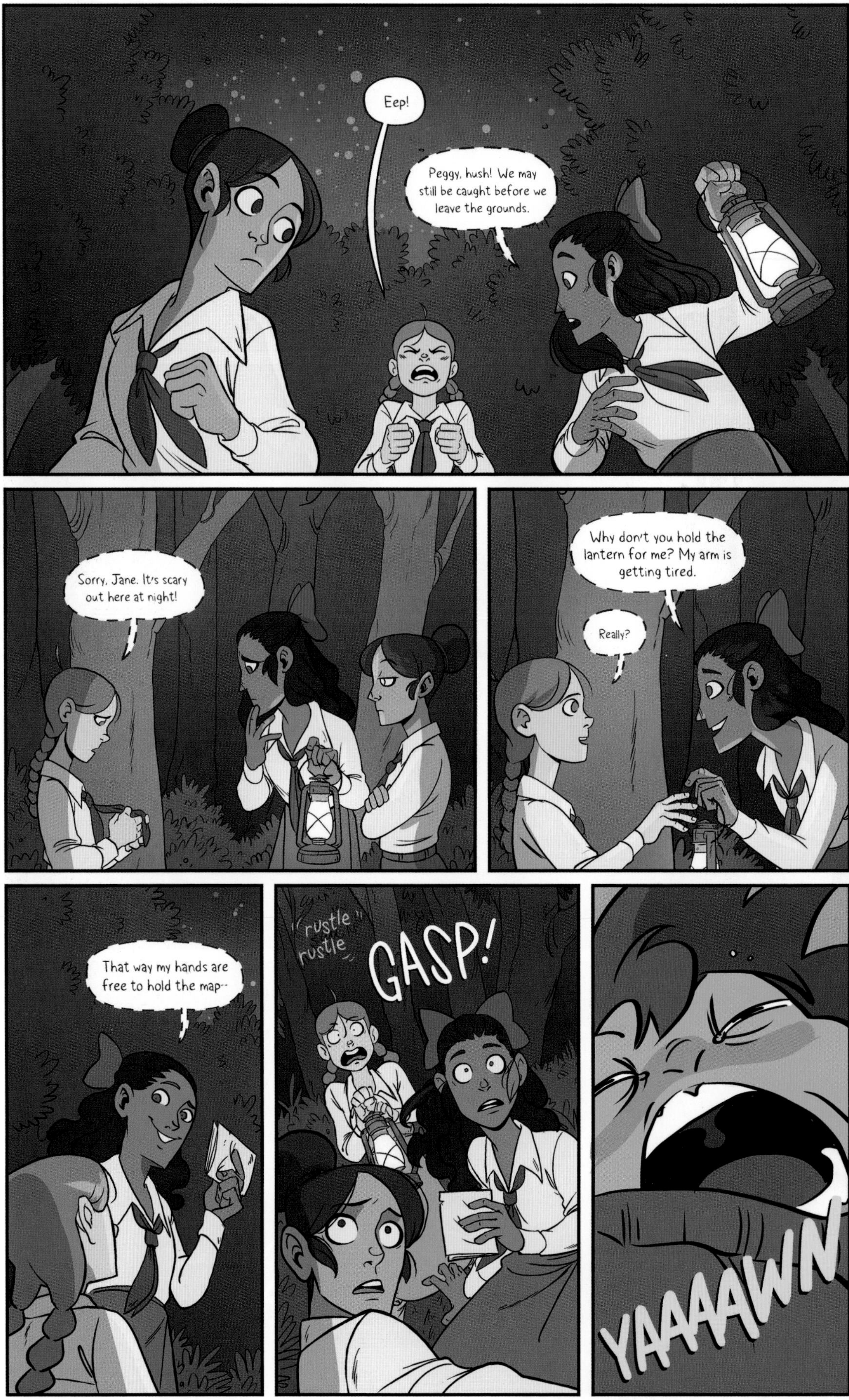
Eep!
Peggy, hush! We may still be caught before we leave the grounds.
Sorry, Jane. It's scary out here at night!
Why don't you hold the lantern for me? My arm is getting tired.
Really?
That way my hands are free to hold the map--
rustle rustle
GASP!
YAAAAWN

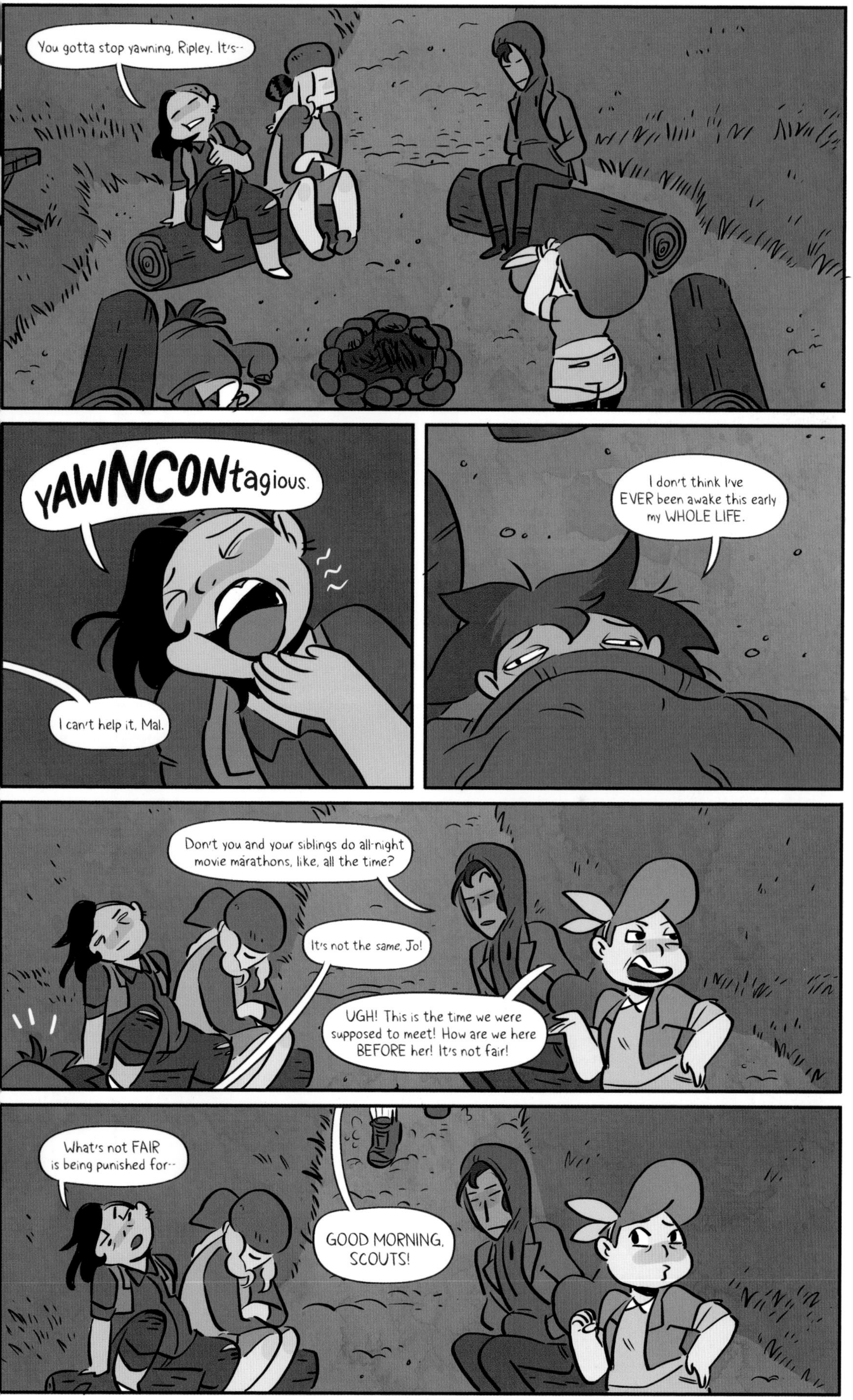

You gotta stop yawning, Ripley. It's--
YAWNCONtagious.
I can't help it, Mal.
I don't think I've EVER been awake this early my WHOLE LIFE.
Don't you and your siblings do all-night movie marathons, like, all the time?
It's not the same, Jo!
UGH! This is the time we were supposed to meet! How are we here BEFORE her! It's not fair!
What's not FAIR is being punished for--
GOOD MORNING, SCOUTS!

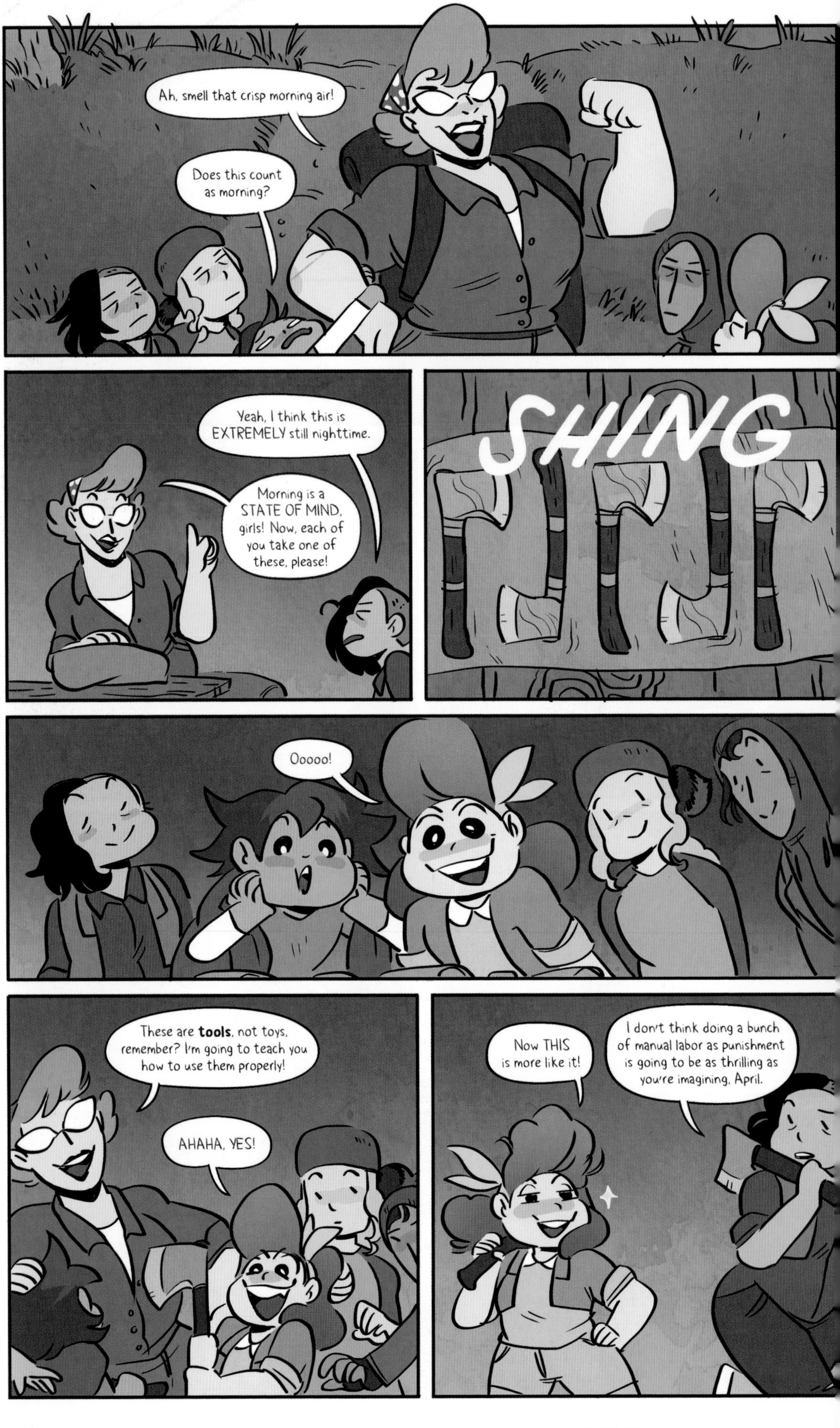
Ah, smell that crisp morning air!
Does this count as morning?
Yeah, I think this is EXTREMELY still nighttime.
Morning is a STATE OF MIND, girls! Now, each of you take one of these, please!
SHING
Ooooo!
These are **tools**, not toys, remember? I'm going to teach you how to use them properly!
AHAHA, YES!
Now THIS is more like it!
I don't think doing a bunch of manual labor as punishment is going to be as thrilling as you're imagining, April.

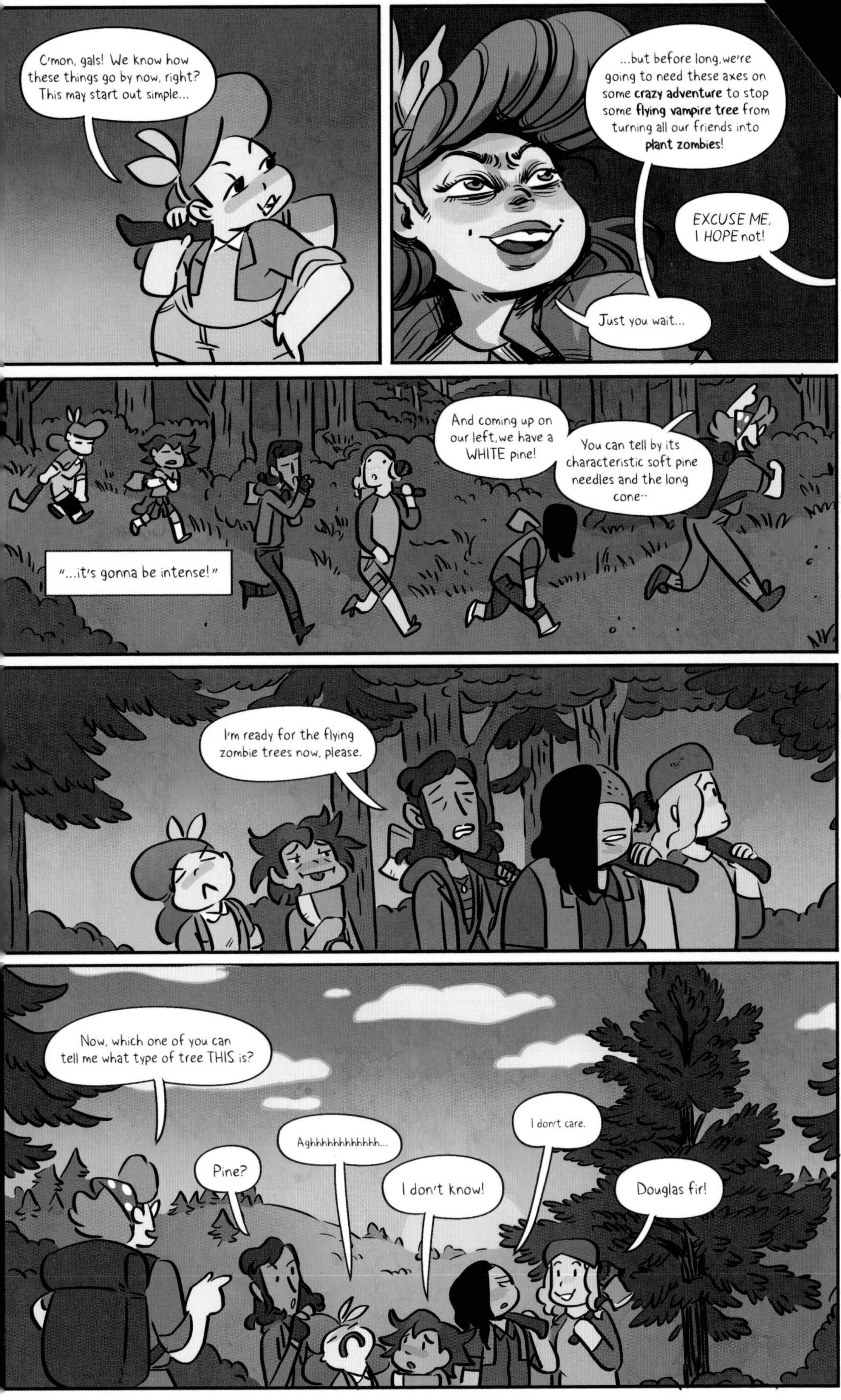
C'mon, gals! We know how these things go by now, right? This may start out simple...
...but before long, we're going to need these axes on some **crazy adventure** to stop some **flying vampire tree** from turning all our friends into **plant zombies**!
EXCUSE ME, I HOPE not!
Just you wait...
And coming up on our left, we have a WHITE pine!
You can tell by its characteristic soft pine needles and the long cone--
"...it's gonna be intense!"
I'm ready for the flying zombie trees now, please.
Now, which one of you can tell me what type of tree THIS is?
Pine?
Aghhhhhhhhhhhh...
I don't know!
I don't care.
Douglas fir!

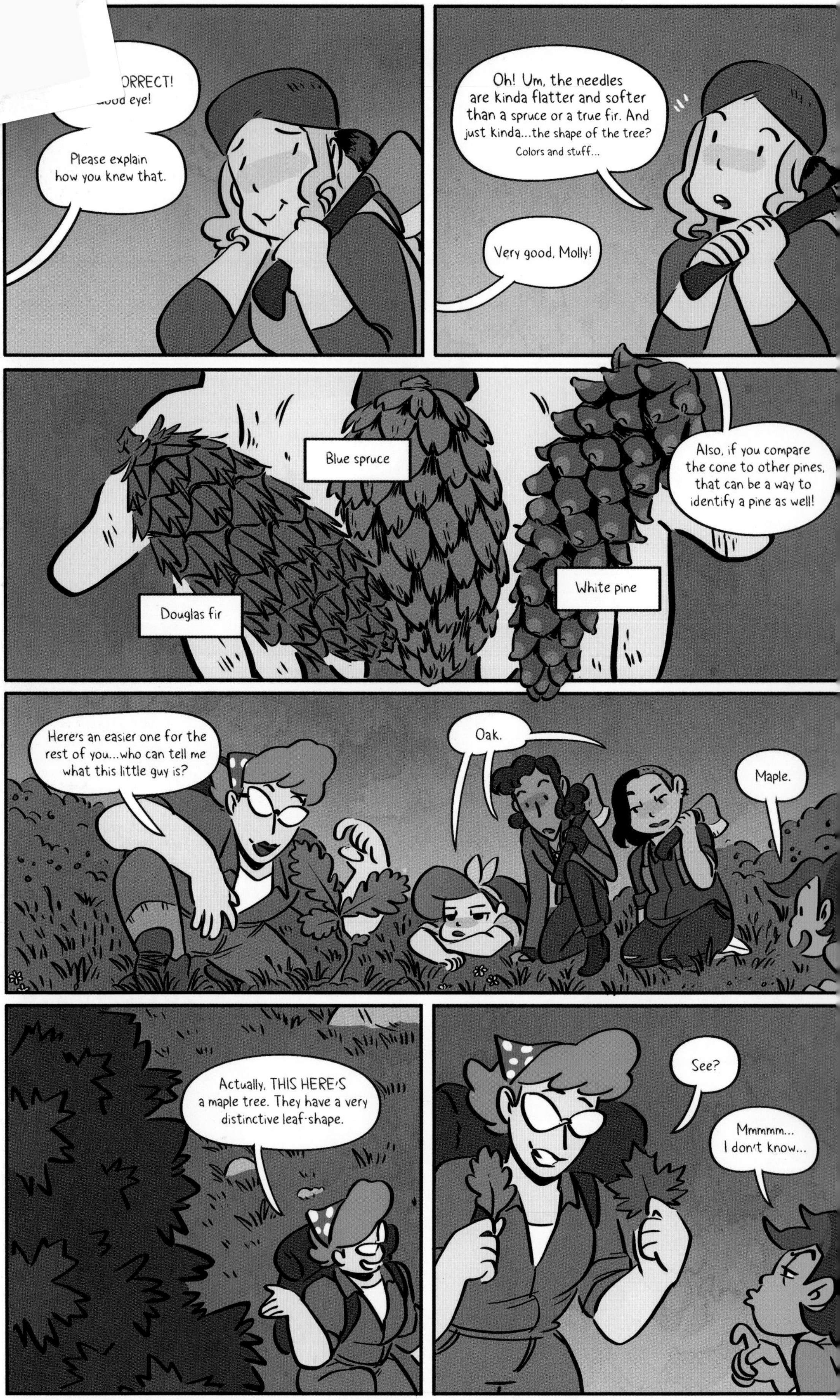
ORRECT!
good eye!
Please explain how you knew that.
Oh! Um, the needles are kinda flatter and softer than a spruce or a true fir. And just kinda...the shape of the tree?
Colors and stuff...
Very good, Molly!
Blue spruce
Douglas fir
White pine
Also, if you compare the cone to other pines, that can be a way to identify a pine as well!
Here's an easier one for the rest of you...who can tell me what this little guy is?
Oak.
Maple.
Actually, THIS HERE'S a maple tree. They have a very distinctive leaf-shape.
See?
Mmmmm... I don't know...

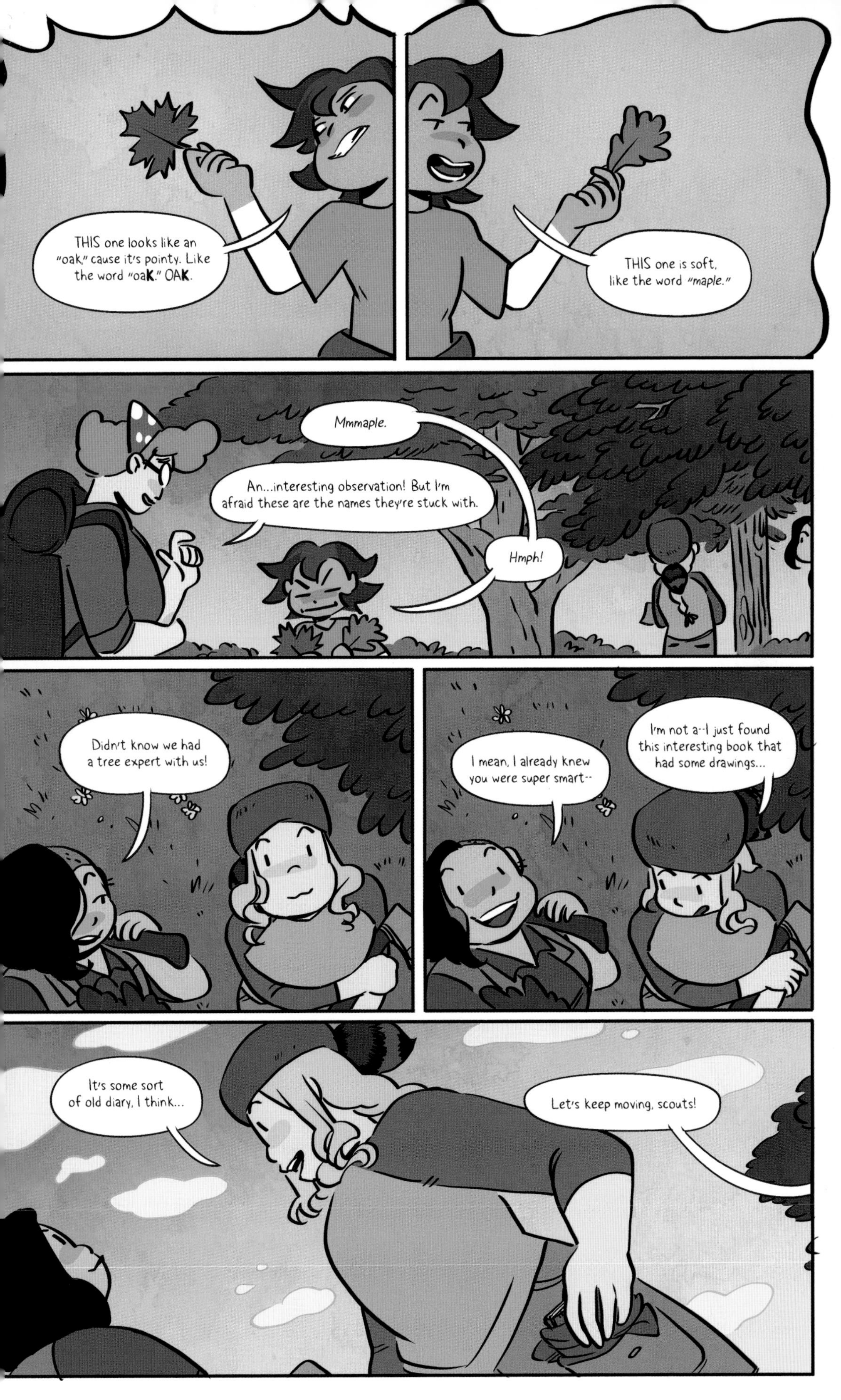
THIS one looks like an "oak," cause it's pointy. Like the word "oaK." OAK.
THIS one is soft, like the word "maple."
Mmmaple.
An...interesting observation! But I'm afraid these are the names they're stuck with.
Hmph!
Didn't know we had a tree expert with us!
I mean, I already knew you were super smart--
I'm not a--I just found this interesting book that had some drawings...
It's some sort of old diary, I think...
Let's keep moving, scouts!

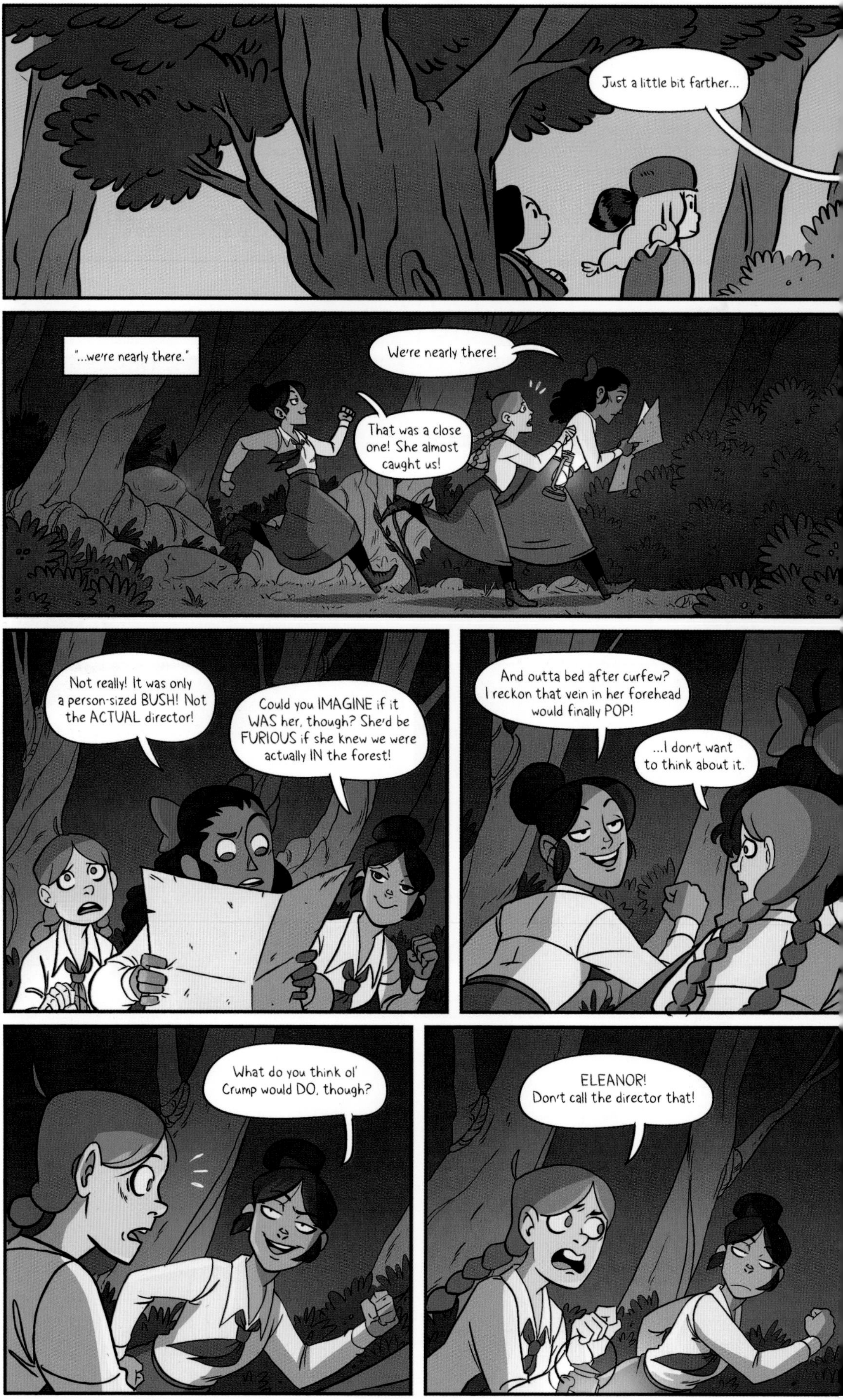
Just a little bit farther...
"...we're nearly there."
We're nearly there!
That was a close one! She almost caught us!
Not really! It was only a person-sized BUSH! Not the ACTUAL director!
Could you IMAGINE if it WAS her, though? She'd be FURIOUS if she knew we were actually IN the forest!
And outta bed after curfew? I reckon that vein in her forehead would finally POP!
...I don't want to think about it.
What do you think ol' Crump would DO, though?
ELEANOR! Don't call the director that!

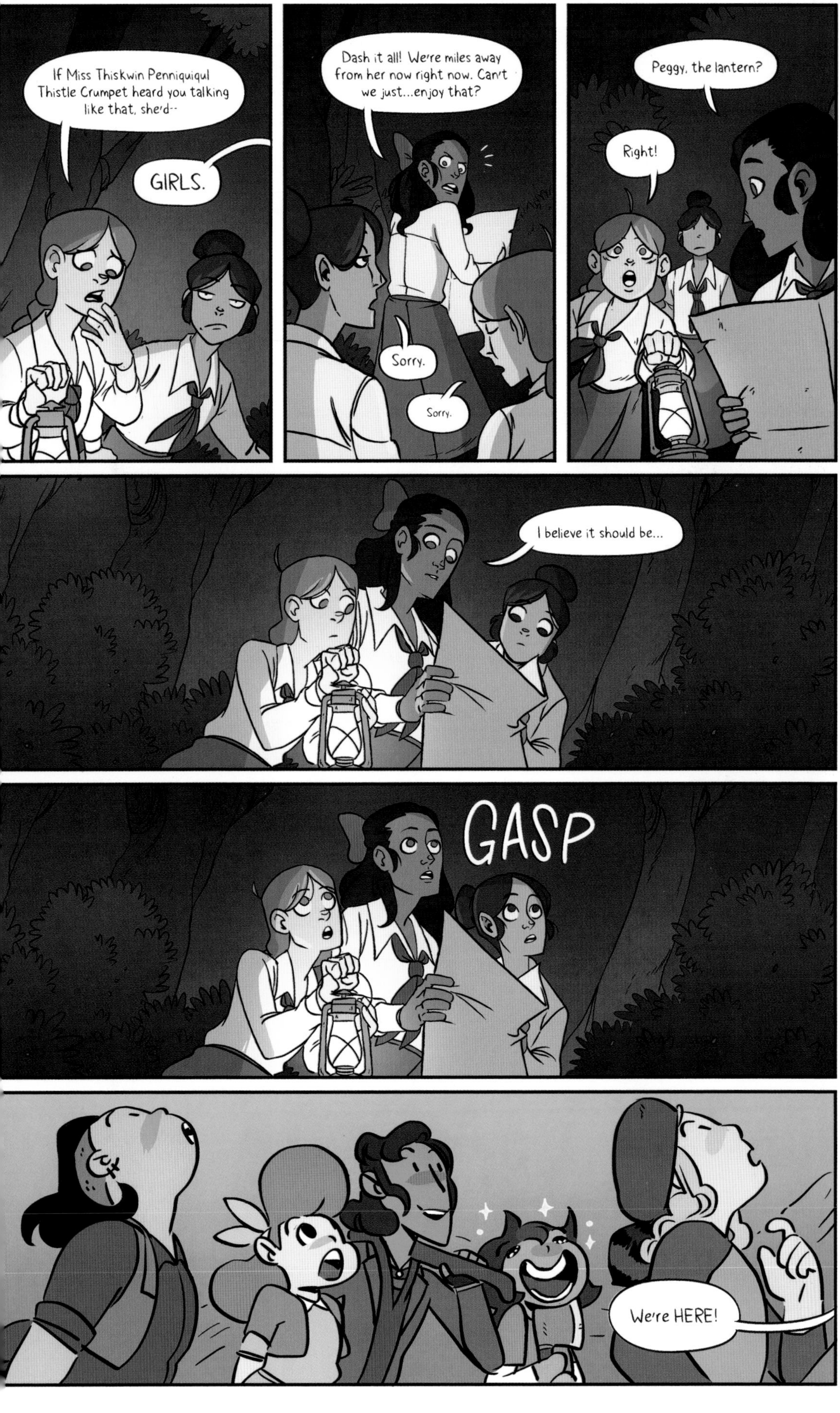
If Miss Thiskwin Penniquiqul Thistle Crumpet heard you talking like that, she'd--
GIRLS.
Dash it all! We're miles away from her now right now. Can't we just...enjoy that?
Sorry.
Sorry.
Peggy, the lantern?
Right!
I believe it should be...
GASP
We're HERE!

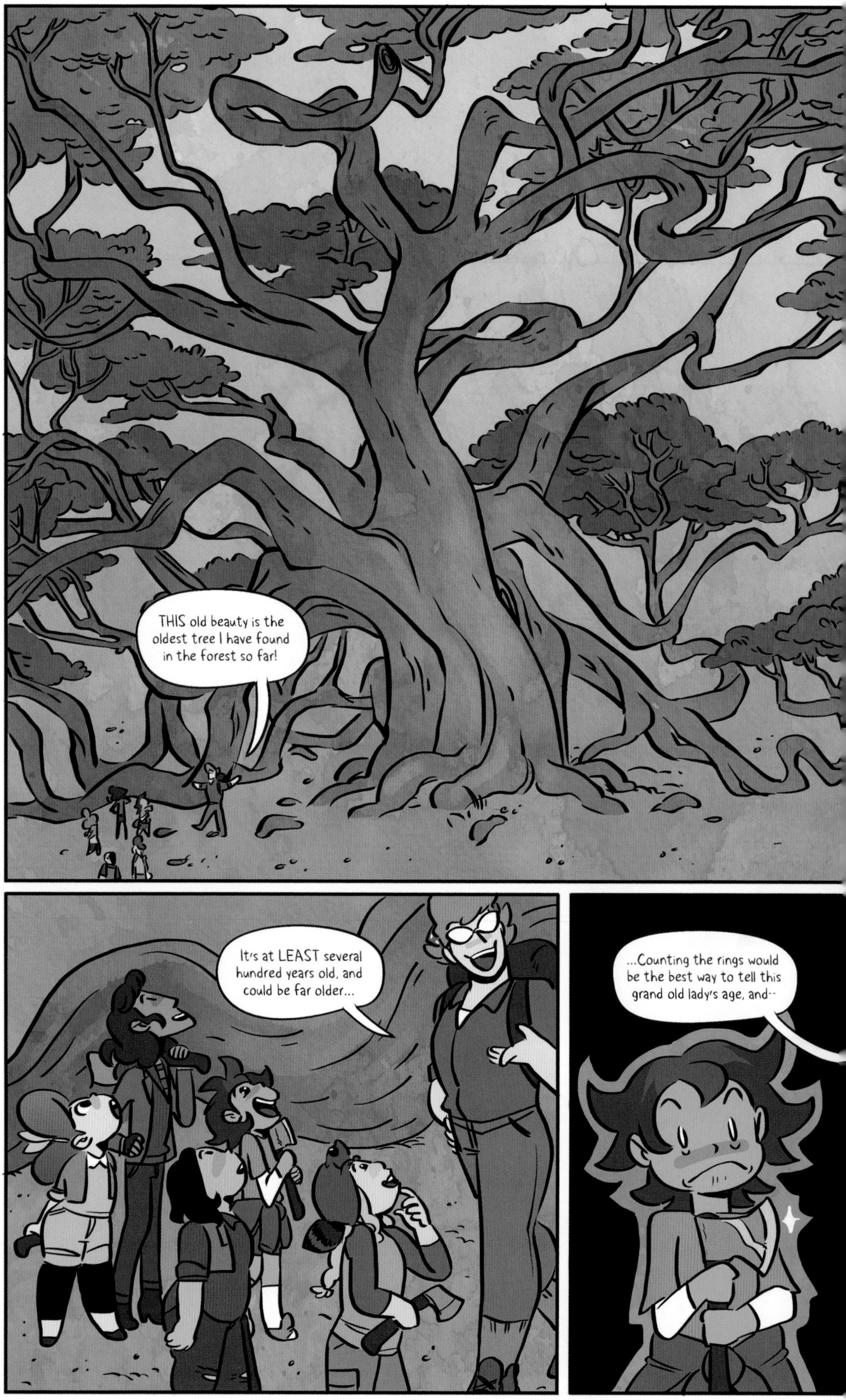
THIS old beauty is the oldest tree I have found in the forest so far!
It's at LEAST several hundred years old, and could be far older...
...Counting the rings would be the best way to tell this grand old lady's age, and--

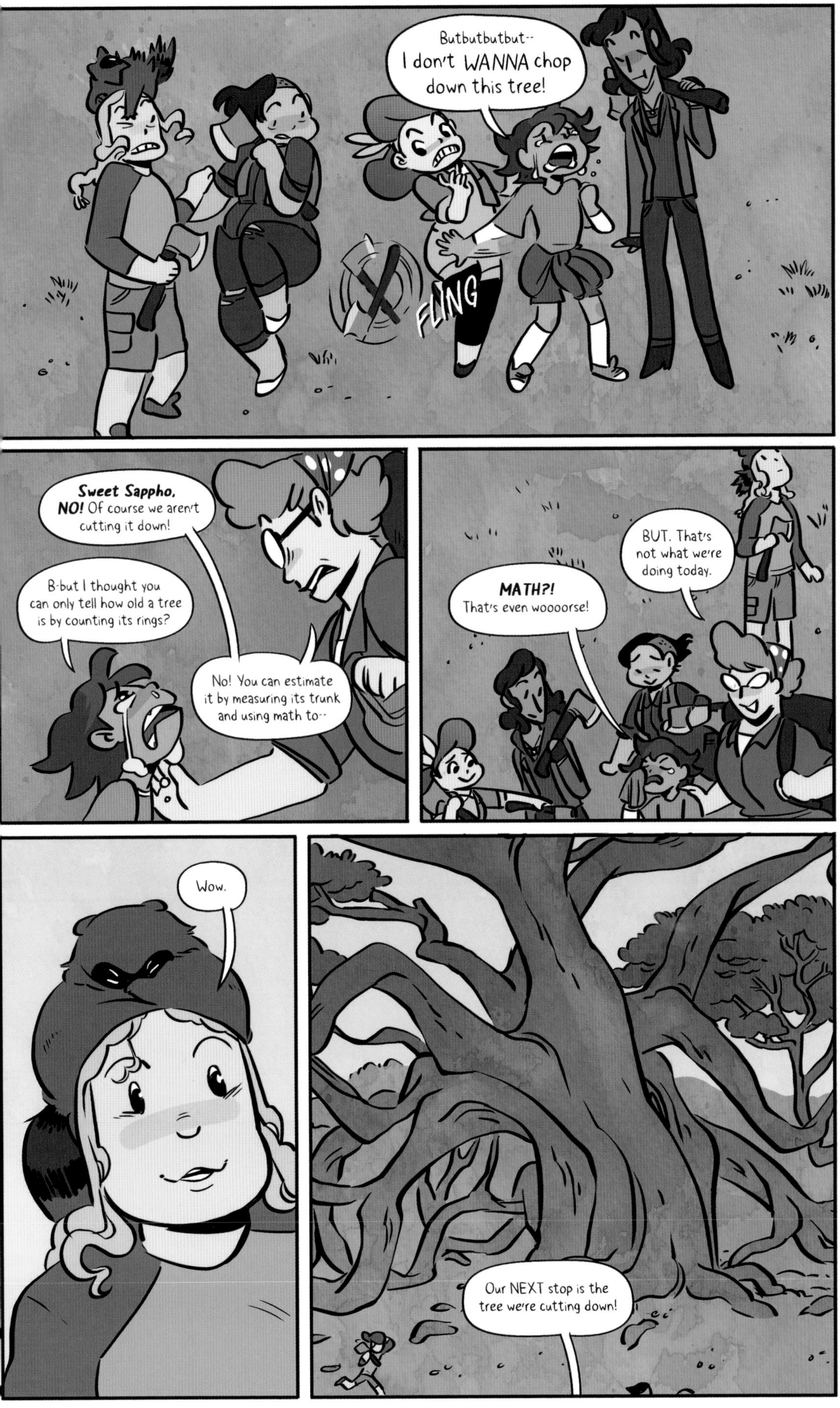
Butbutbutbut--
I don't WANNA chop down this tree!
FLING
Sweet Sappho, NO! Of course we aren't cutting it down!
B-but I thought you can only tell how old a tree is by counting its rings?
No! You can estimate it by measuring its trunk and using math to--
MATH?! That's even woooorse!
BUT. That's not what we're doing today.
Wow.
Our NEXT stop is the tree we're cutting down!

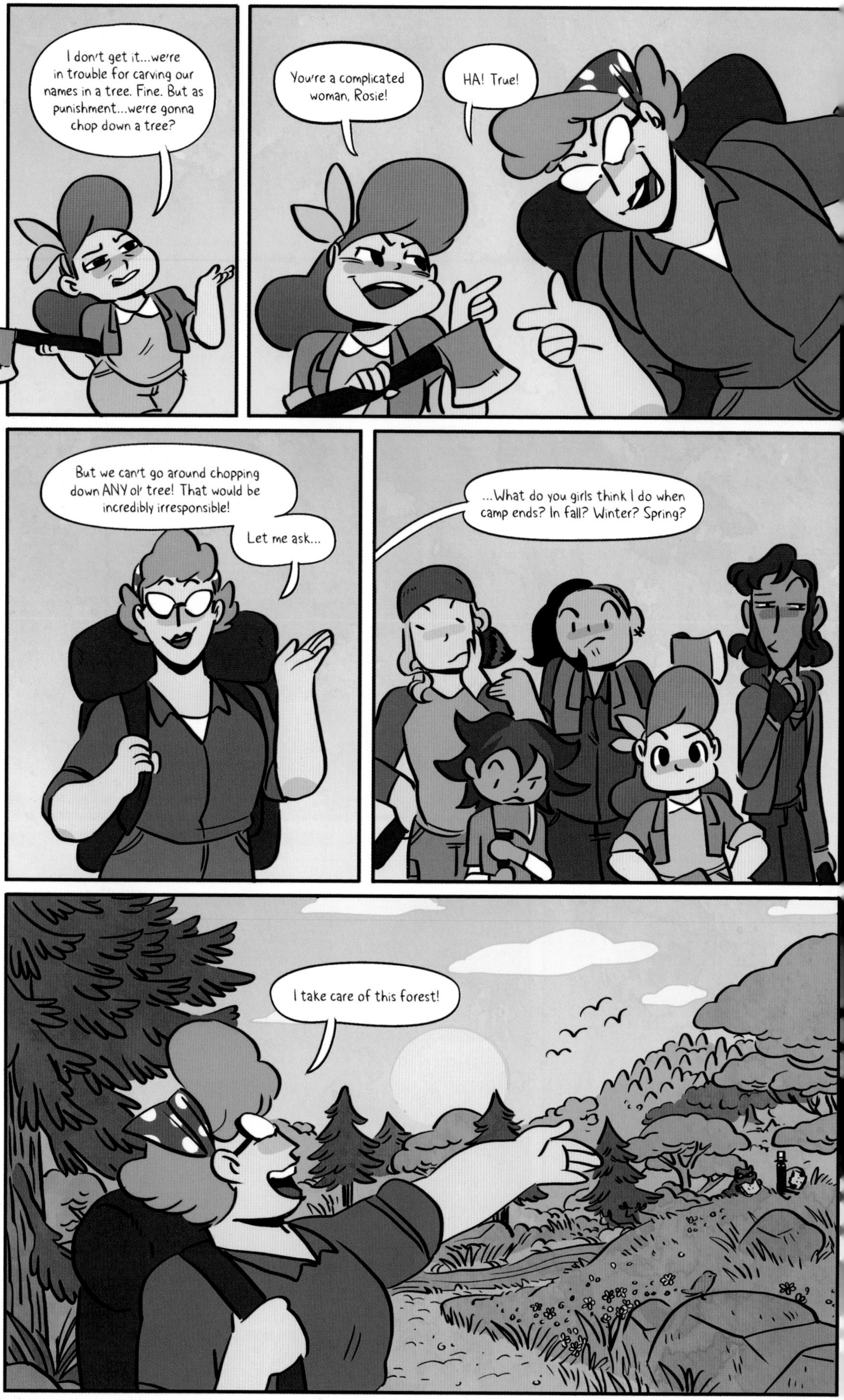
I don't get it...we're in trouble for carving our names in a tree. Fine. But as punishment...we're gonna chop down a tree?
You're a complicated woman, Rosie!
HA! True!
But we can't go around chopping down ANY ol' tree! That would be incredibly irresponsible!
Let me ask...
...What do you girls think I do when camp ends? In fall? Winter? Spring?
I take care of this forest!

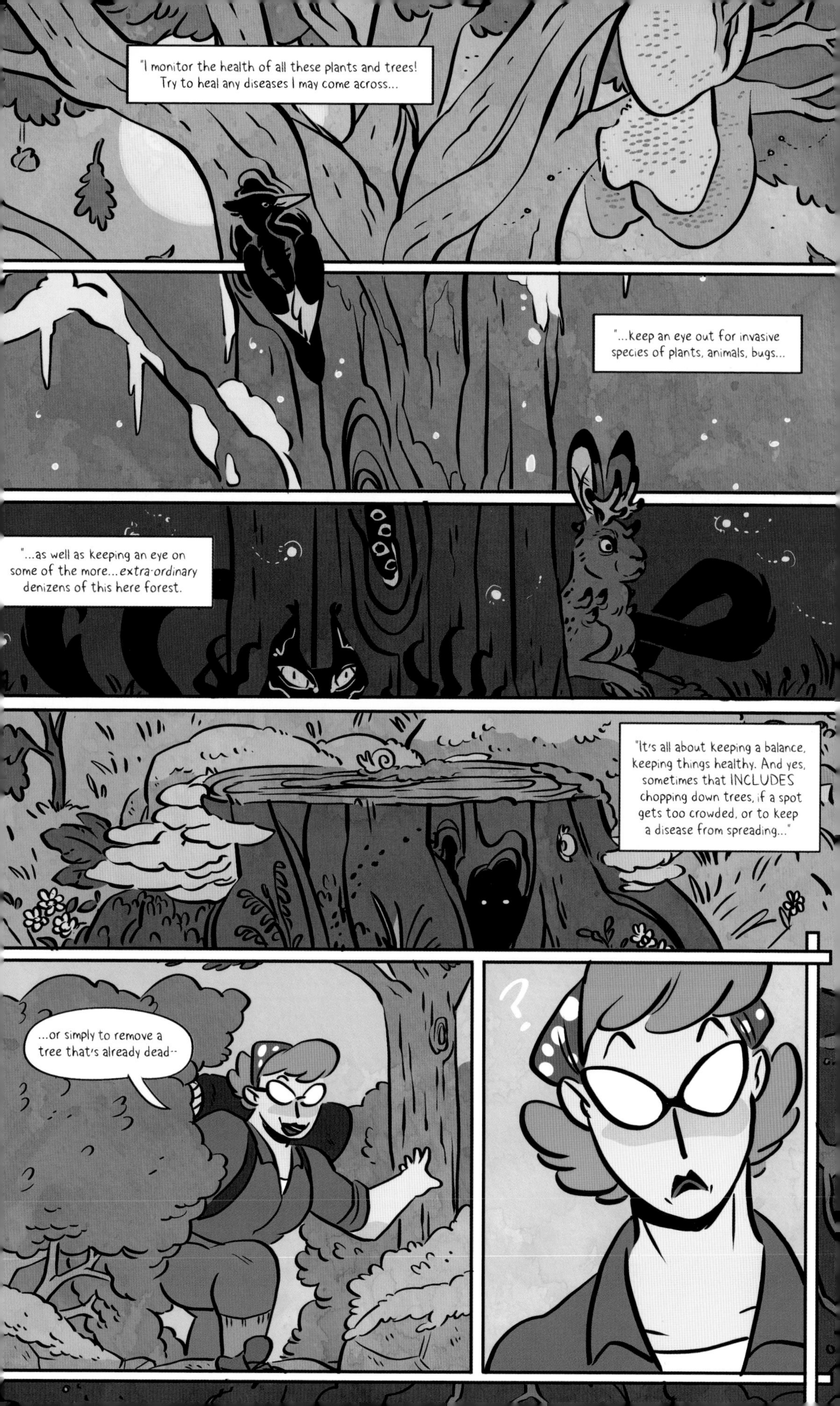
"I monitor the health of all these plants and trees! Try to heal any diseases I may come across...
"...keep an eye out for invasive species of plants, animals, bugs...
"...as well as keeping an eye on some of the more... extra-ordinary denizens of this here forest.
"It's all about keeping a balance, keeping things healthy. And yes, sometimes that INCLUDES chopping down trees, if a spot gets too crowded, or to keep a disease from spreading..."
...or simply to remove a tree that's already dead--
?

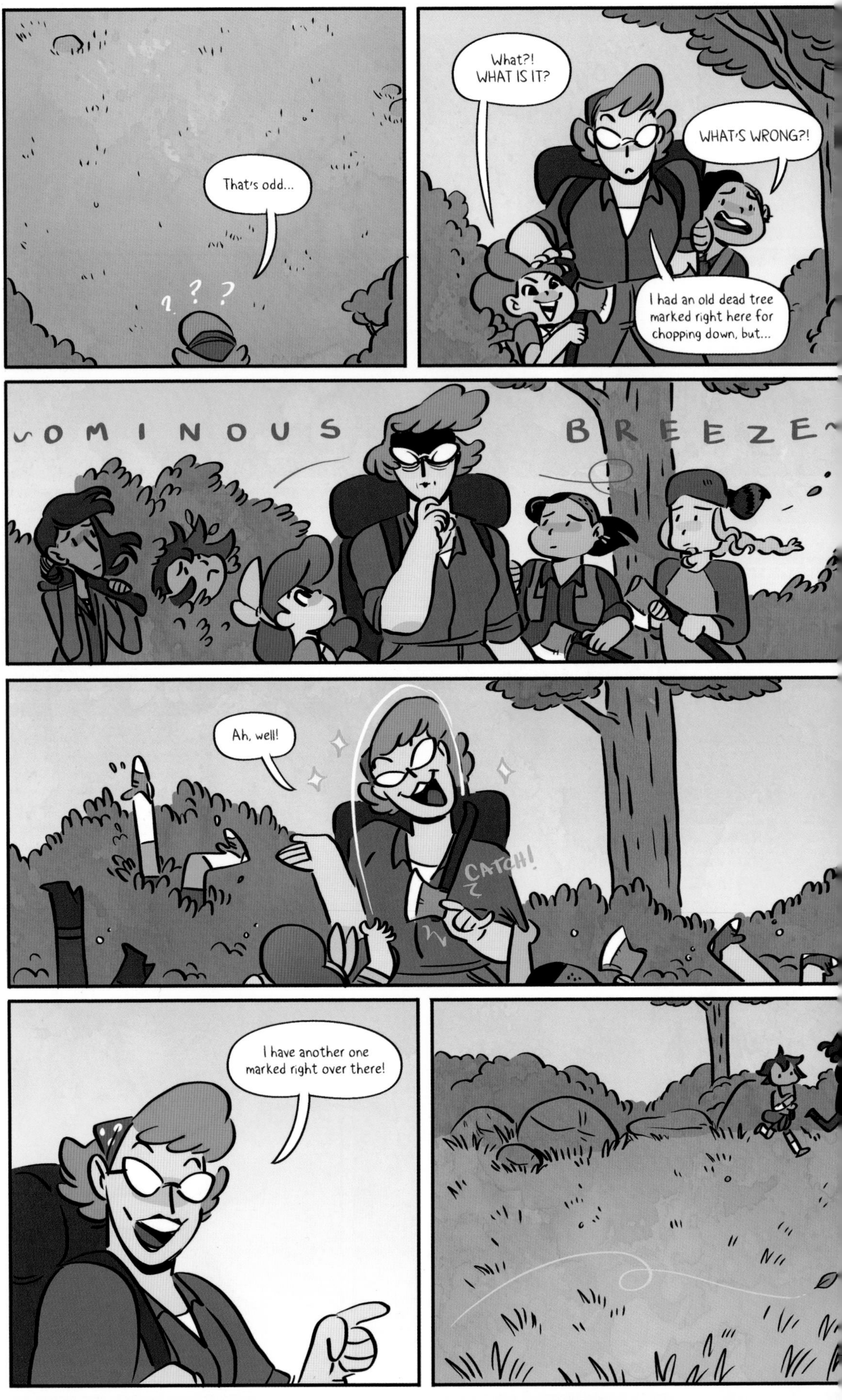

That's odd...
? ? ?
What?! WHAT IS IT?
WHAT'S WRONG?!
I had an old dead tree marked right here for chopping down, but...
OMINOUS BREEZE
Ah, well!
CATCH!
I have another one marked right over there!

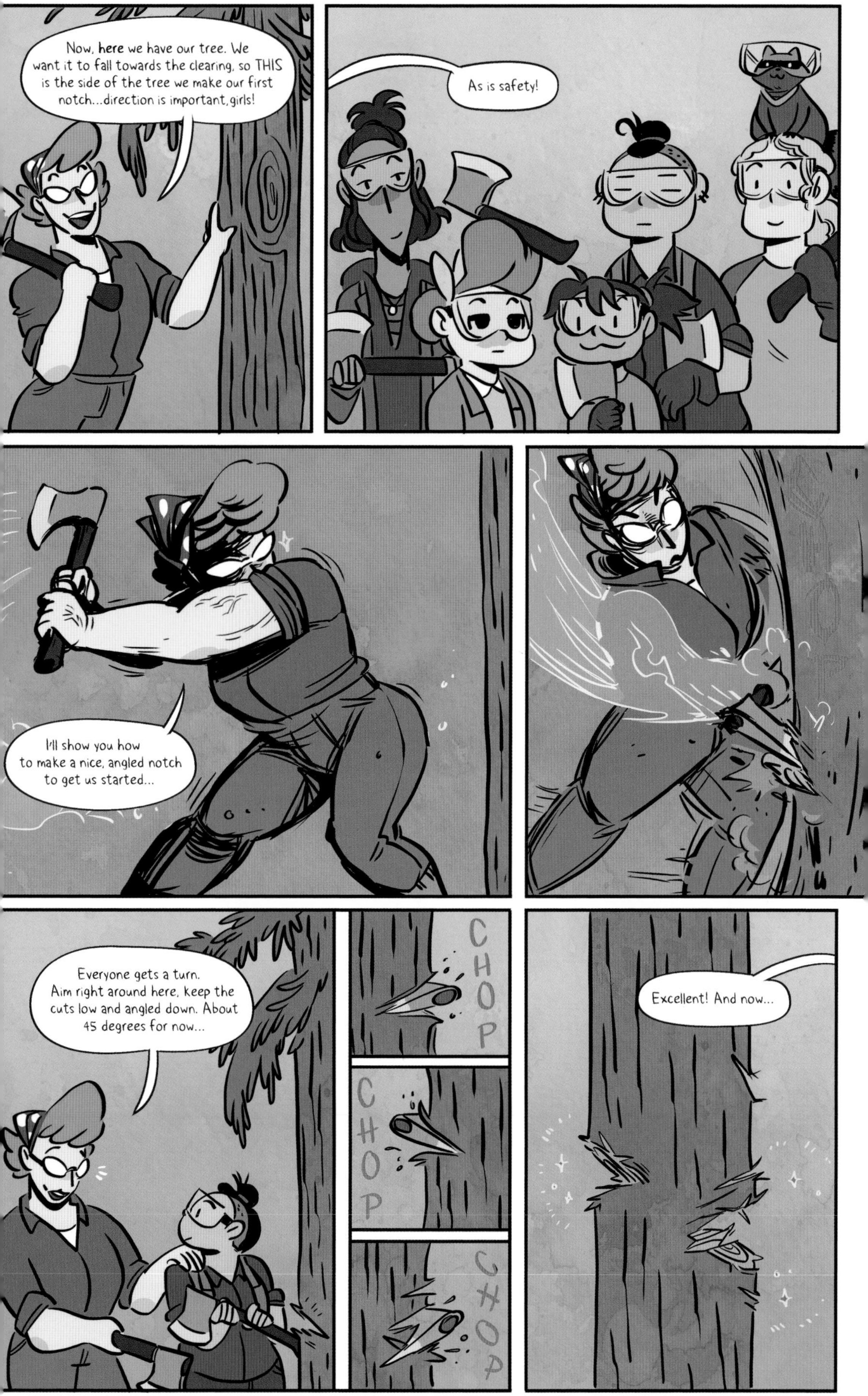
Now, **here** we have our tree. We want it to fall towards the clearing, so THIS is the side of the tree we make our first notch...direction is important, girls!
As is safety!
I'll show you how to make a nice, angled notch to get us started...
Everyone gets a turn. Aim right around here, keep the cuts low and angled down. About 45 degrees for now...
CHOP
CHOP
CHOP
Excellent! And now...

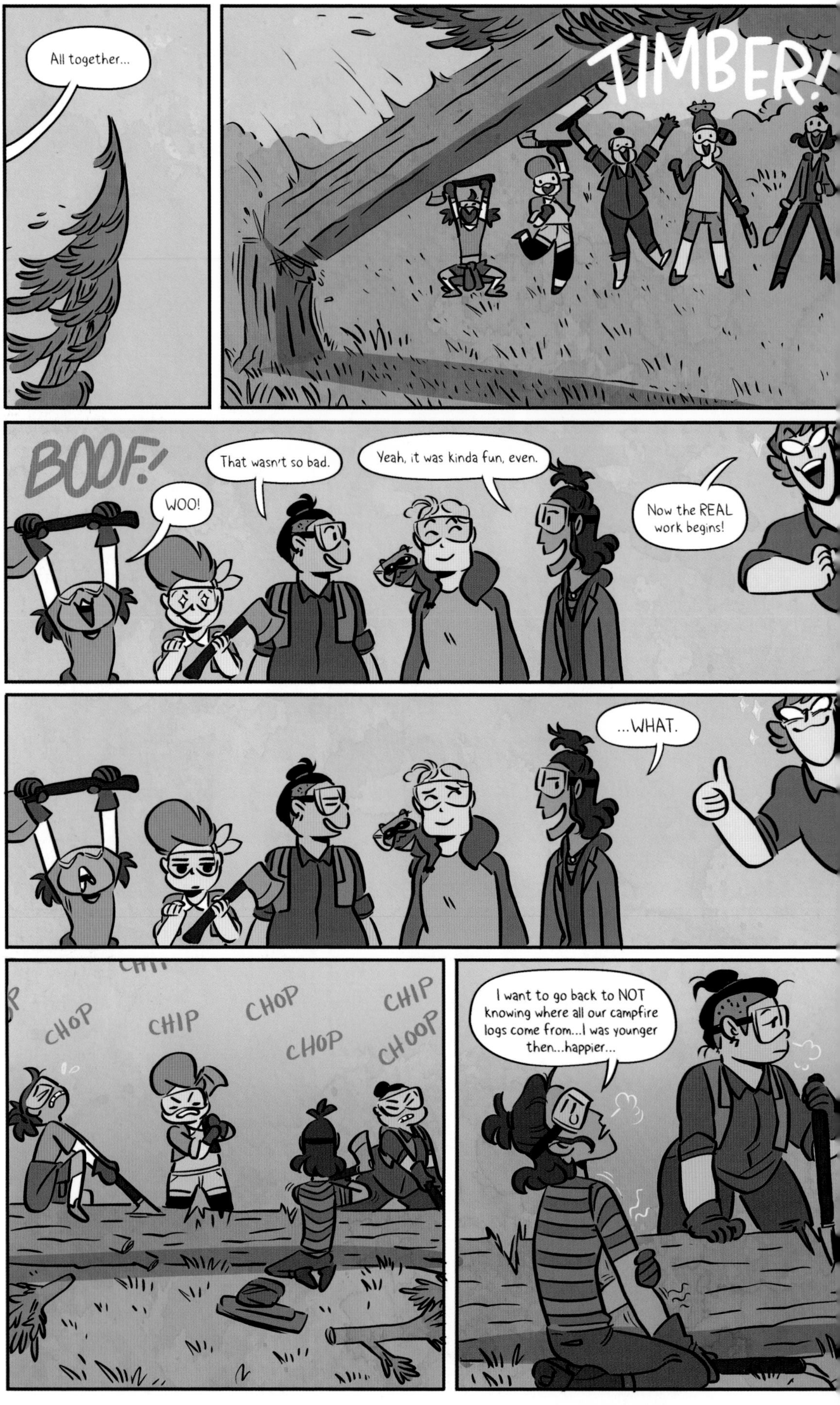

All together...
TIMBER!
BOOF!
WOO!
That wasn't so bad.
Yeah, it was kinda fun, even.
Now the REAL work begins!
...WHAT.
CHOP
CHIP
CHOP
CHIP
CHOP
CHOOP
I want to go back to NOT knowing where all our campfire logs come from...I was younger then...happier...

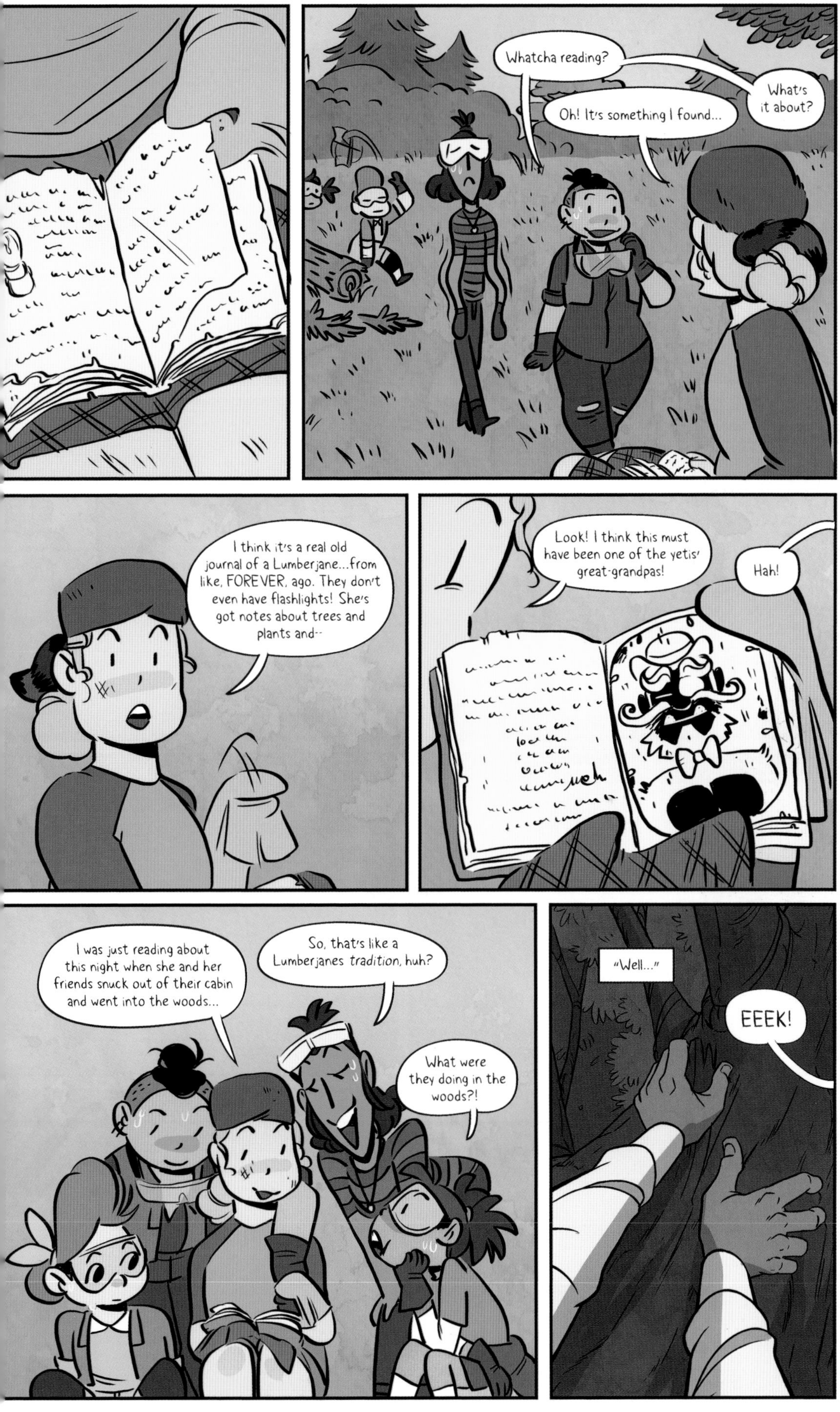
Whatcha reading?
What's it about?
Oh! It's something I found...
I think it's a real old journal of a Lumberjane...from like, FOREVER, ago. They don't even have flashlights! She's got notes about trees and plants and--
Look! I think this must have been one of the yetis' great-grandpas!
Hah!
I was just reading about this night when she and her friends snuck out of their cabin and went into the woods...
So, that's like a Lumberjanes *tradition*, huh?
What were they doing in the woods?!
"Well..."
EEEK!

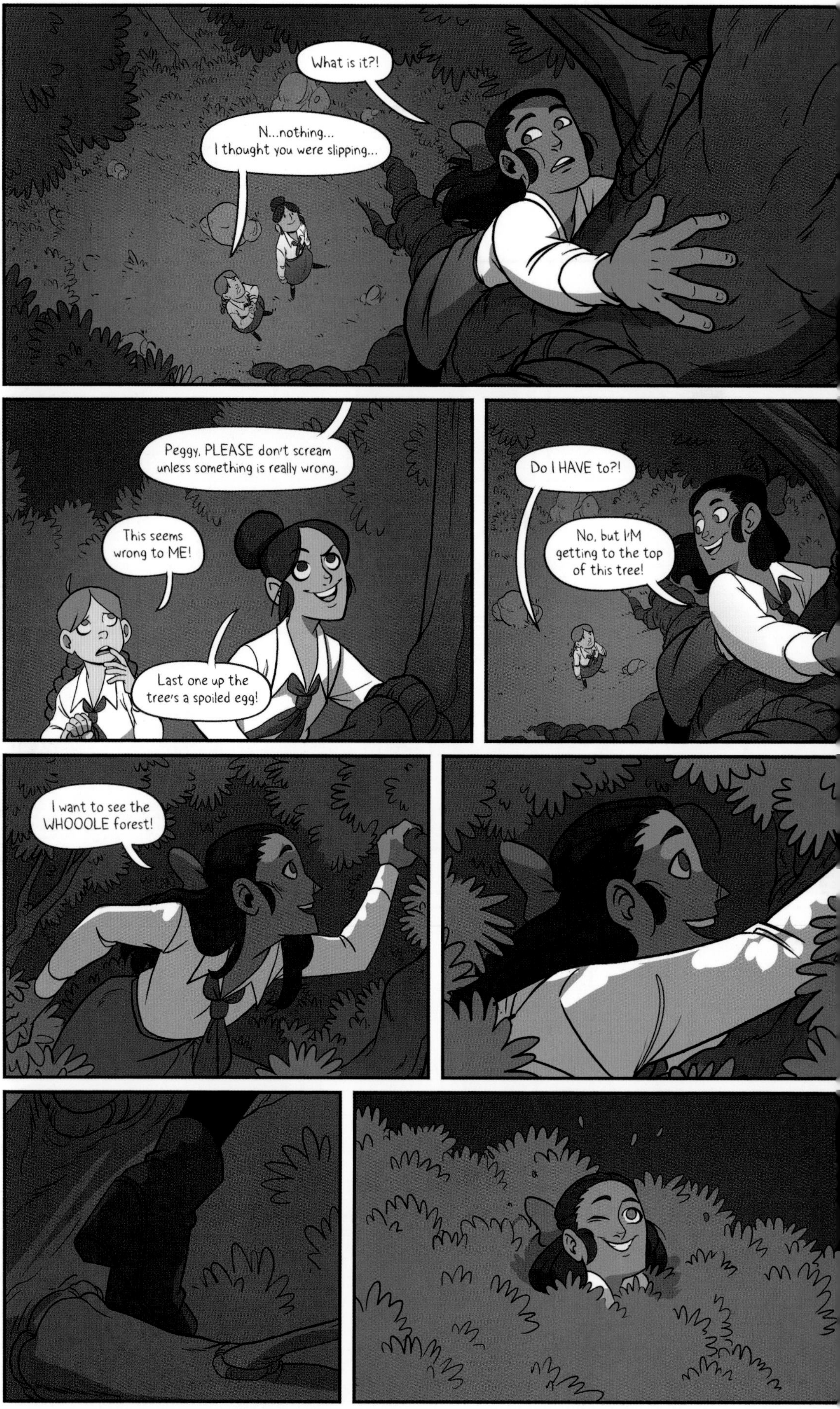
What is it?!
N...nothing... I thought you were slipping...
Peggy, PLEASE don't scream unless something is really wrong.
This seems wrong to ME!
Last one up the tree's a spoiled egg!
Do I HAVE to?!
No, but I'M getting to the top of this tree!
I want to see the WHOOOLE forest!

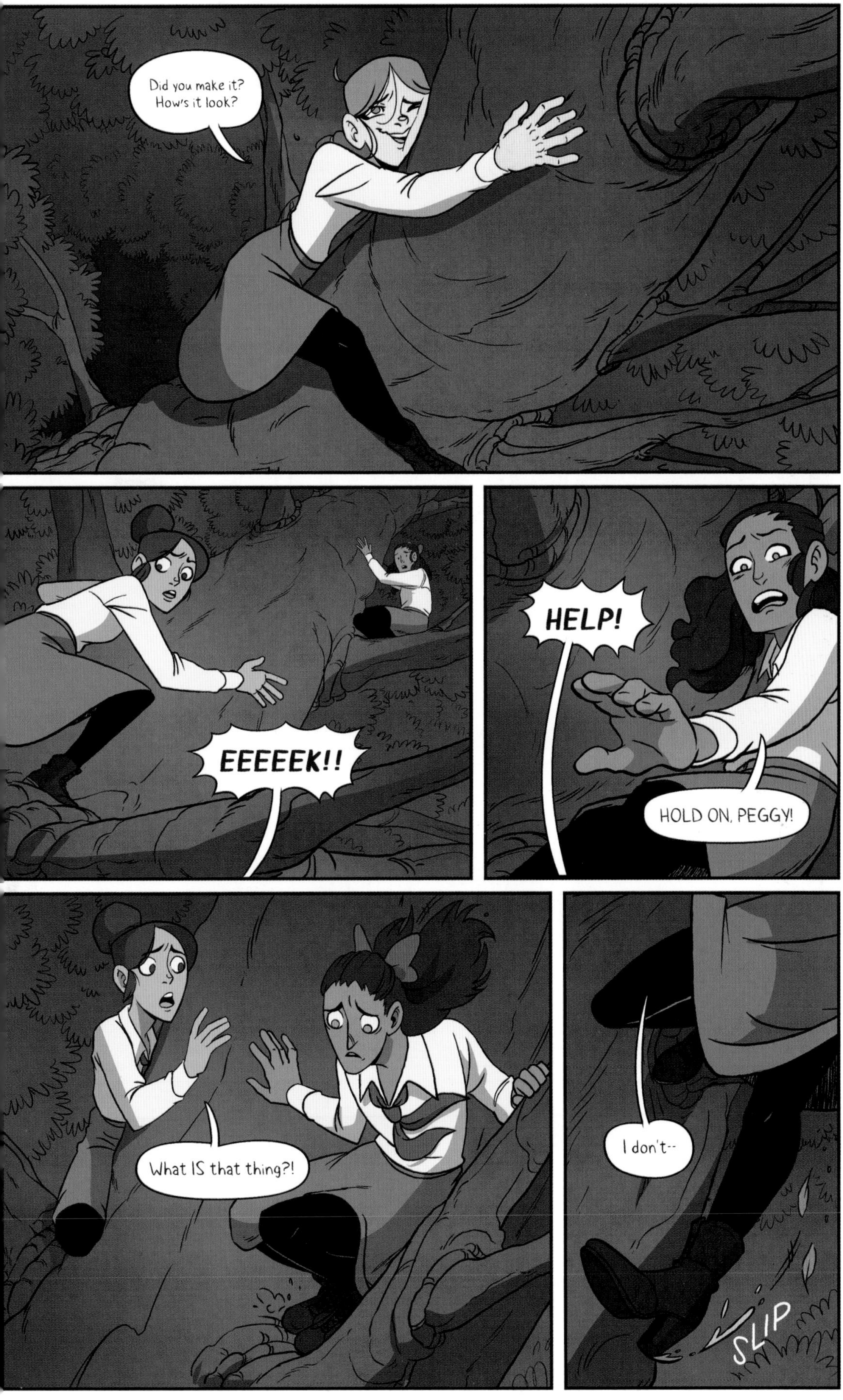
Did you make it? How's it look?
EEEEEK!!
HELP!
HOLD ON, PEGGY!
What IS that thing?!
I don't--
SLIP

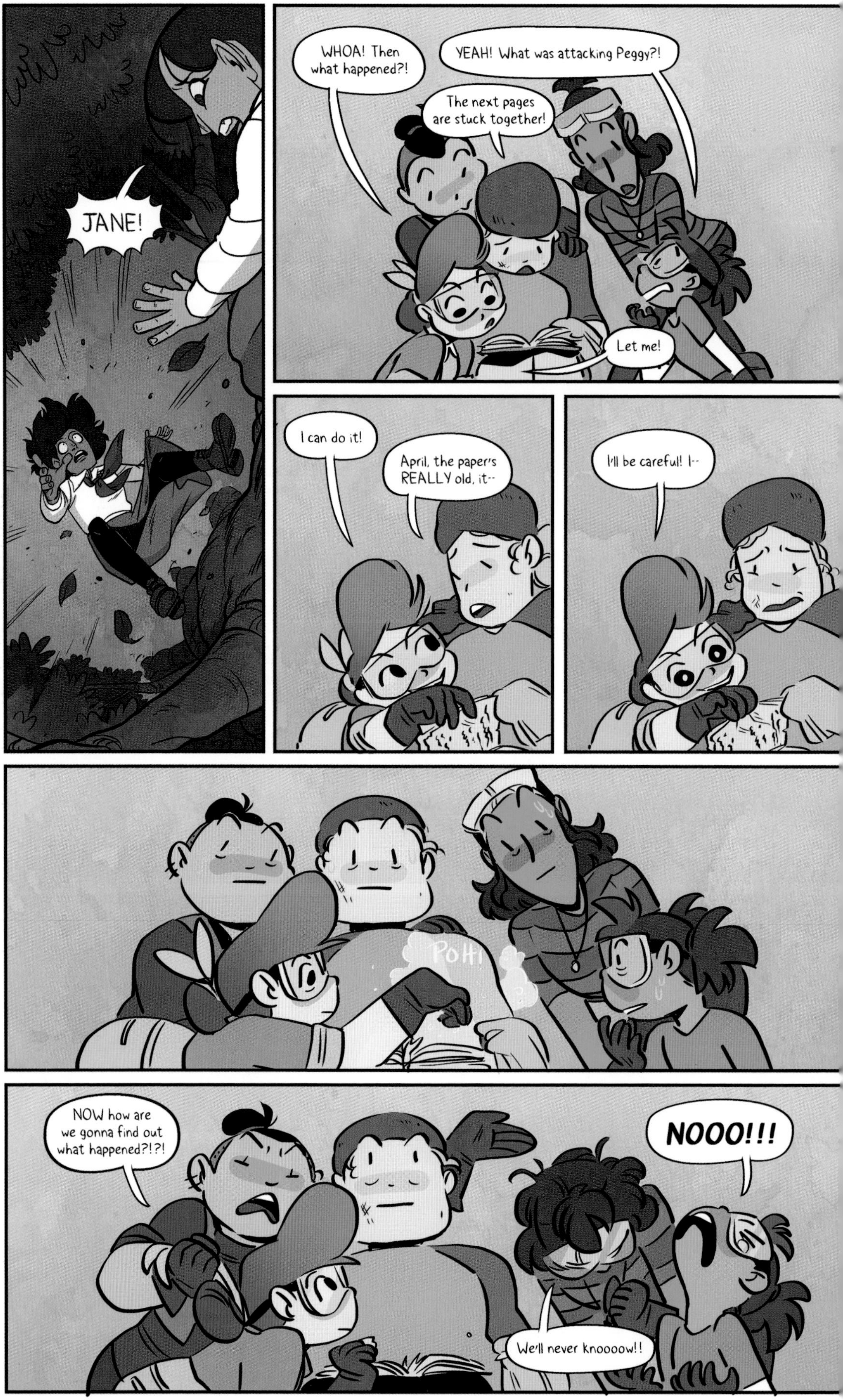
JANE!
WHOA! Then what happened?!
YEAH! What was attacking Peggy?!
The next pages are stuck together!
Let me!
I can do it!
April, the paper's REALLY old, it--
I'll be careful! I--
POHI
NOW how are we gonna find out what happened?!?!
NOOO!!!
We'll never knoooow!!

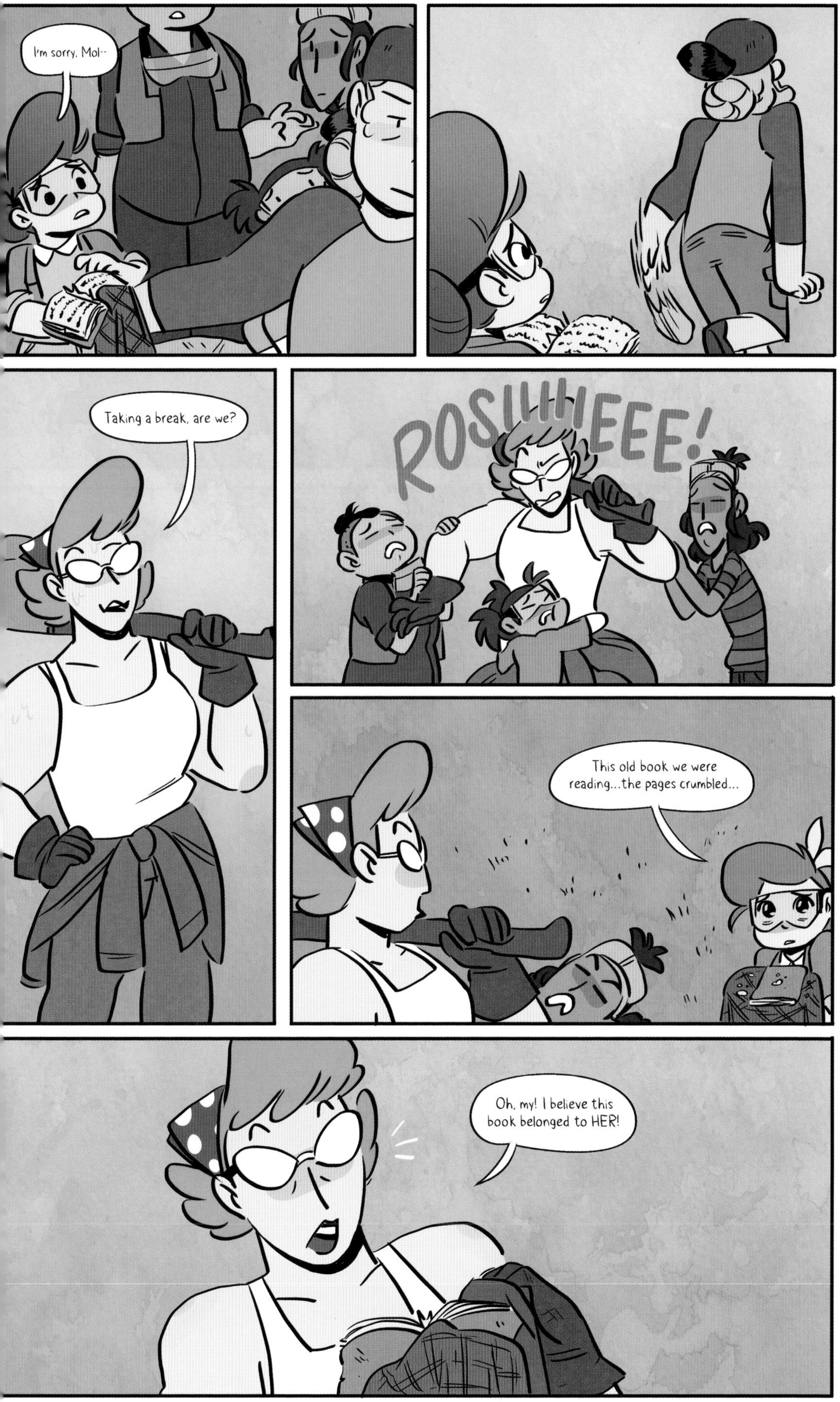
I'm sorry, Mol--
Taking a break, are we?
ROSIIIIIEEE!
This old book we were reading...the pages crumbled...
Oh, my! I believe this book belonged to HER!

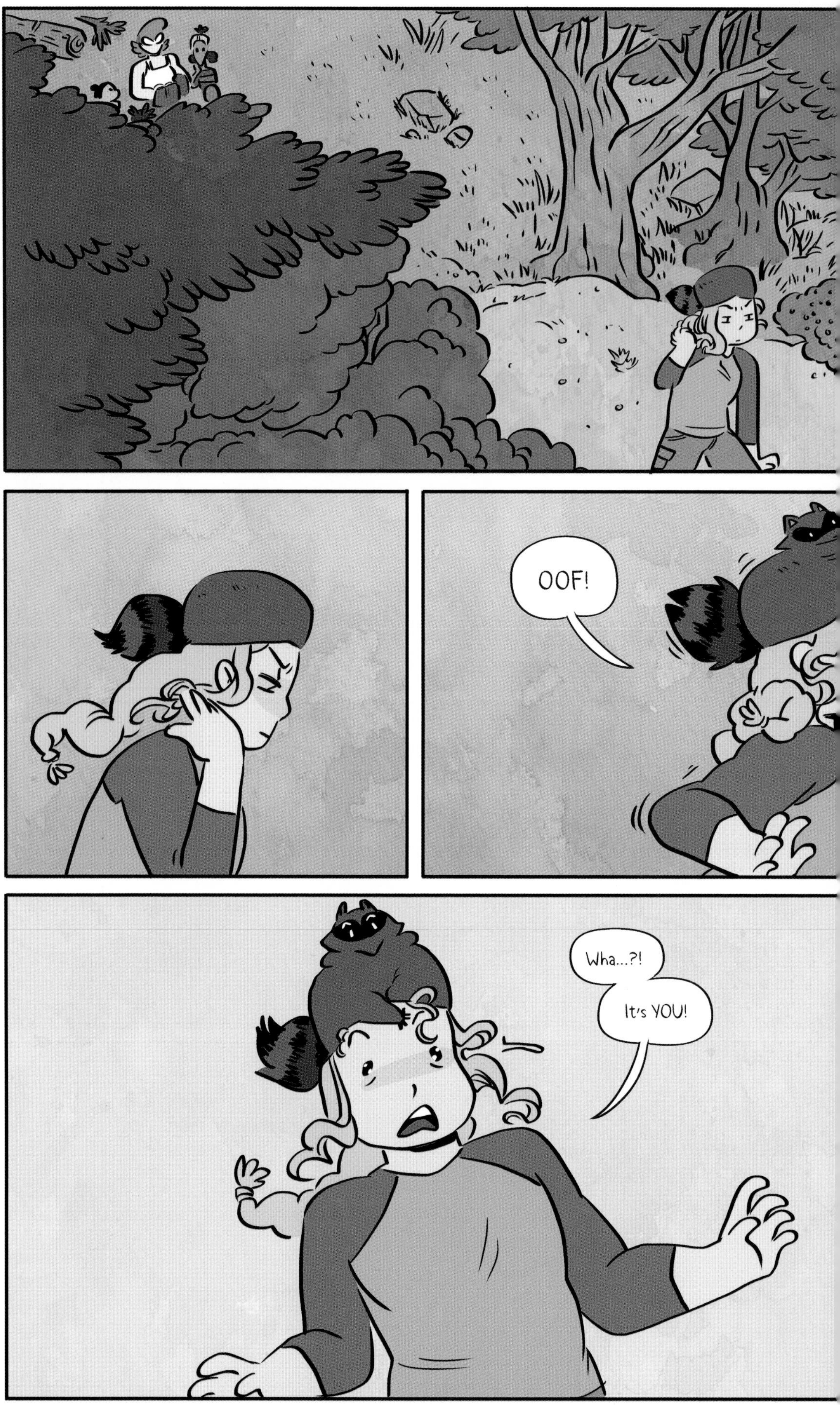
OOF!
Wha...?!
It's YOU!

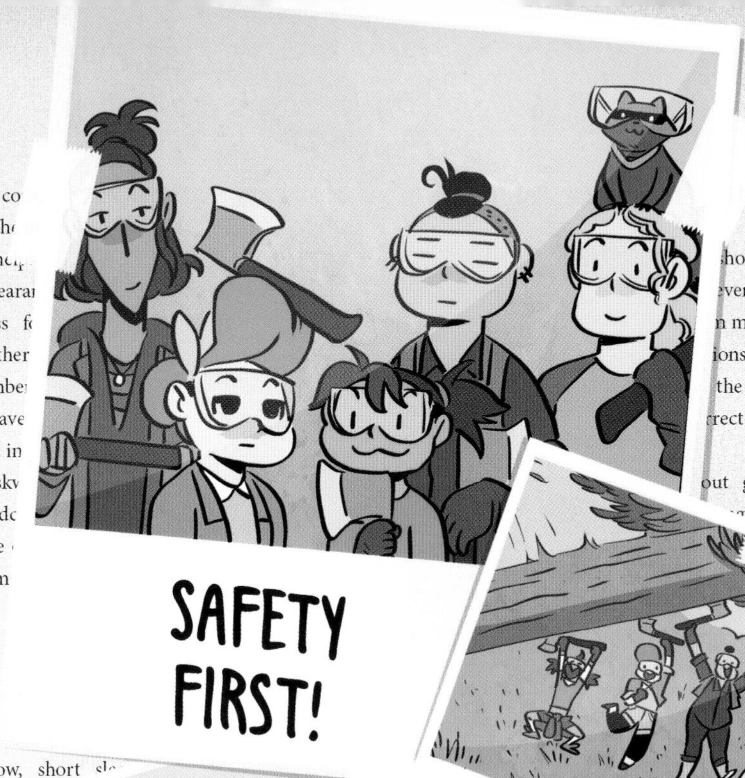
SAFETY FIRST!

will co

Th

It h

appeara

dress f

Further

Lumbe

to have

part in

Thiskv

Hardc

have

them

…E UNIFORM

…hould be worn at camp …events when Lumberjanes …n may also be worn at other …ions. It should be worn as a … the uniform dress with …rrect shoes, and stocking or

…out grows her uniform or …ther Lumberjane. …a she has … her … her

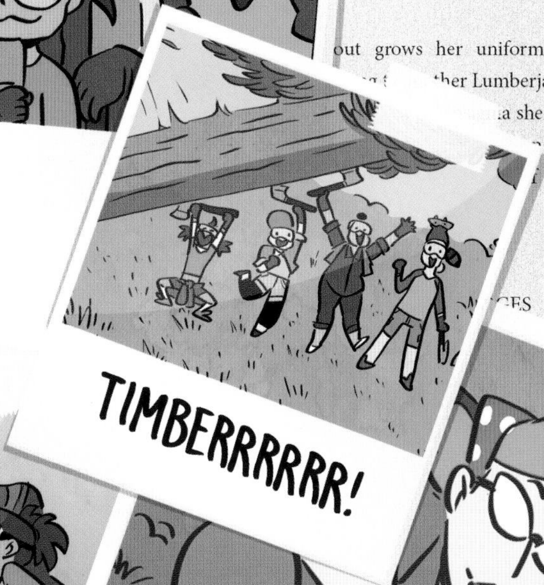
TIMBERRRRRR!

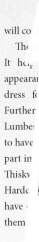

The … yellow, short sl… emb… the w… choos… slacks, … made o… out-of-do… green bere… the colla… Shoes m… heels, rou… …ings or socks shou… …with the shoes or wi… the uniform. Ne… …ces, bracelets, or other jewelry do … belong with a Lumberjane uniform.

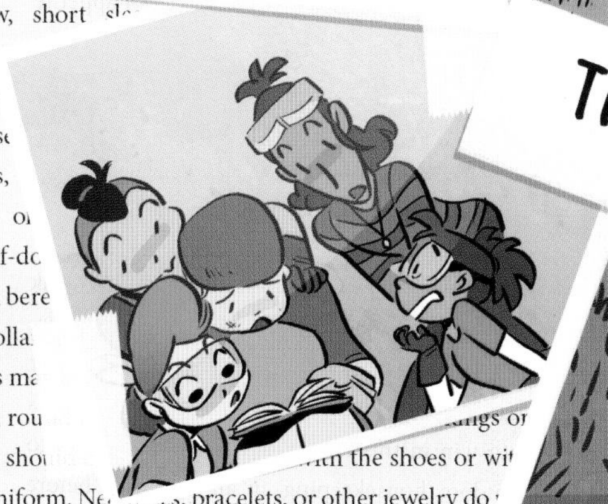

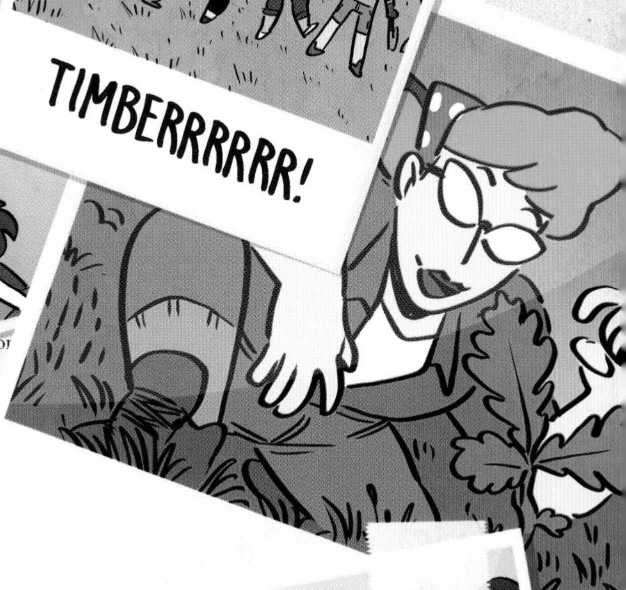

HOW TO WEAR THE UNIFORM

To look well in a uniform demands first of … uniform be kept in good condition—clean … pressed. See that the skirt is the right length for your own height and build, that the belt is adjusted to your waist, that your shoes and stockings are in keeping with the uniform, that you watch your posture and carry yourself with dignity and grace. If the beret is removed indoors, be sure that your hair is neat and kept in place with an inconspicuous clip or ribbon. When you wear a Lumberjane uniform you are identified as a member of this organization and you should be doubly careful to conduct yourself in a way that will show everyone that courtesy and thoughtfulness are part of being a Lumberjane. People are likely to judge a whole nation by the selfishness of a few individuals, to criticize a whole family because of the misconduct of one member, and to feel unkindly toward an organization because of the

The unifor… helps to cre… in a group. … active life th… another bond… future, and pr… in order to b… Lumberjane pr… Penniquiqul Thi… …core Lady Types, but m… …es will wish to have one. They can either bu… …, or make it themselves from materials available at the trading post.

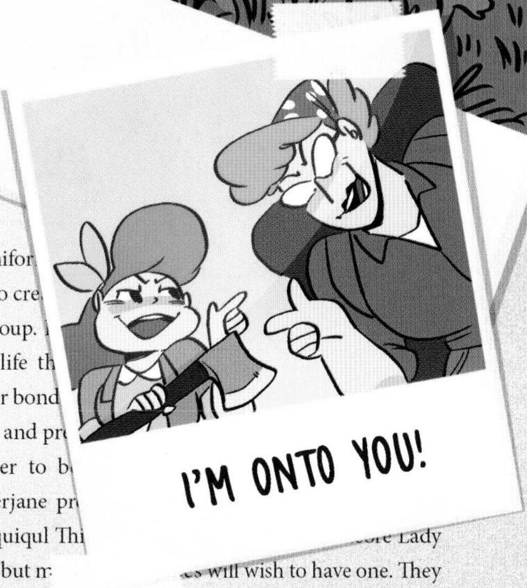
I'M ONTO YOU!

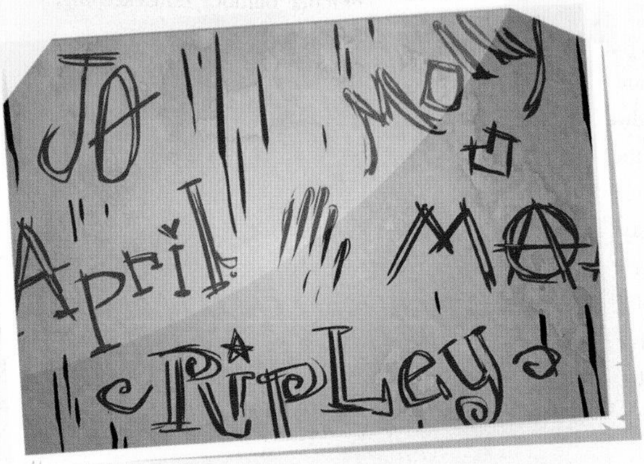
Jo
Molly
April
Mal
Ripley

LUMBERJANES FIELD MANUAL

CHAPTER SEVENTY

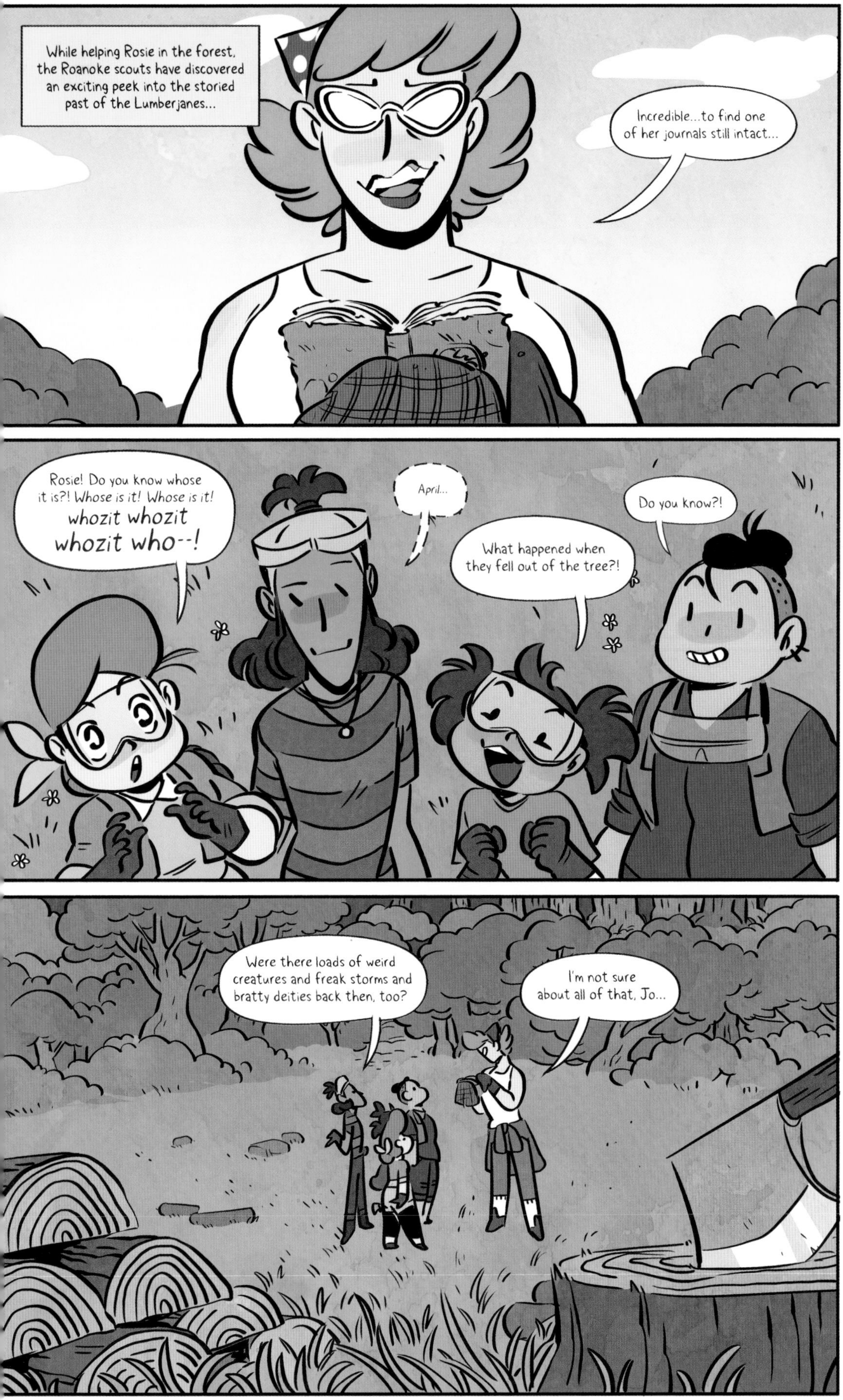
While helping Rosie in the forest, the Roanoke scouts have discovered an exciting peek into the storied past of the Lumberjanes...
Incredible...to find one of her journals still intact...
Rosie! Do you know whose it is?! Whose is it! Whose is it! whozit whozit whozit who--!
April...
What happened when they fell out of the tree?!
Do you know?!
Were there loads of weird creatures and freak storms and bratty deities back then, too?
I'm not sure about all of that, Jo...

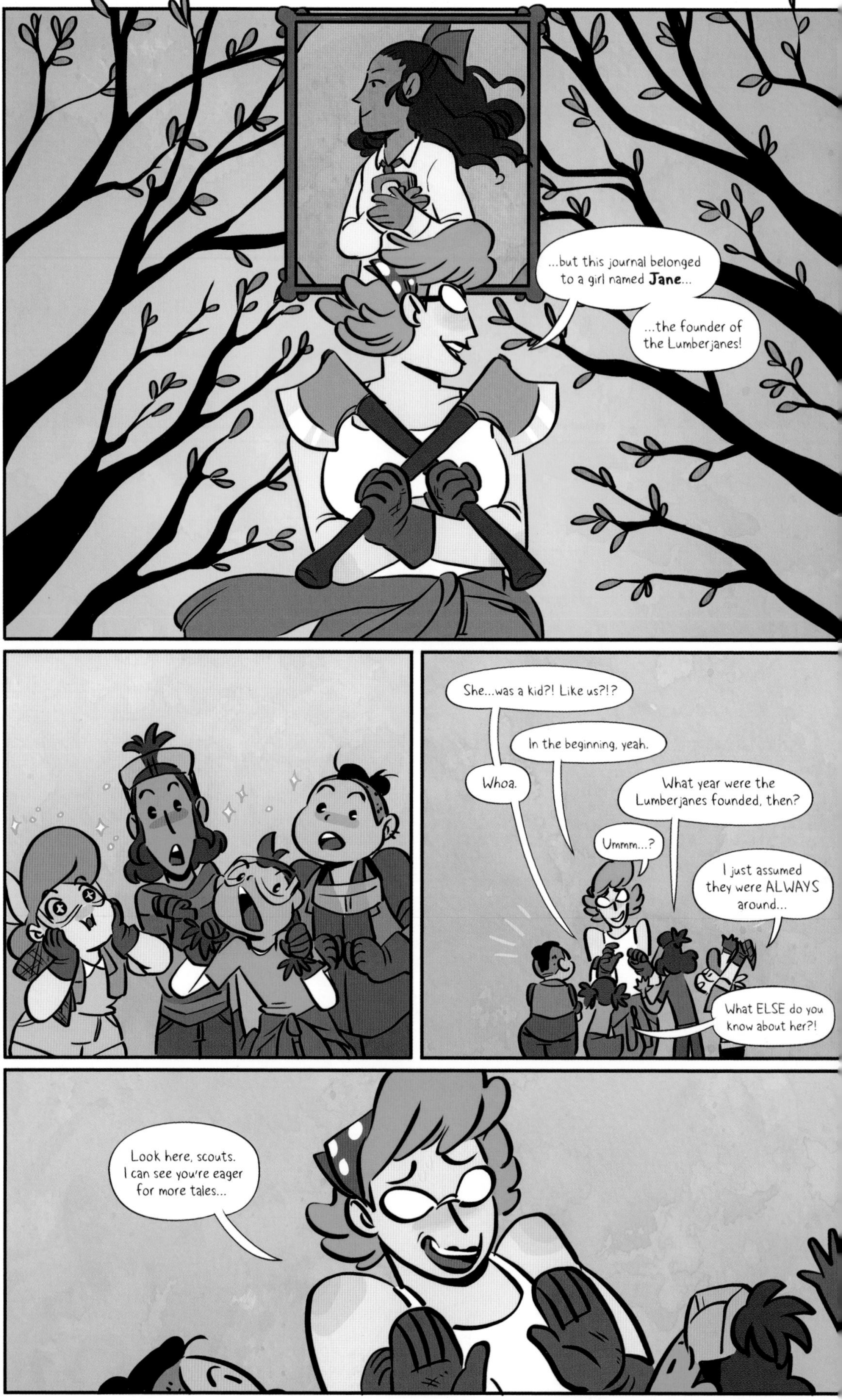
...but this journal belonged to a girl named **Jane**...
...the founder of the Lumberjanes!
She...was a kid?! Like us?!?
In the beginning, yeah.
Whoa.
What year were the Lumberjanes founded, then?
Ummm...?
I just assumed they were ALWAYS around...
What ELSE do you know about her?!
Look here, scouts. I can see you're eager for more tales...

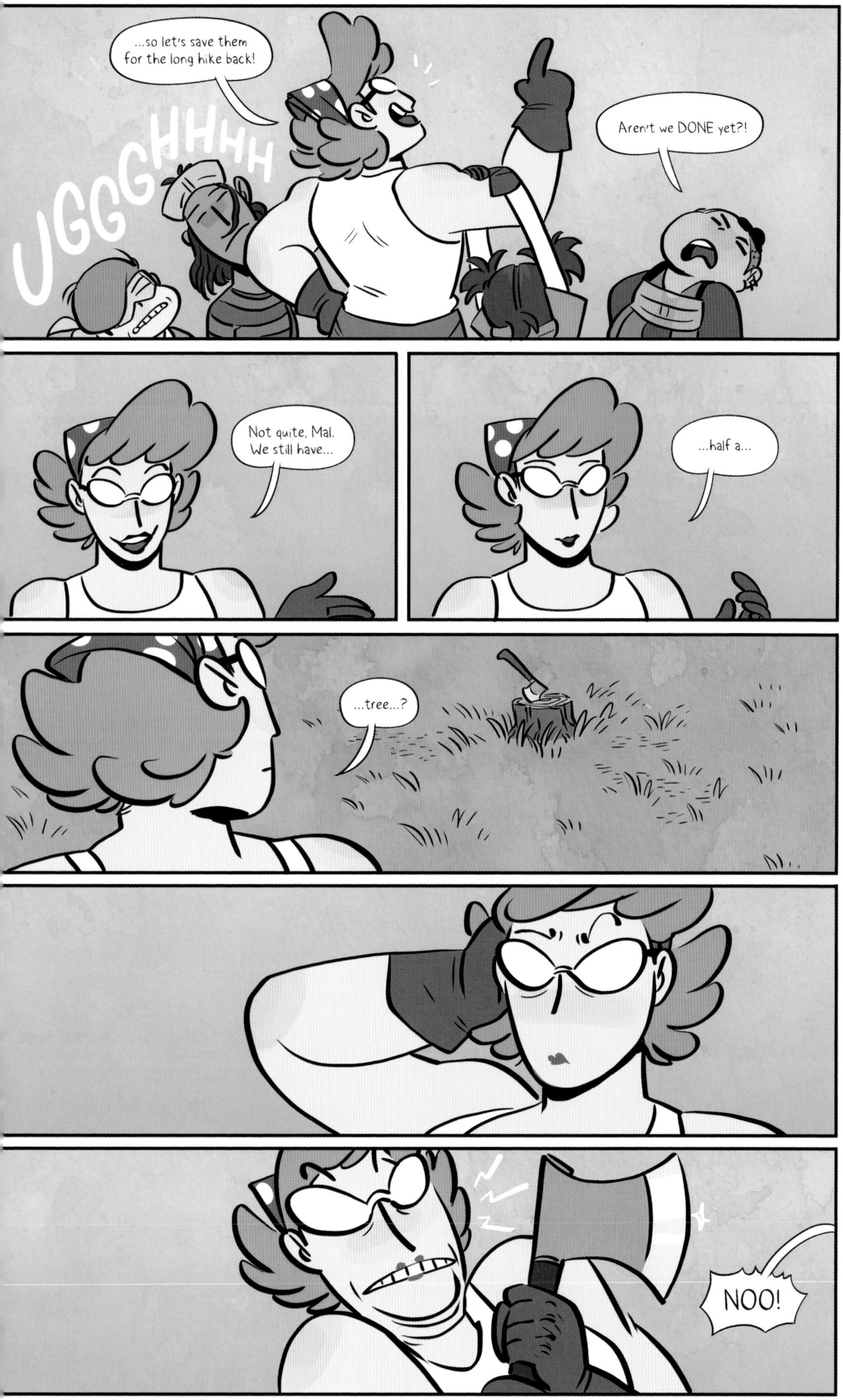

...so let's save them for the long hike back!
UGGGHHHHH
Aren't we DONE yet?!
Not quite, Mal. We still have...
...half a...
...tree...?
NOO!

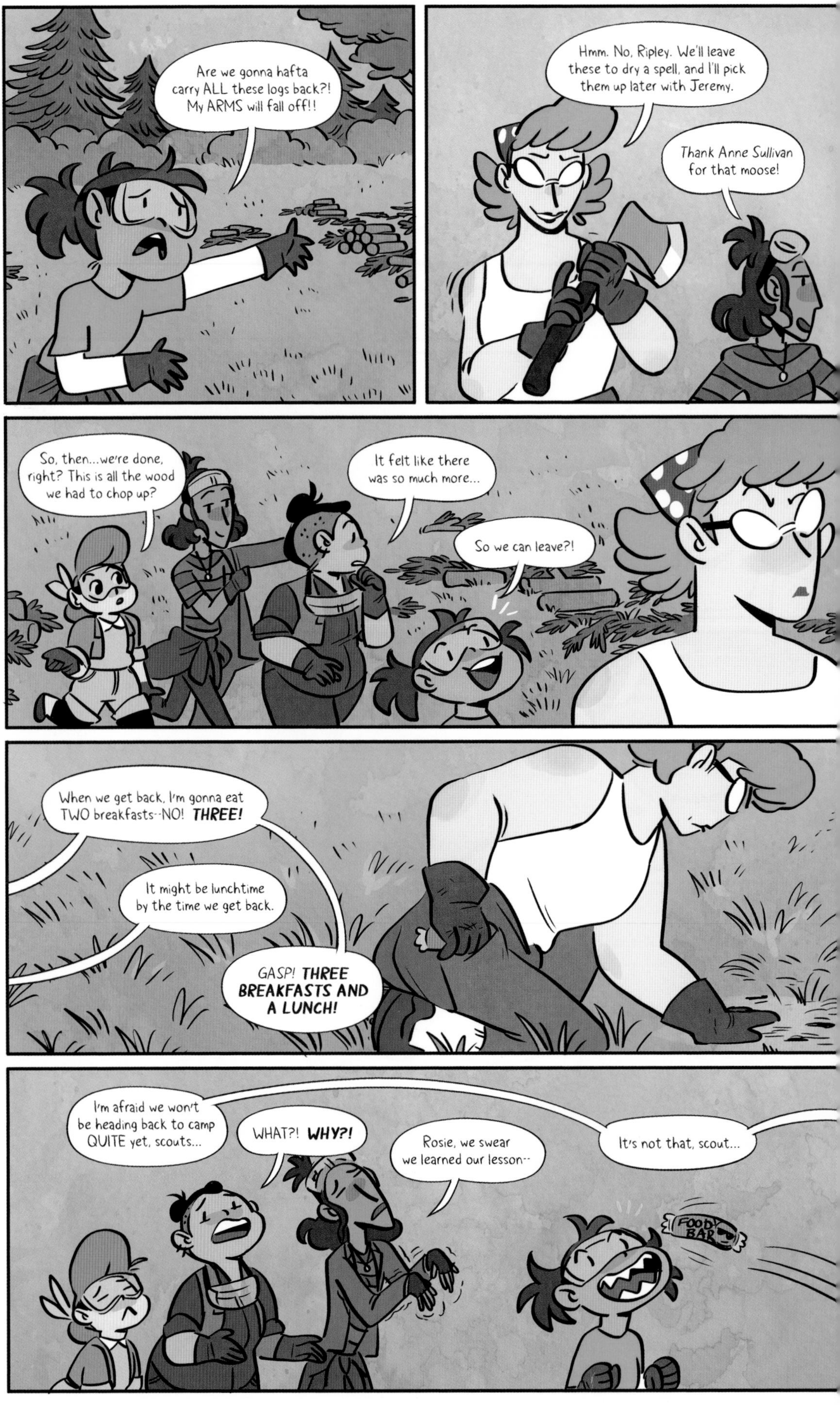
Are we gonna hafta carry ALL these logs back?! My ARMS will fall off!!
Hmm. No, Ripley. We'll leave these to dry a spell, and I'll pick them up later with Jeremy.
Thank Anne Sullivan for that moose!
So, then...we're done, right? This is all the wood we had to chop up?
It felt like there was so much more...
So we can leave?!
When we get back, I'm gonna eat TWO breakfasts--NO! **THREE!**
It might be lunchtime by the time we get back.
GASP! **THREE BREAKFASTS AND A LUNCH!**
I'm afraid we won't be heading back to camp QUITE yet, scouts...
WHAT?! **WHY?!**
Rosie, we swear we learned our lesson--
It's not that, scout...
FOOD BAR

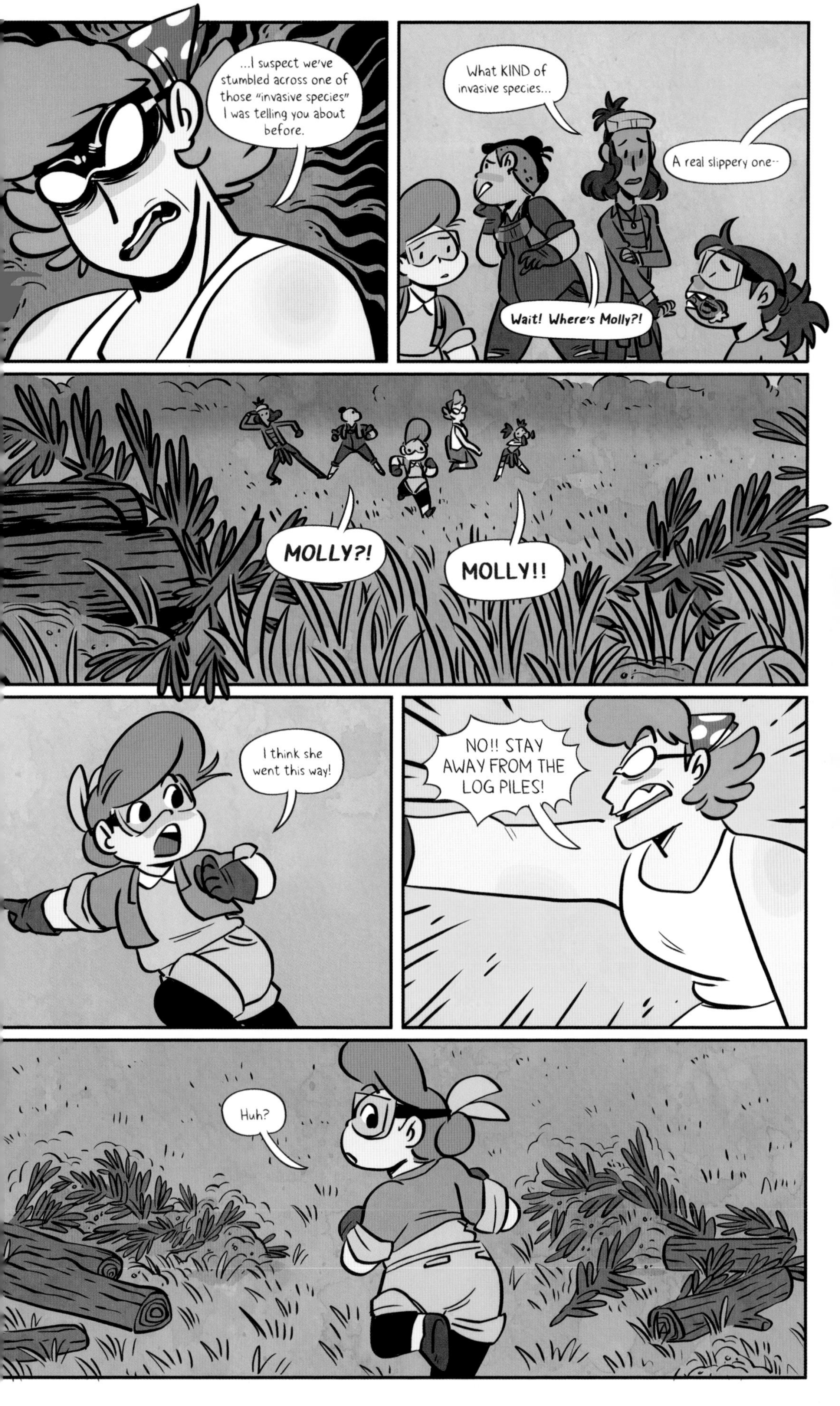
...I suspect we've stumbled across one of those "invasive species" I was telling you about before.
What KIND of invasive species...
A real slippery one--
Wait! Where's Molly?!
MOLLY?!
MOLLY!!
I think she went this way!
NO!! STAY AWAY FROM THE LOG PILES!
Huh?

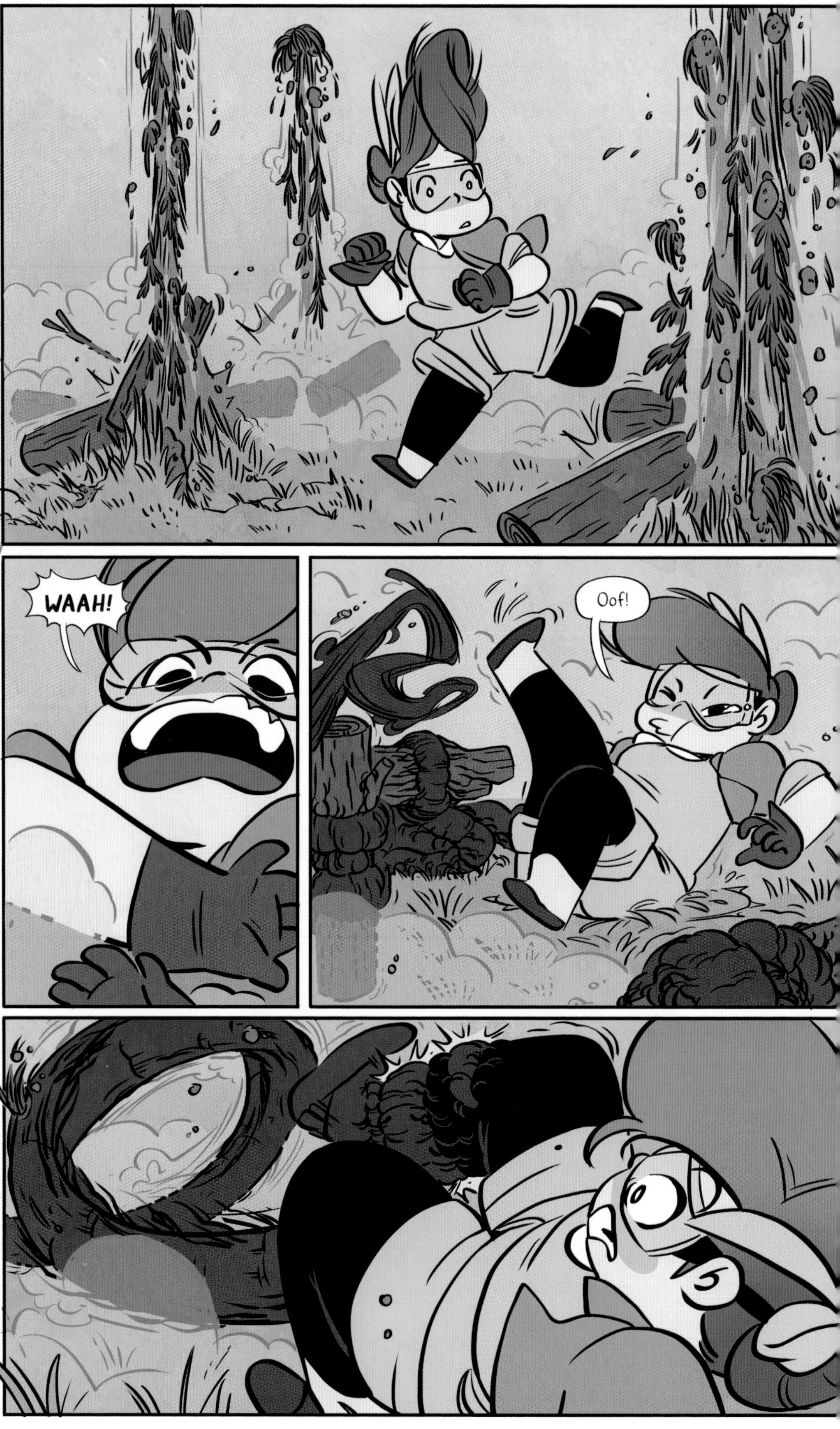
WAAH!
Oof!

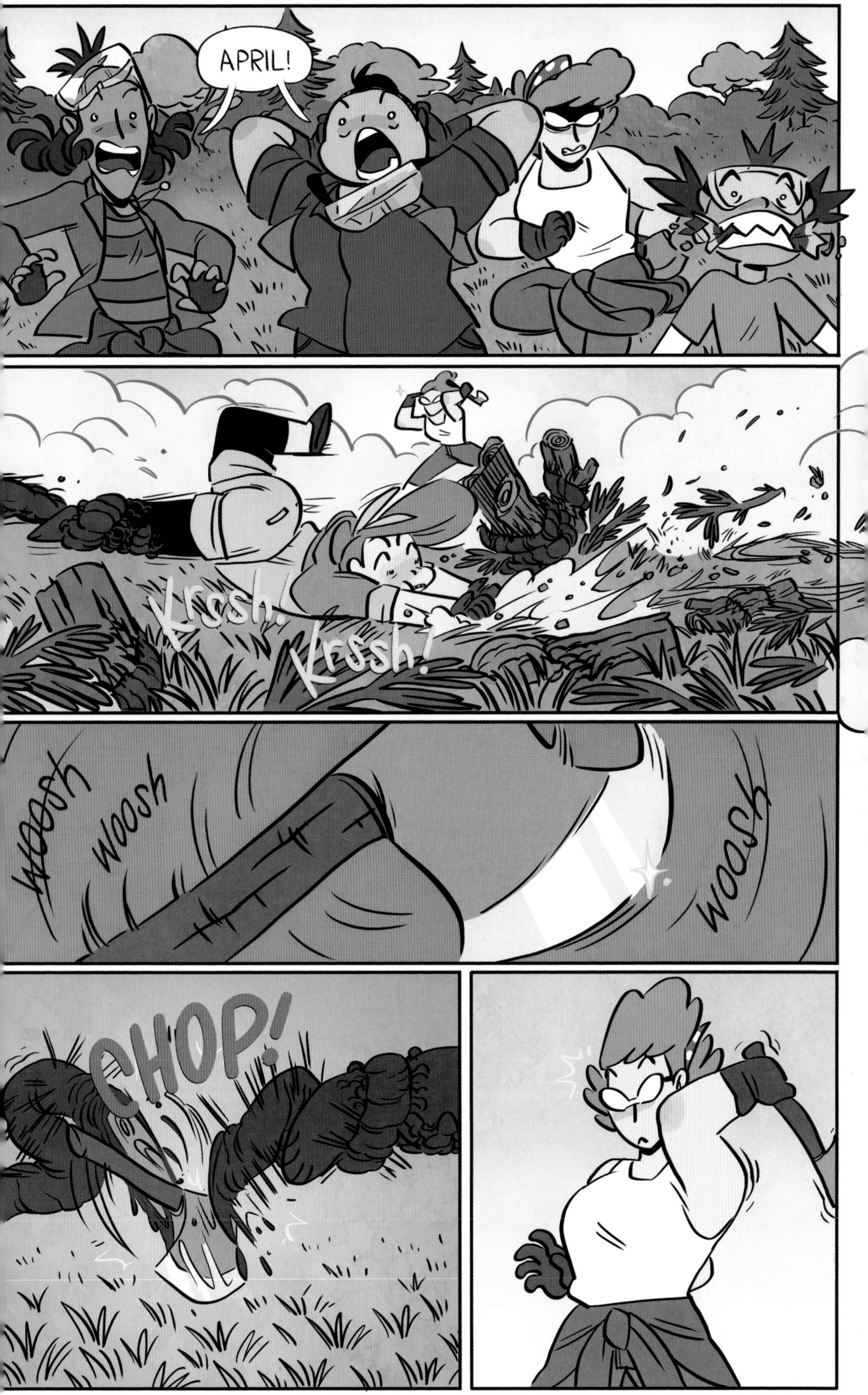
APRIL!
Krssh! Krssh!
woosh
woosh
woosh
CHOP!

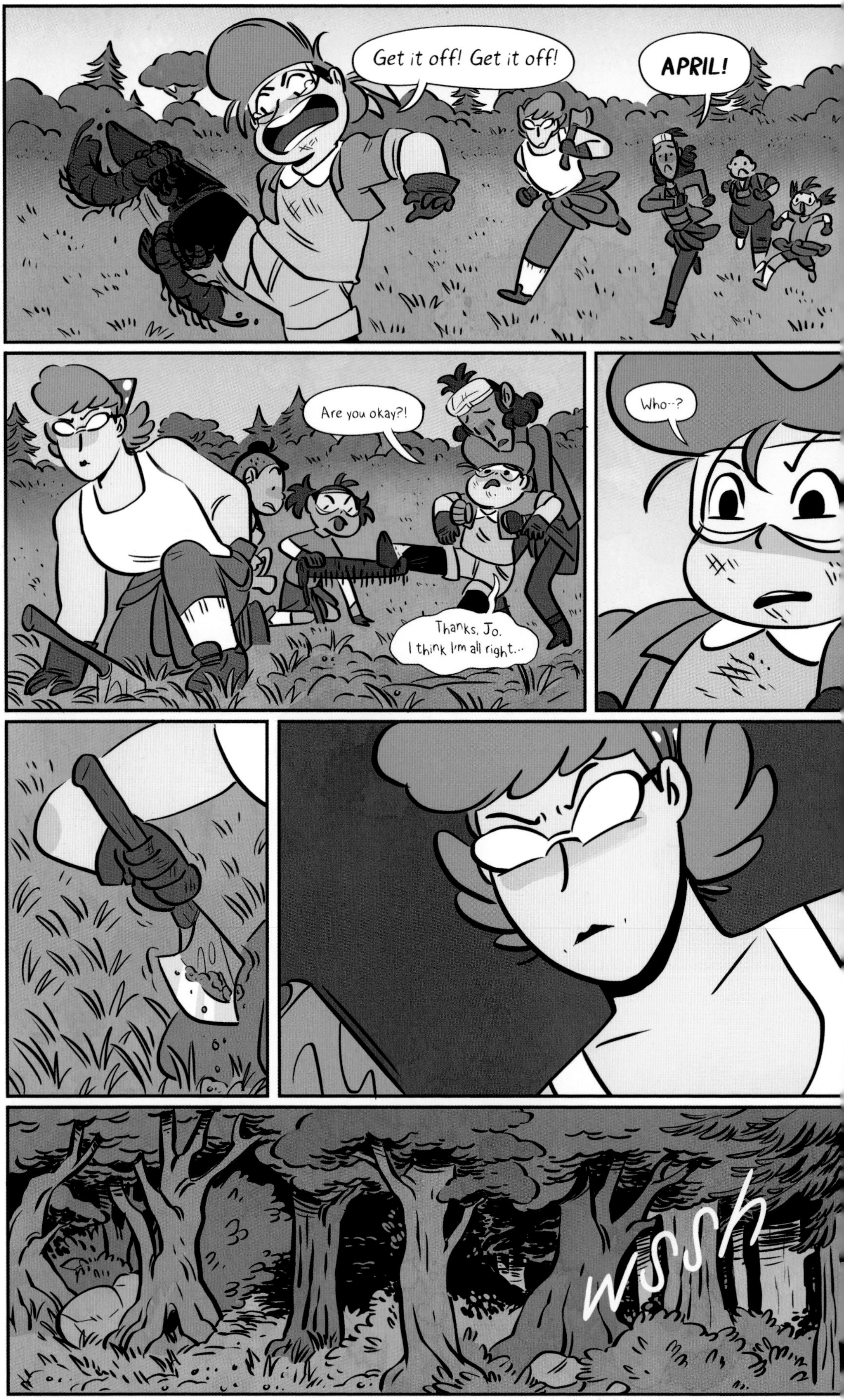
Get it off! Get it off!
APRIL!
Are you okay?!
Thanks, Jo.
I think I'm all right...
Who--?
wssh

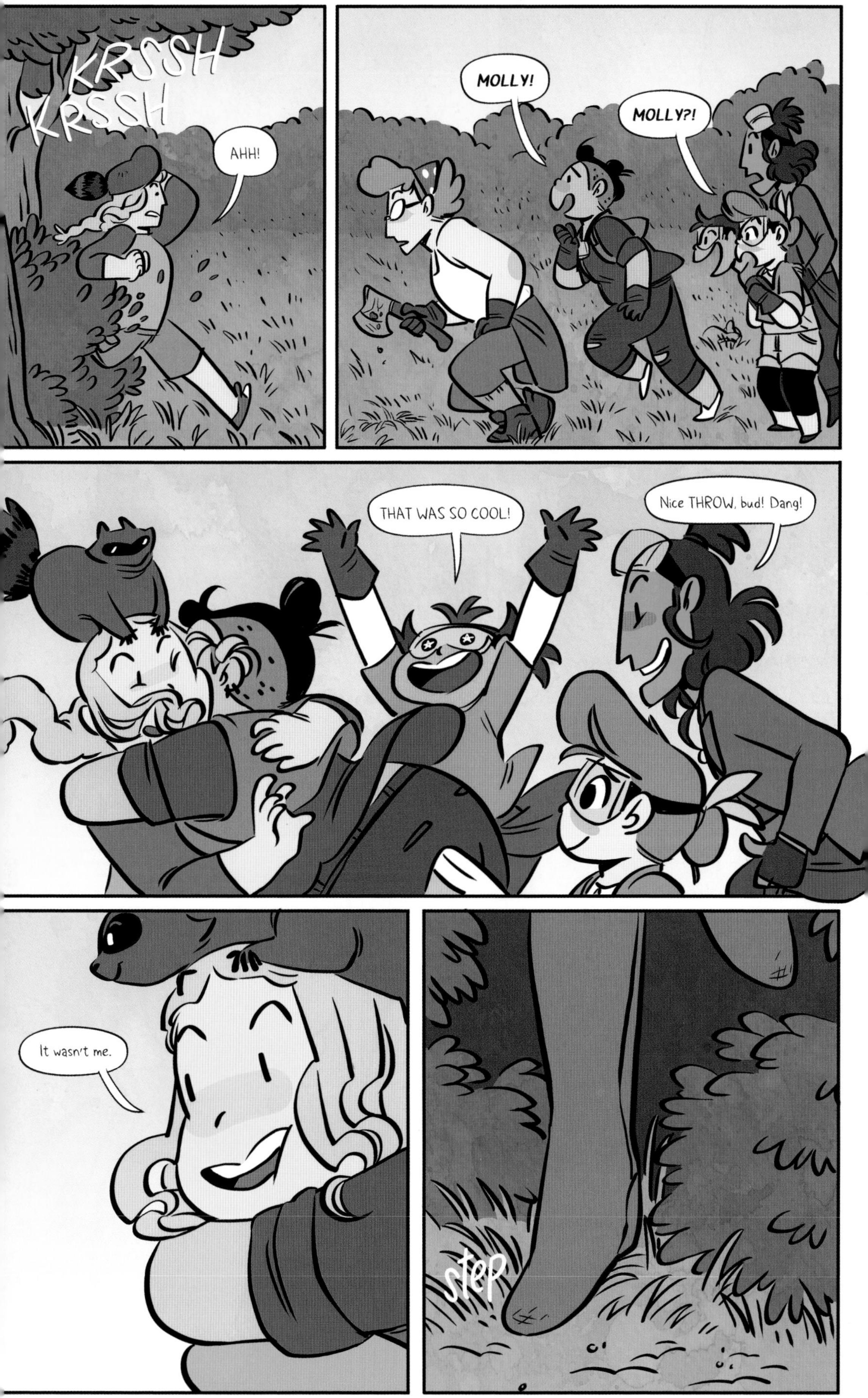
KRSSH
KRSSH
AHH!
MOLLY!
MOLLY?!
THAT WAS SO COOL!
Nice THROW, bud! Dang!
It wasn't me.
step

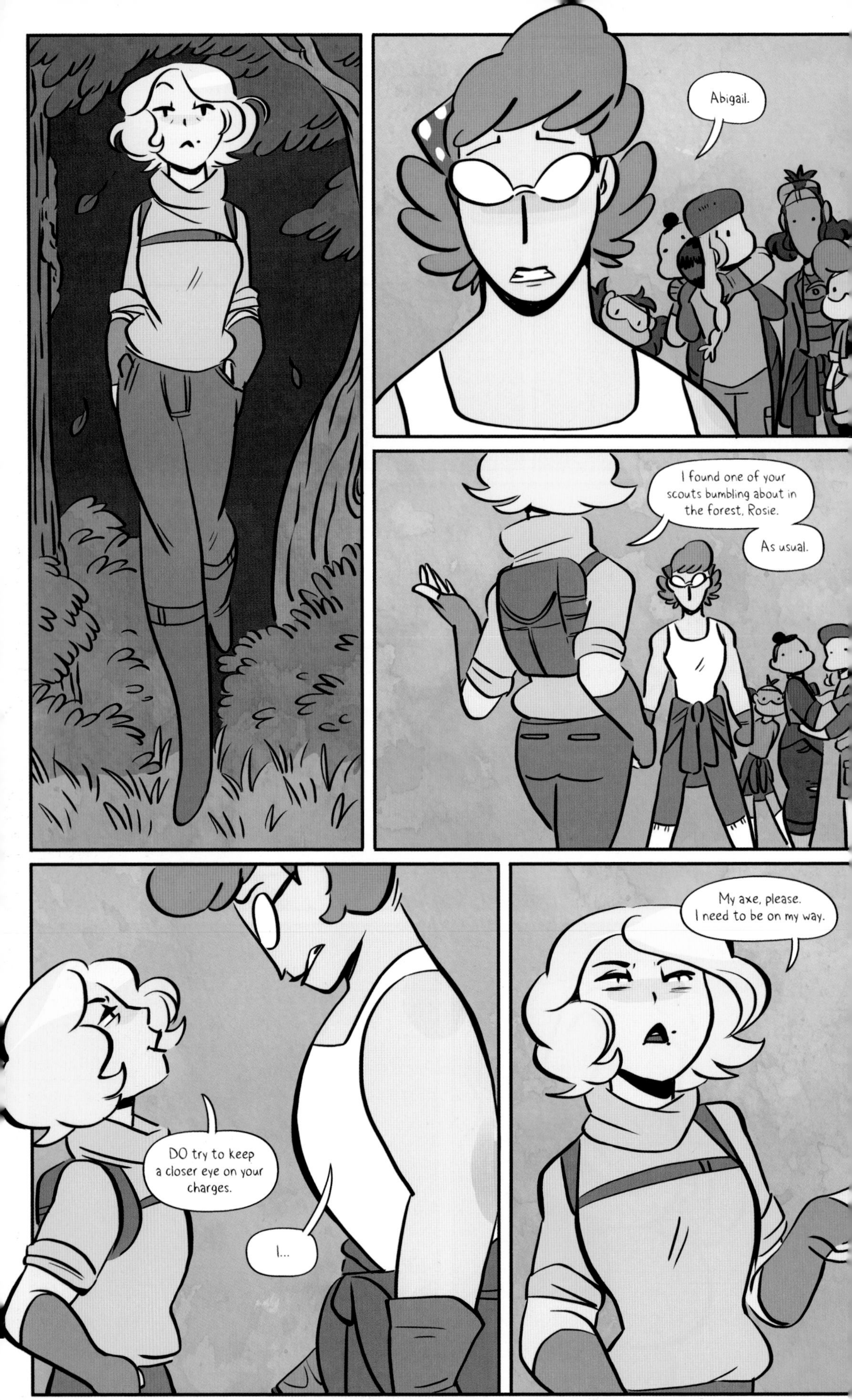
Abigail.
I found one of your scouts bumbling about in the forest, Rosie.
As usual.
DO try to keep a closer eye on your charges.
I...
My axe, please. I need to be on my way.

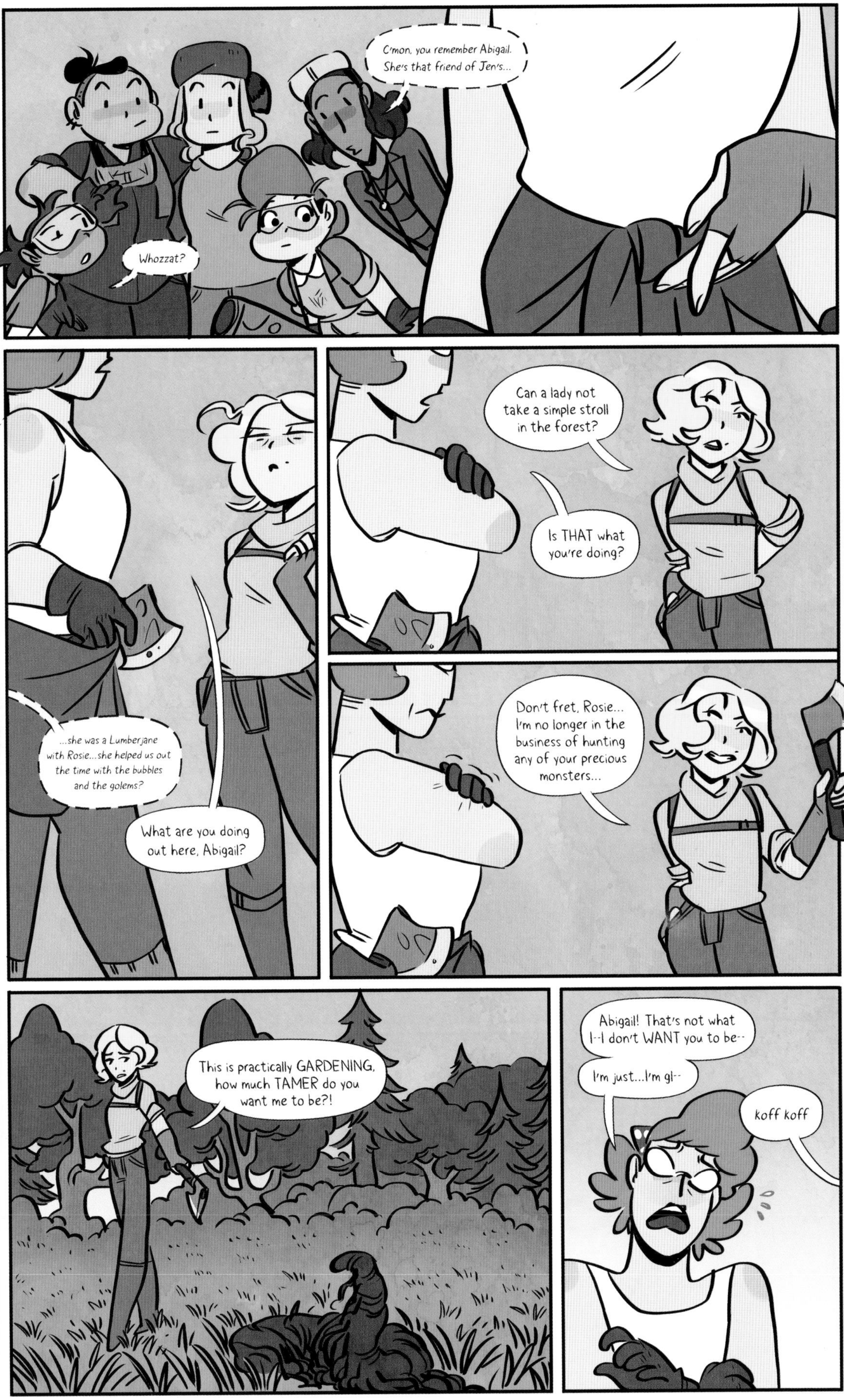
C'mon, you remember Abigail. She's that friend of Jen's...
Whozzat?
...she was a Lumberjane with Rosie...she helped us out the time with the bubbles and the golems?
What are you doing out here, Abigail?
Can a lady not take a simple stroll in the forest?
Is THAT what you're doing?
Don't fret, Rosie... I'm no longer in the business of hunting any of your precious monsters...
This is practically GARDENING, how much TAMER do you want me to be?!
Abigail! That's not what I--I don't WANT you to be--
I'm just...I'm gl--
koff koff

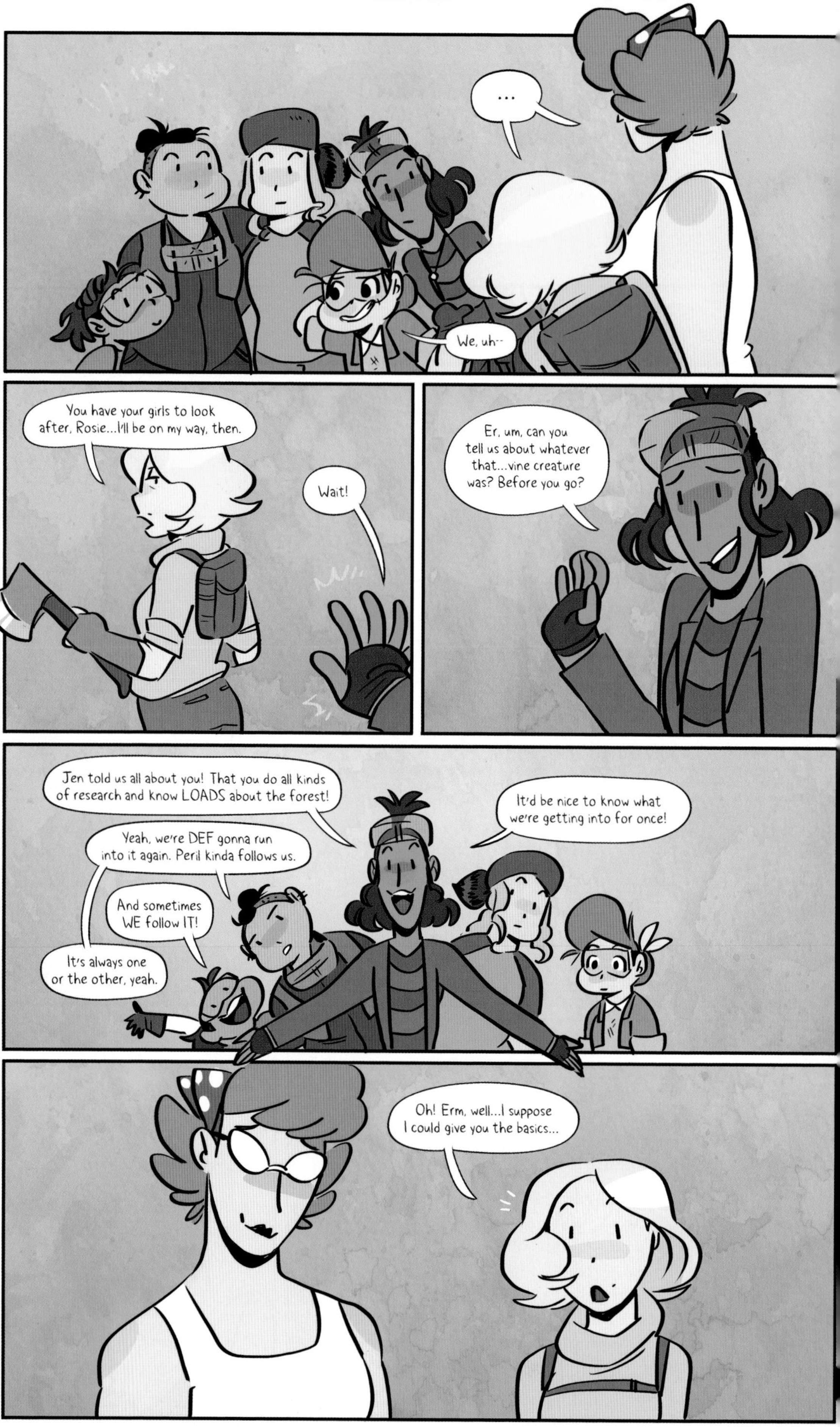
...
We, uh--
You have your girls to look after, Rosie...I'll be on my way, then.
Wait!
Er, um, can you tell us about whatever that...vine creature was? Before you go?
Jen told us all about you! That you do all kinds of research and know LOADS about the forest!
It'd be nice to know what we're getting into for once!
Yeah, we're DEF gonna run into it again. Peril kinda follows us.
And sometimes WE follow IT!
It's always one or the other, yeah.
Oh! Erm, well...I suppose I could give you the basics...

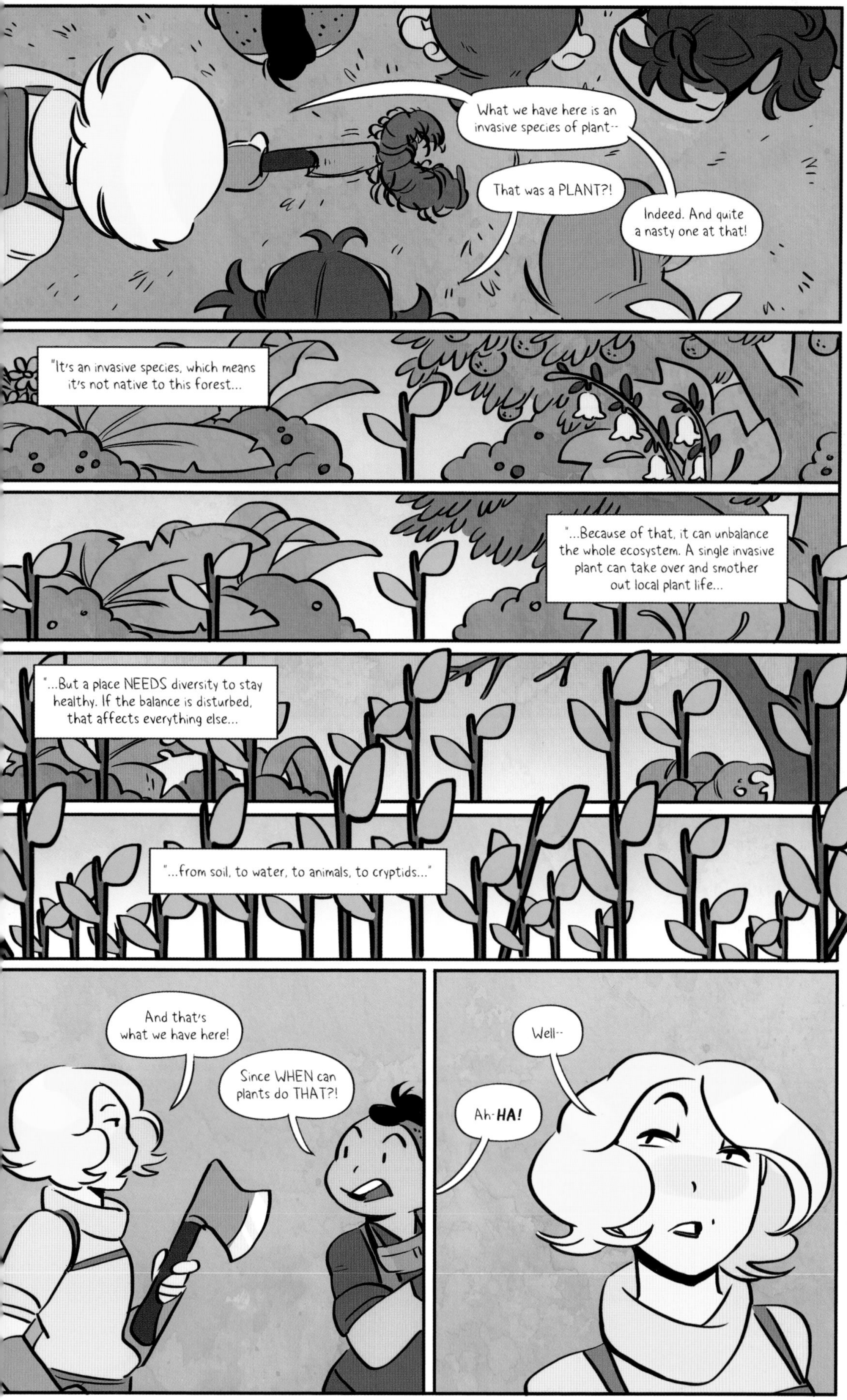
What we have here is an invasive species of plant--
That was a PLANT?!
Indeed. And quite a nasty one at that!
"It's an invasive species, which means it's not native to this forest...
"...Because of that, it can unbalance the whole ecosystem. A single invasive plant can take over and smother out local plant life...
"...But a place NEEDS diversity to stay healthy. If the balance is disturbed, that affects everything else...
"...from soil, to water, to animals, to cryptids..."
And that's what we have here!
Since WHEN can plants do THAT?!
Well--
Ah-HA!

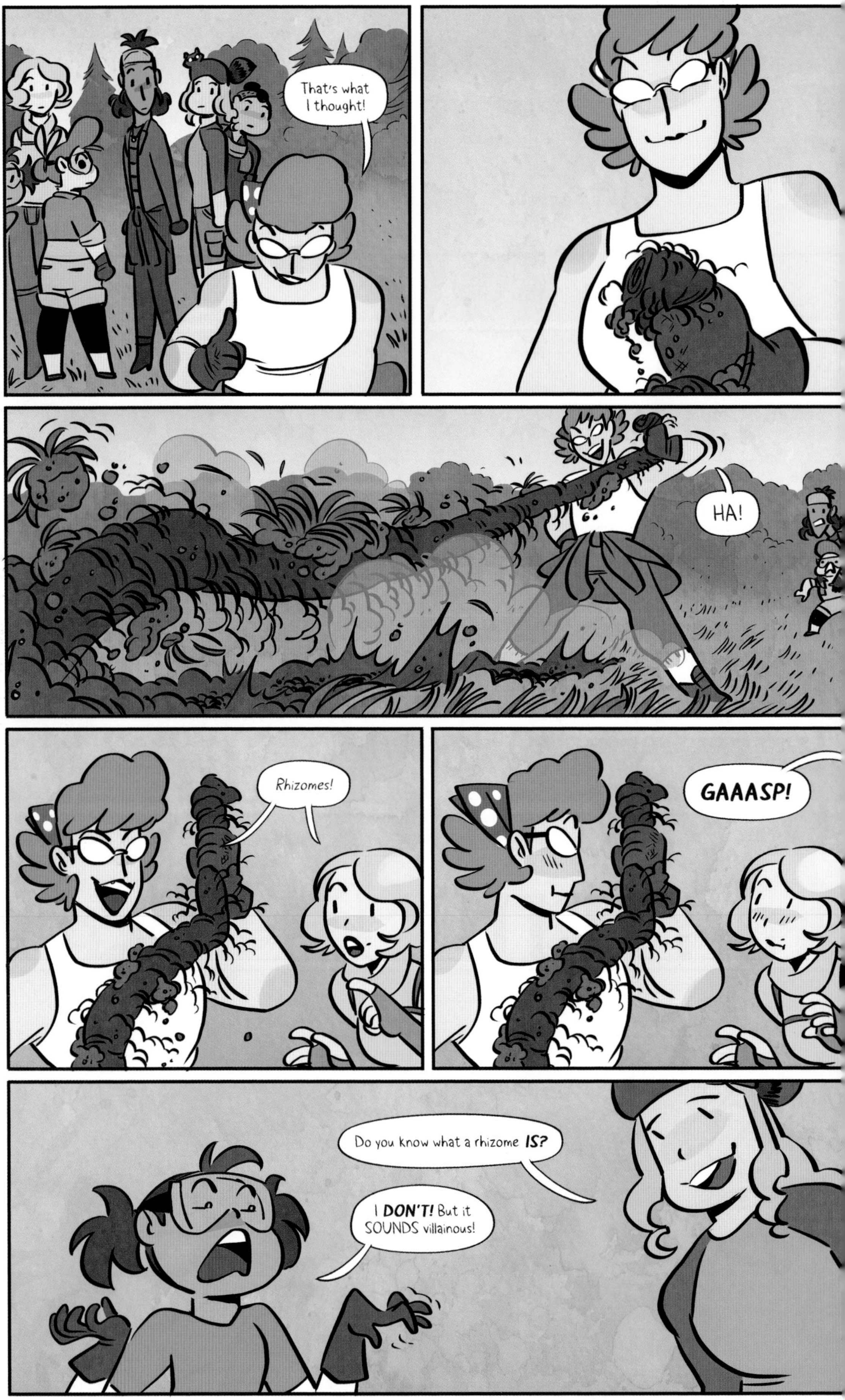
That's what I thought!
HA!
Rhizomes!
GAAASP!
Do you know what a rhizome IS?
I DON'T! But it SOUNDS villainous!

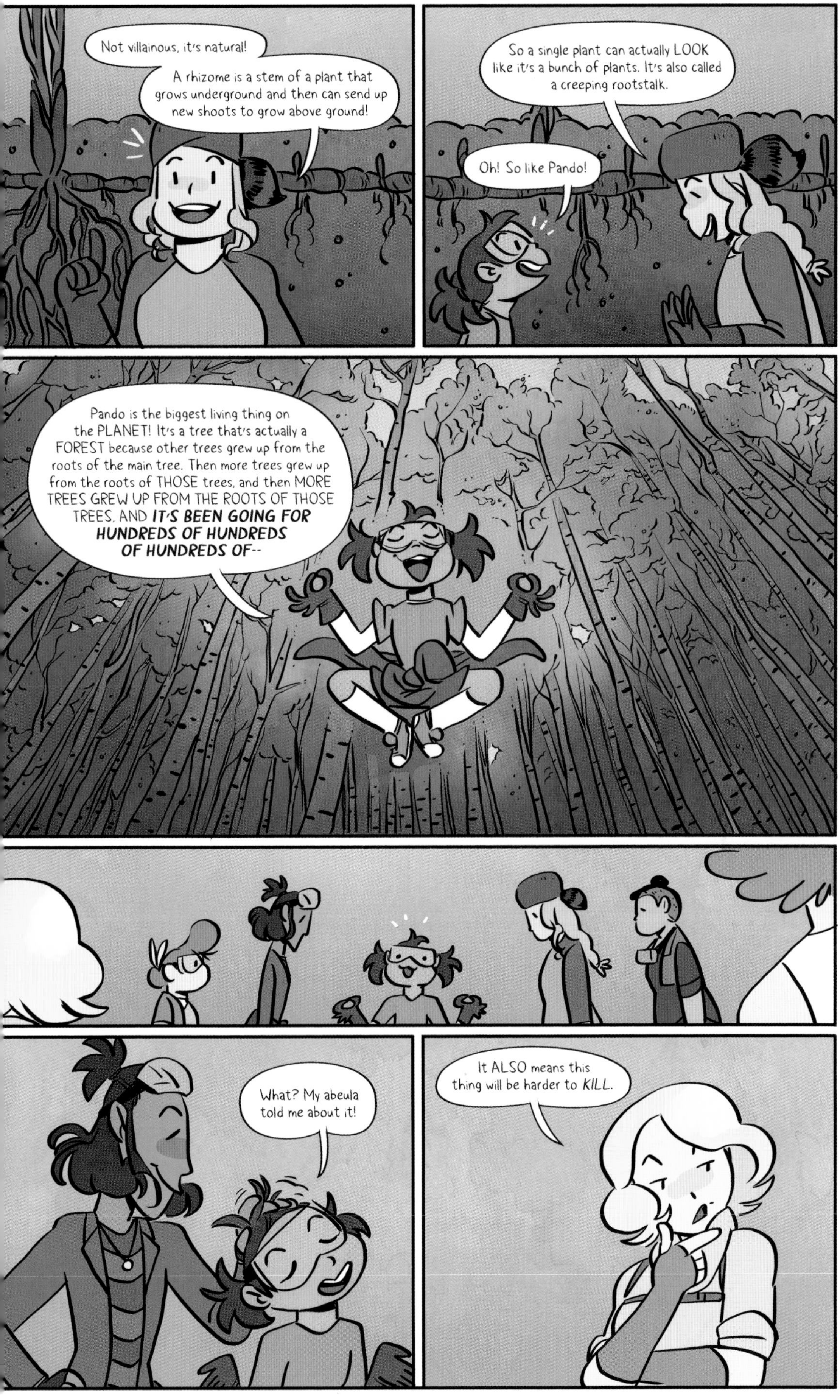
Not villainous, it's natural!
A rhizome is a stem of a plant that grows underground and then can send up new shoots to grow above ground!
So a single plant can actually LOOK like it's a bunch of plants. It's also called a creeping rootstalk.
Oh! So like Pando!
Pando is the biggest living thing on the PLANET! It's a tree that's actually a FOREST because other trees grew up from the roots of the main tree. Then more trees grew up from the roots of THOSE trees, and then MORE TREES GREW UP FROM THE ROOTS OF THOSE TREES, AND ***IT'S BEEN GOING FOR HUNDREDS OF HUNDREDS OF HUNDREDS OF--***
What? My abeula told me about it!
It ALSO means this thing will be harder to *KILL*.

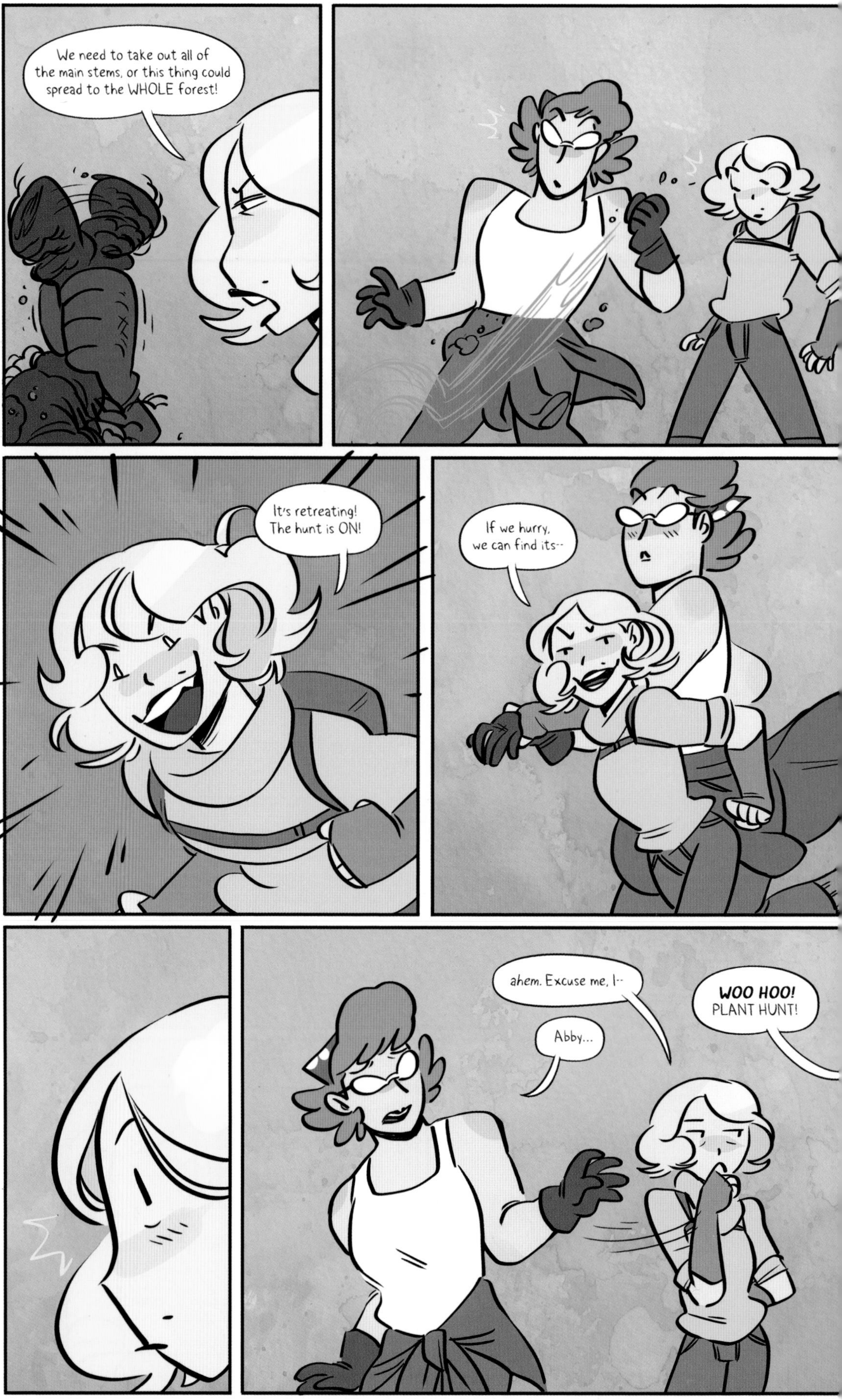
We need to take out all of the main stems, or this thing could spread to the WHOLE forest!
It's retreating! The hunt is ON!
If we hurry, we can find its--
ahem. Excuse me, I--
Abby...
WOO HOO! PLANT HUNT!

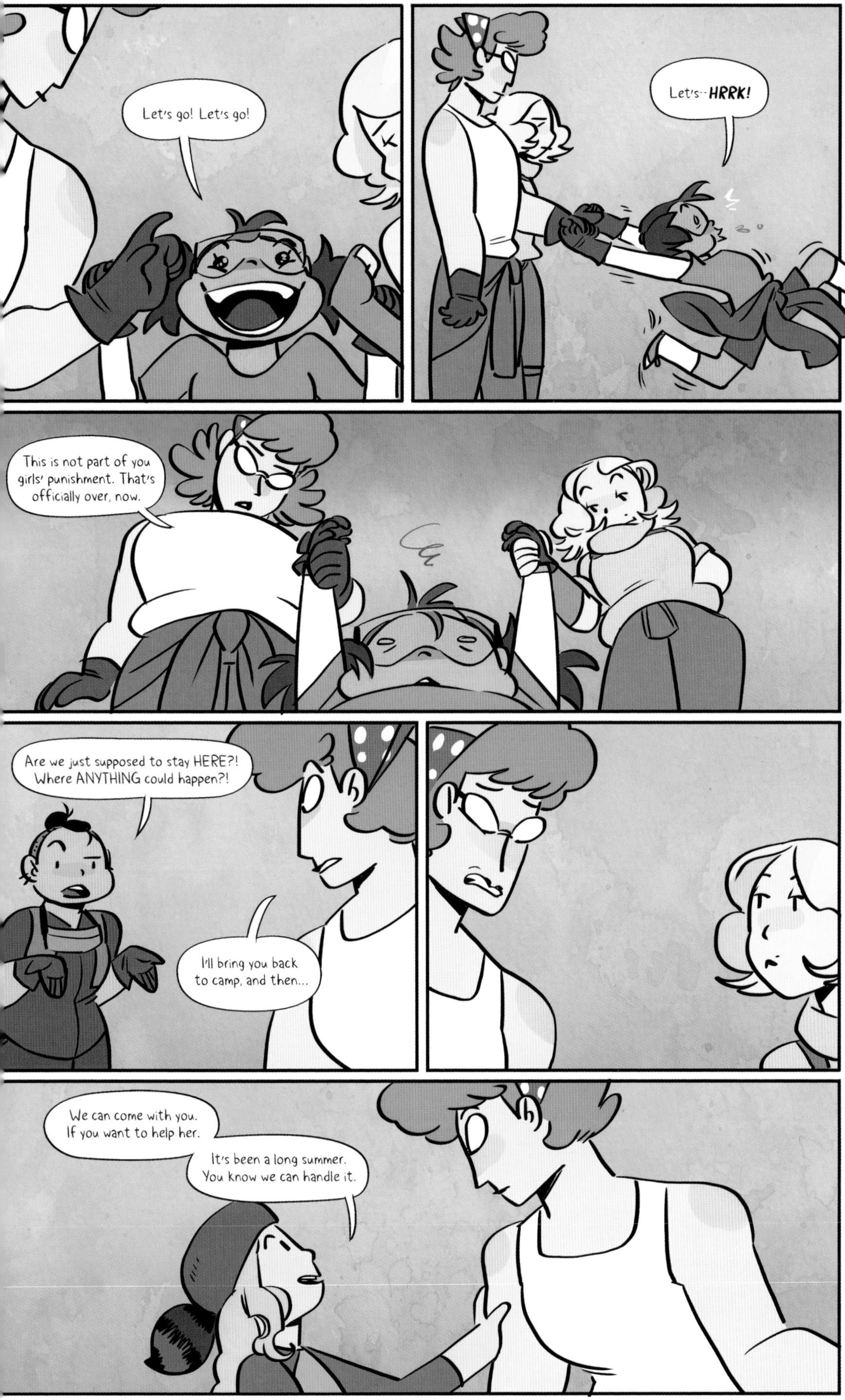
Let's go! Let's go!
Let's--HRRK!
This is not part of you girls' punishment. That's officially over, now.
Are we just supposed to stay HERE?! Where ANYTHING could happen?!
I'll bring you back to camp, and then...
We can come with you. If you want to help her.
It's been a long summer. You know we can handle it.

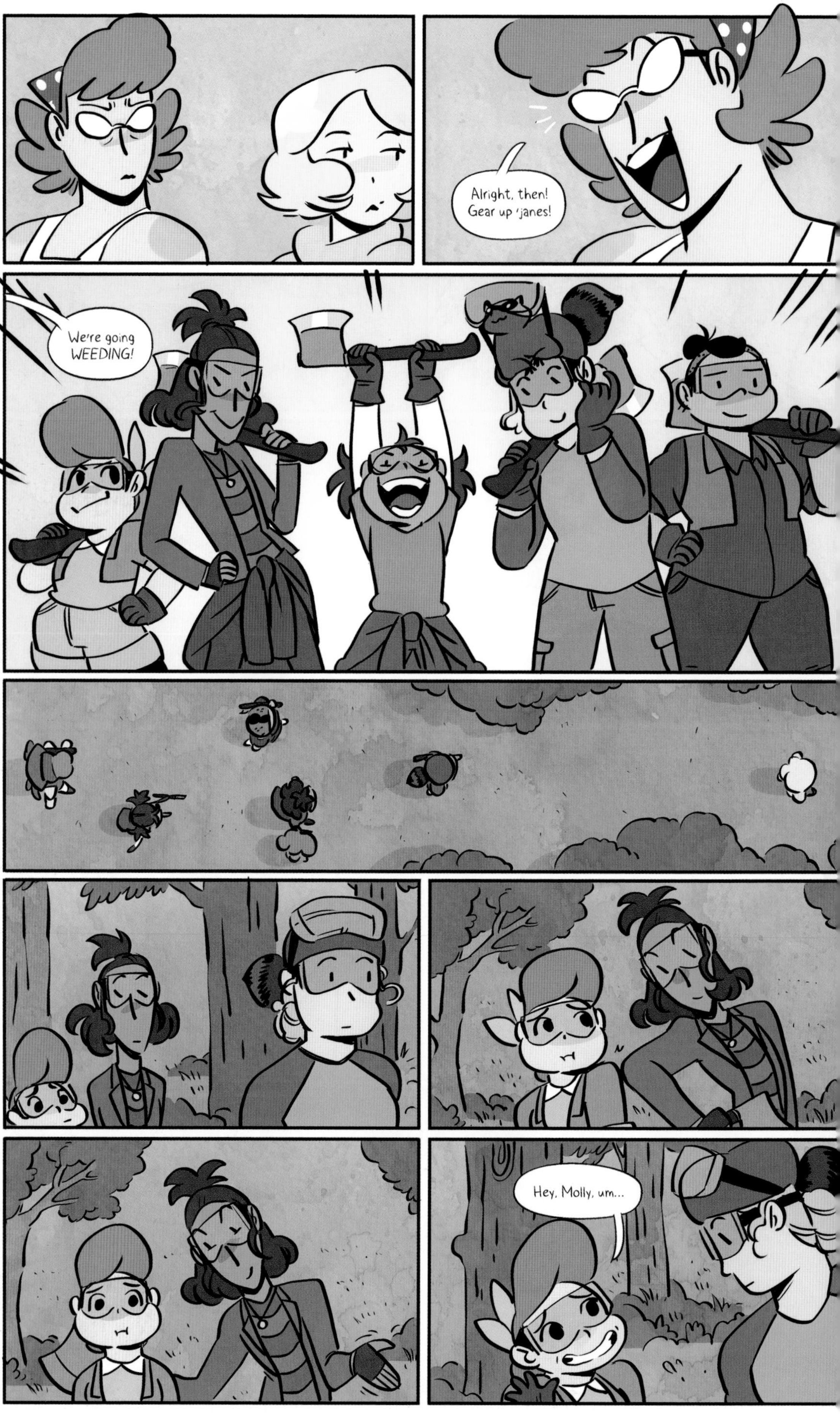
Alright, then!
Gear up 'janes!
We're going
WEEDING!
Hey, Molly, um...

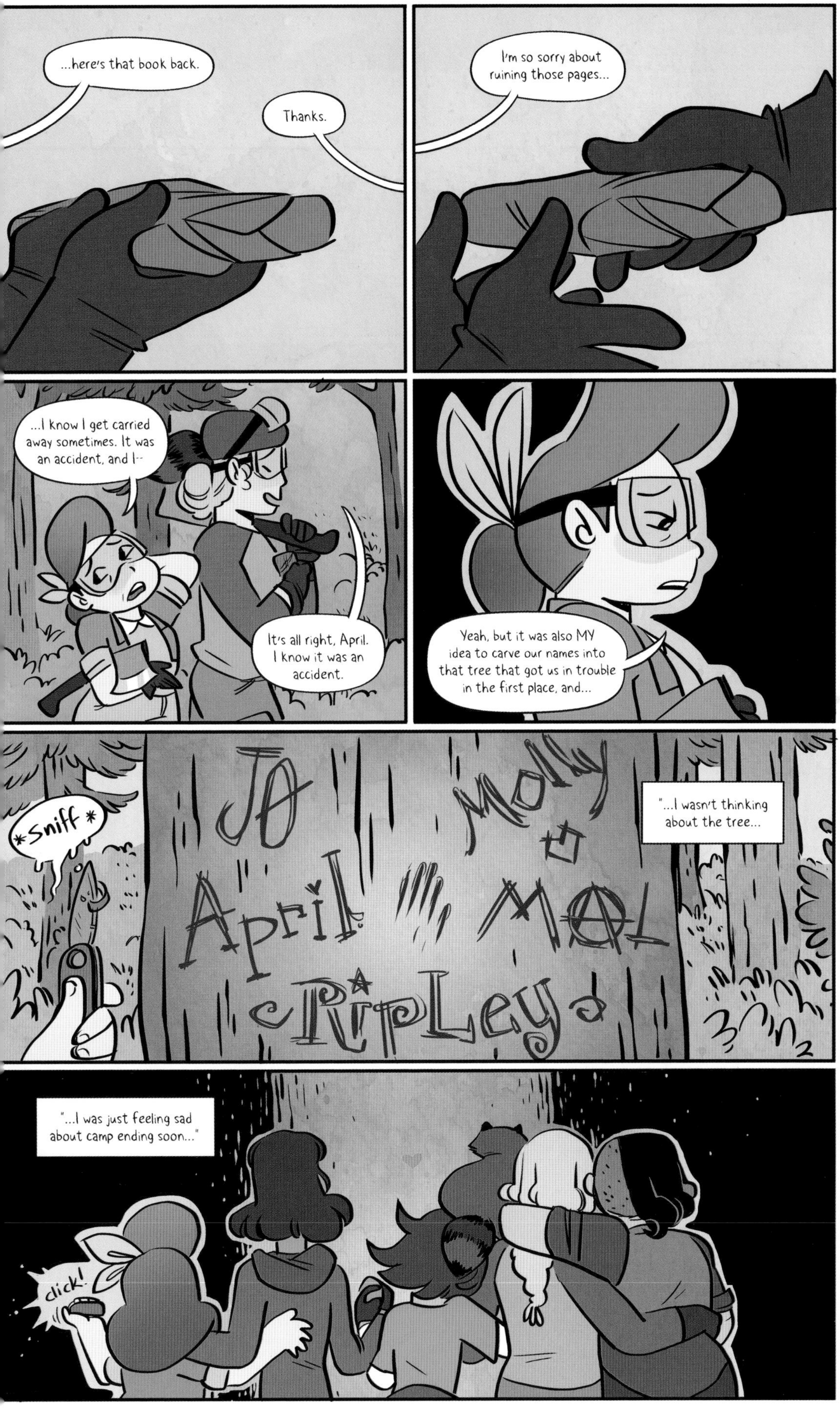
...here's that book back.
Thanks.
I'm so sorry about ruining those pages...
...I know I get carried away sometimes. It was an accident, and I--
It's all right, April. I know it was an accident.
Yeah, but it was also MY idea to carve our names into that tree that got us in trouble in the first place, and...
Sniff
JO
Molly
April
MAL
RipLey
"...I wasn't thinking about the tree...
"...I was just feeling sad about camp ending soon..."
click!

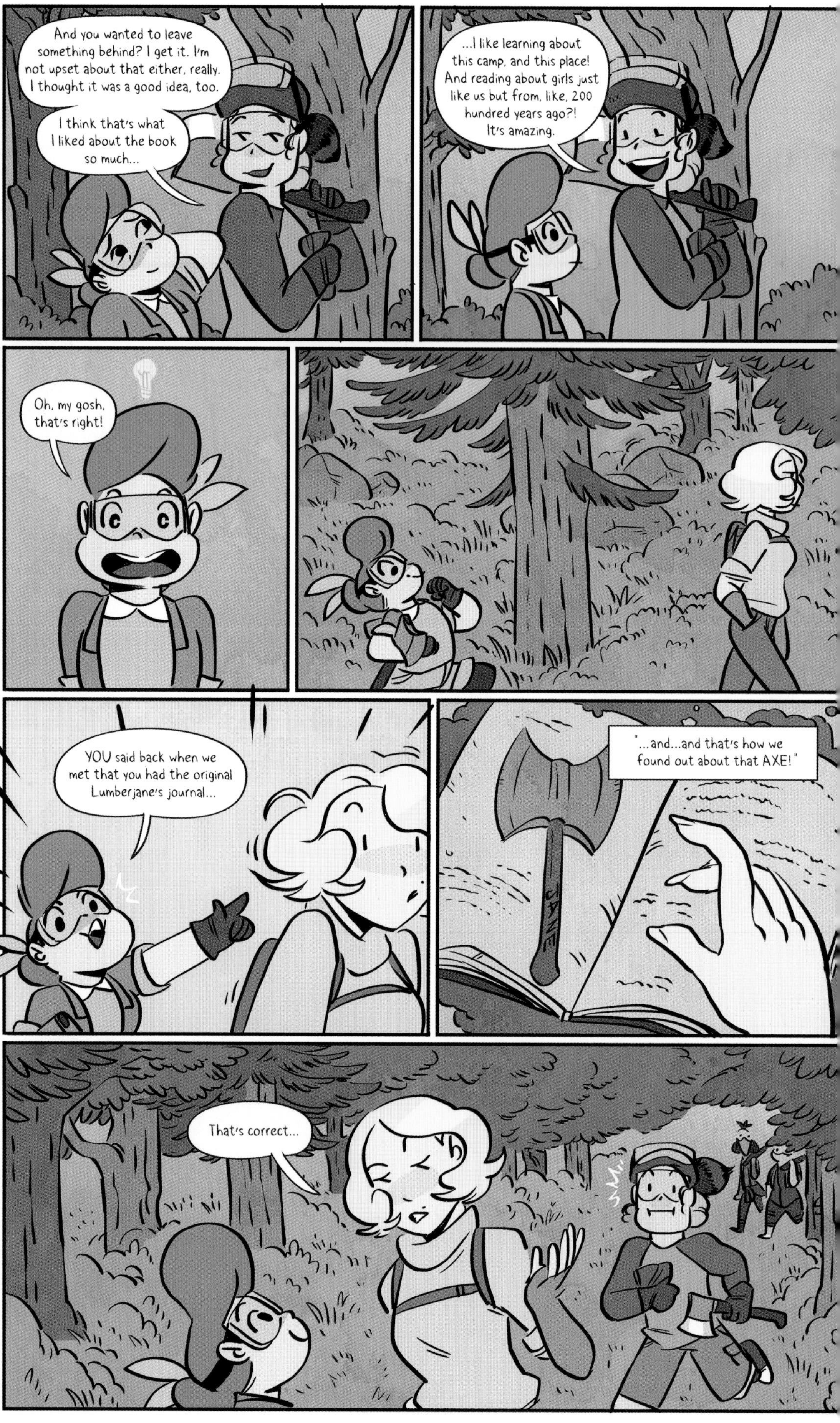
And you wanted to leave something behind? I get it. I'm not upset about that either, really. I thought it was a good idea, too.
I think that's what I liked about the book so much...
...I like learning about this camp, and this place! And reading about girls just like us but from, like, 200 hundred years ago?! It's amazing.
Oh, my gosh, that's right!
YOU said back when we met that you had the original Lumberjane's journal...
"...and...and that's how we found out about that AXE!"
JANE
That's correct...

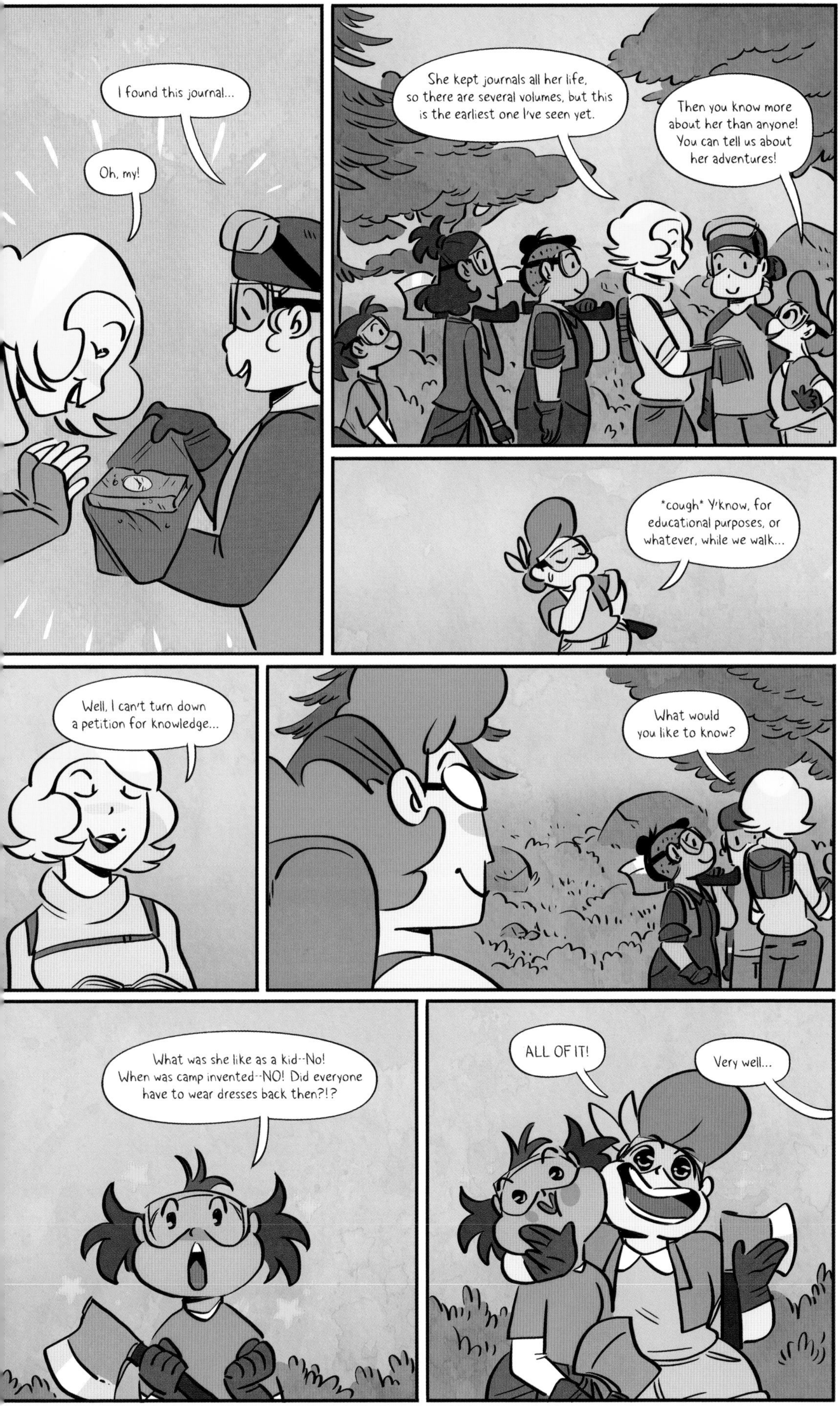
I found this journal...
Oh, my!
She kept journals all her life, so there are several volumes, but this is the earliest one I've seen yet.
Then you know more about her than anyone! You can tell us about her adventures!
cough Y'know, for educational purposes, or whatever, while we walk...
Well, I can't turn down a petition for knowledge...
What would you like to know?
What was she like as a kid--No! When was camp invented--NO! Did everyone have to wear dresses back then?!?
ALL OF IT!
Very well...

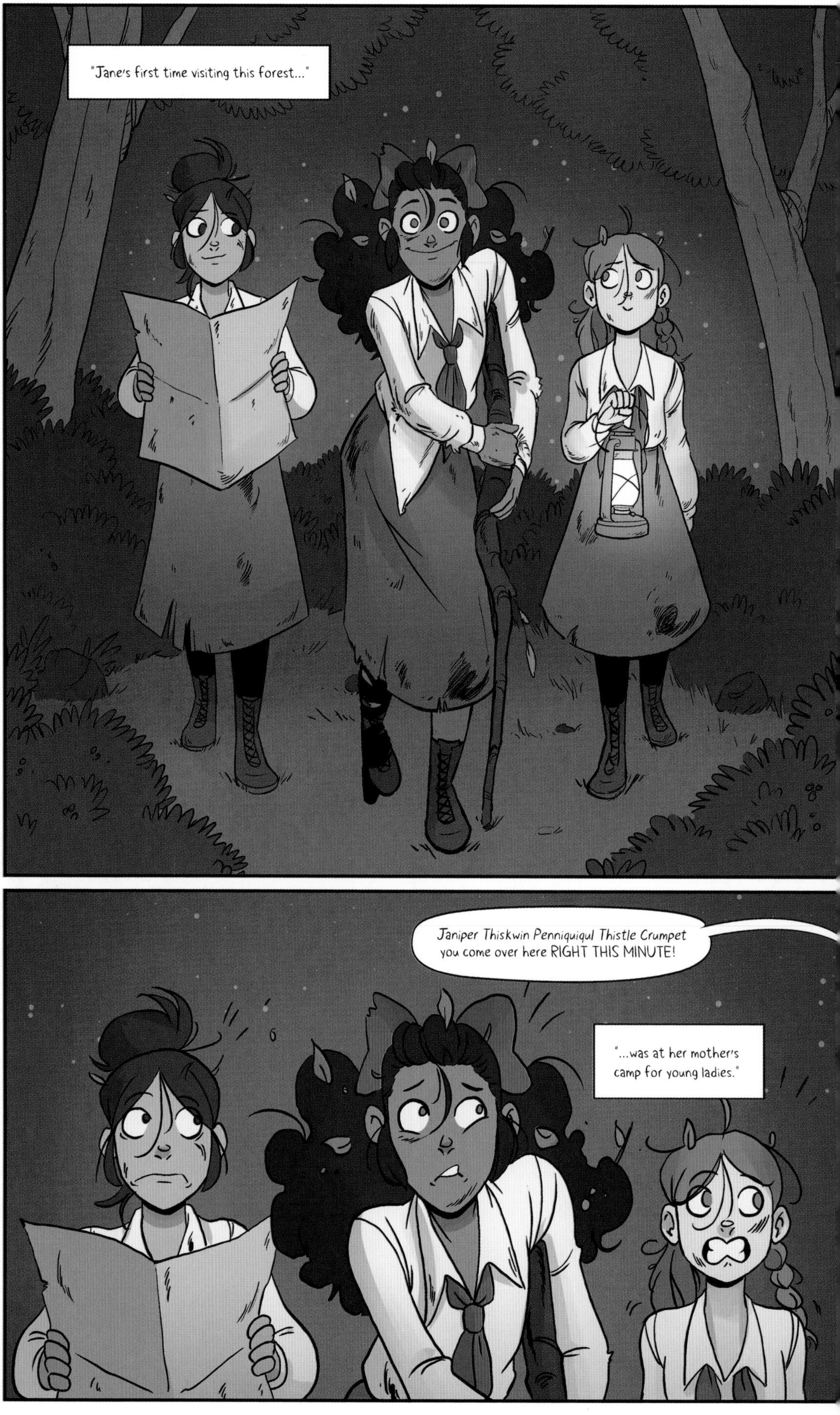
"Jane's first time visiting this forest..."
Janiper Thiskwin Penniquiqul Thistle Crumpet you come over here RIGHT THIS MINUTE!
"...was at her mother's camp for young ladies."

will co
The
It he
appearar
dress fo
Further
Lumber
to have
part in
Thiskw
Hardc
have
thems

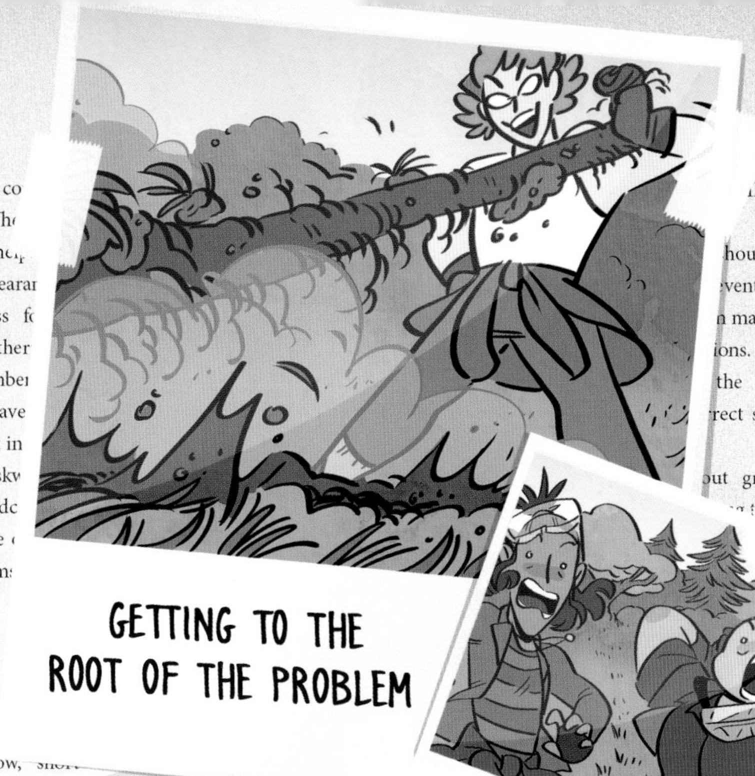
GETTING TO THE
ROOT OF THE PROBLEM

E UNIFORM

hould be worn at camp
events when Lumberjanes
n may also be worn at other
ions. It should be worn as a
the uniform dress with
rect shoes, and stocking or

out grows her uniform or
ther Lumberjane.
a she has
her
her

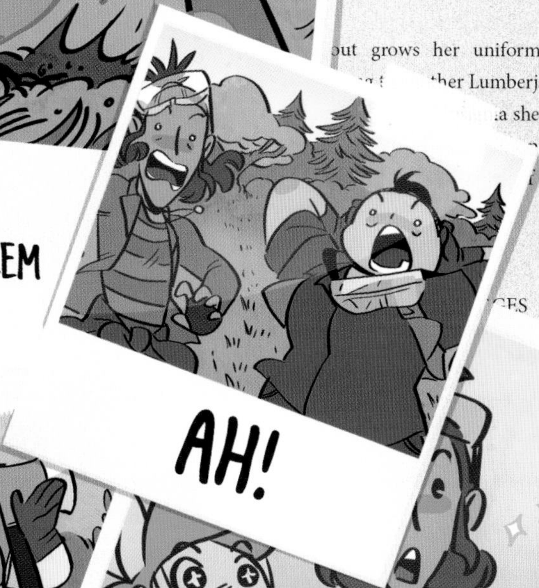
AH!

The
yellow,
emb
the w
choos
slacks,
made o
out-of-do
green bere
the colla
Shoes ma
heels, rou ... ings or
socks sho ... with the shoes or wi
the uniform. Ne... bracelets, or other jewelry do
belong with a Lumberjane uniform.

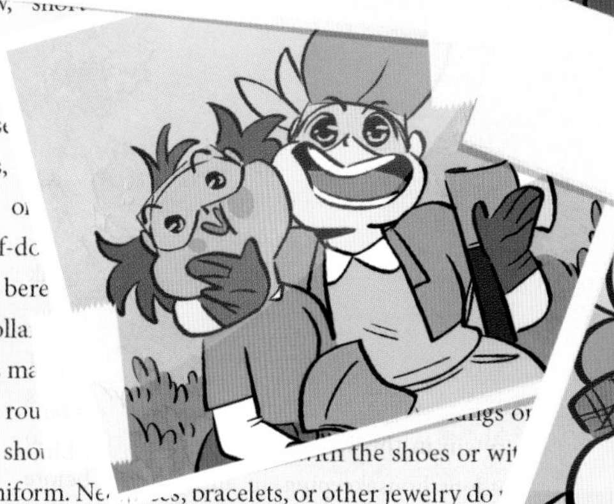

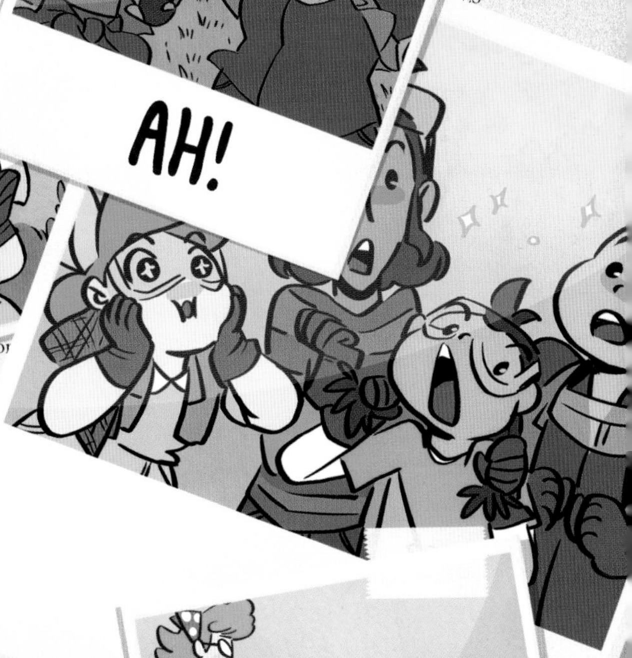

HOW TO WEAR THE UNIFORM

To look well in a uniform demands first of ... uniform be kept in good condition—clean ... pressed. See that the skirt is the right length for your own height and build, that the belt is adjusted to your waist, that your shoes and stockings are in keeping with the uniform, that you watch your posture and carry yourself with dignity and grace. If the beret is removed indoors, be sure that your hair is neat and kept in place with an inconspicuous clip or ribbon. When you wear a Lumberjane uniform you are identified as a member of this organization and you should be doubly careful to conduct yourself in a way that will show everyone that courtesy and thoughtfulness are part of being a Lumberjane. People are likely to judge a whole nation by the selfishness of a few individuals, to criticize a whole family because of the misconduct of one member, and to feel unkindly toward an organization because of the

The unifor
helps to cre
in a group.
active life th
another bond
future, and pr
in order to b
Lumberjane pr
Penniquiqul Thi ... ore Lady
Types, but m... s will wish to have one. They
can either bu... , or make it themselves from
materials available at the trading post.

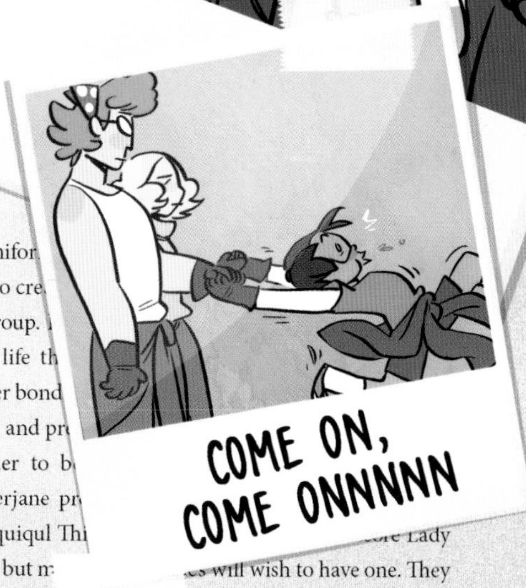
COME ON,
COME ONNNNN

LUMBERJANES FIELD MANUAL

CHAPTER
SEVENTY-ONE

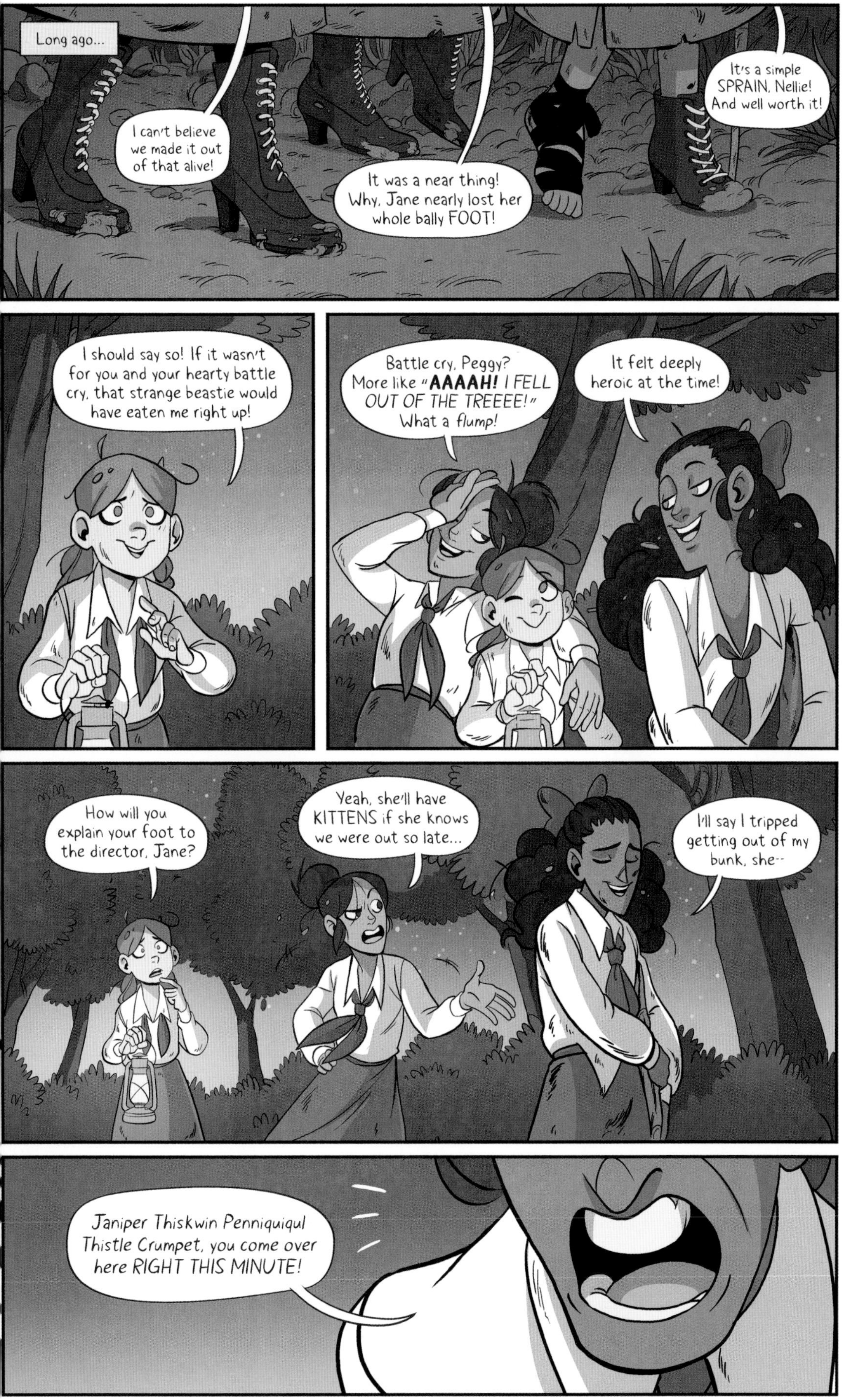
Long ago...
I can't believe we made it out of that alive!
It was a near thing! Why, Jane nearly lost her whole bally FOOT!
It's a simple SPRAIN, Nellie! And well worth it!
I should say so! If it wasn't for you and your hearty battle cry, that strange beastie would have eaten me right up!
Battle cry, Peggy? More like "AAAAH! I FELL OUT OF THE TREEEE!" What a flump!
It felt deeply heroic at the time!
How will you explain your foot to the director, Jane?
Yeah, she'll have KITTENS if she knows we were out so late...
I'll say I tripped getting out of my bunk, she--
Janiper Thiskwin Penniquiqul Thistle Crumpet, you come over here RIGHT THIS MINUTE!

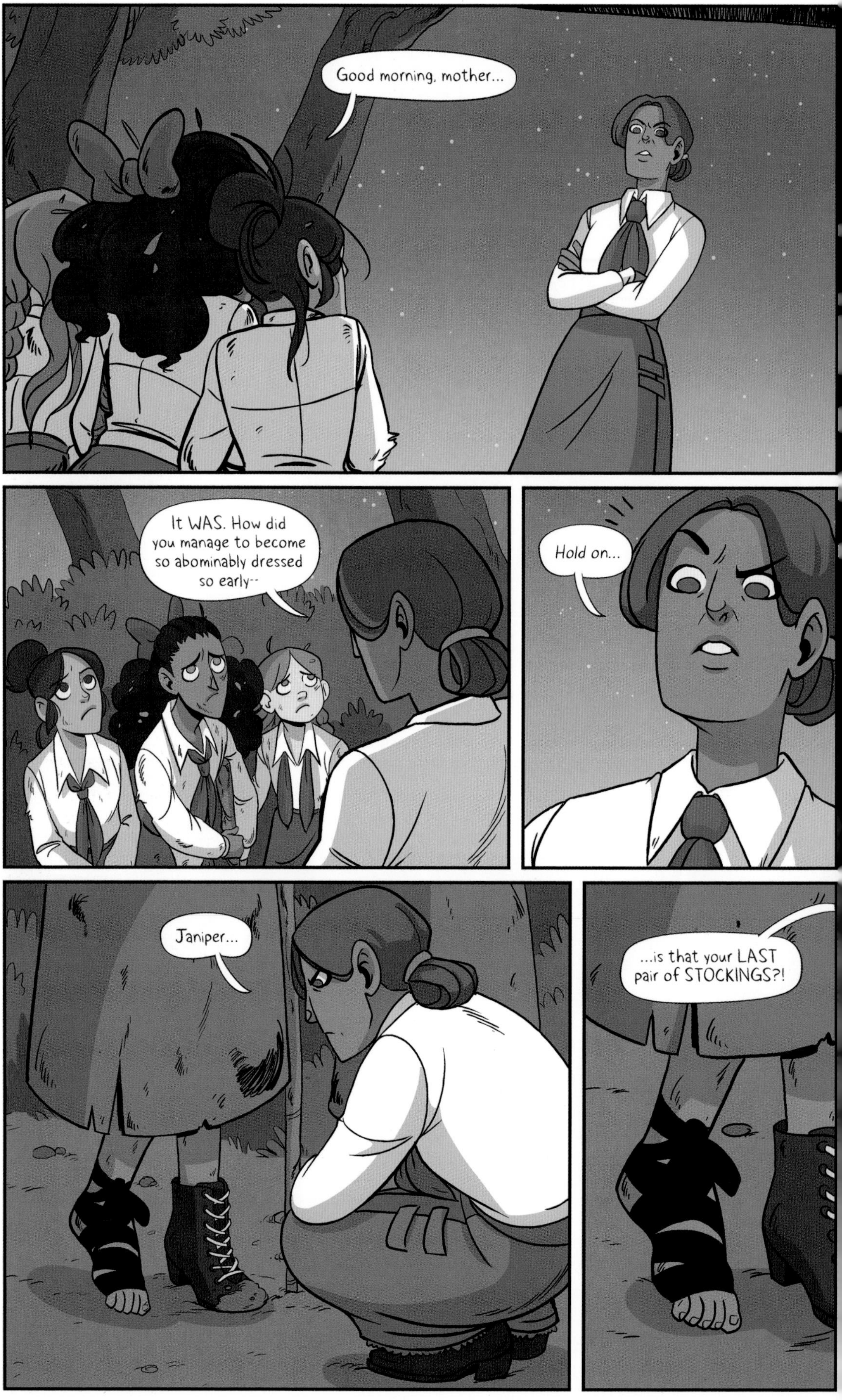
Good morning, mother...
It WAS. How did you manage to become so abominably dressed so early--
Hold on...
Janiper...
...is that your LAST pair of STOCKINGS?!

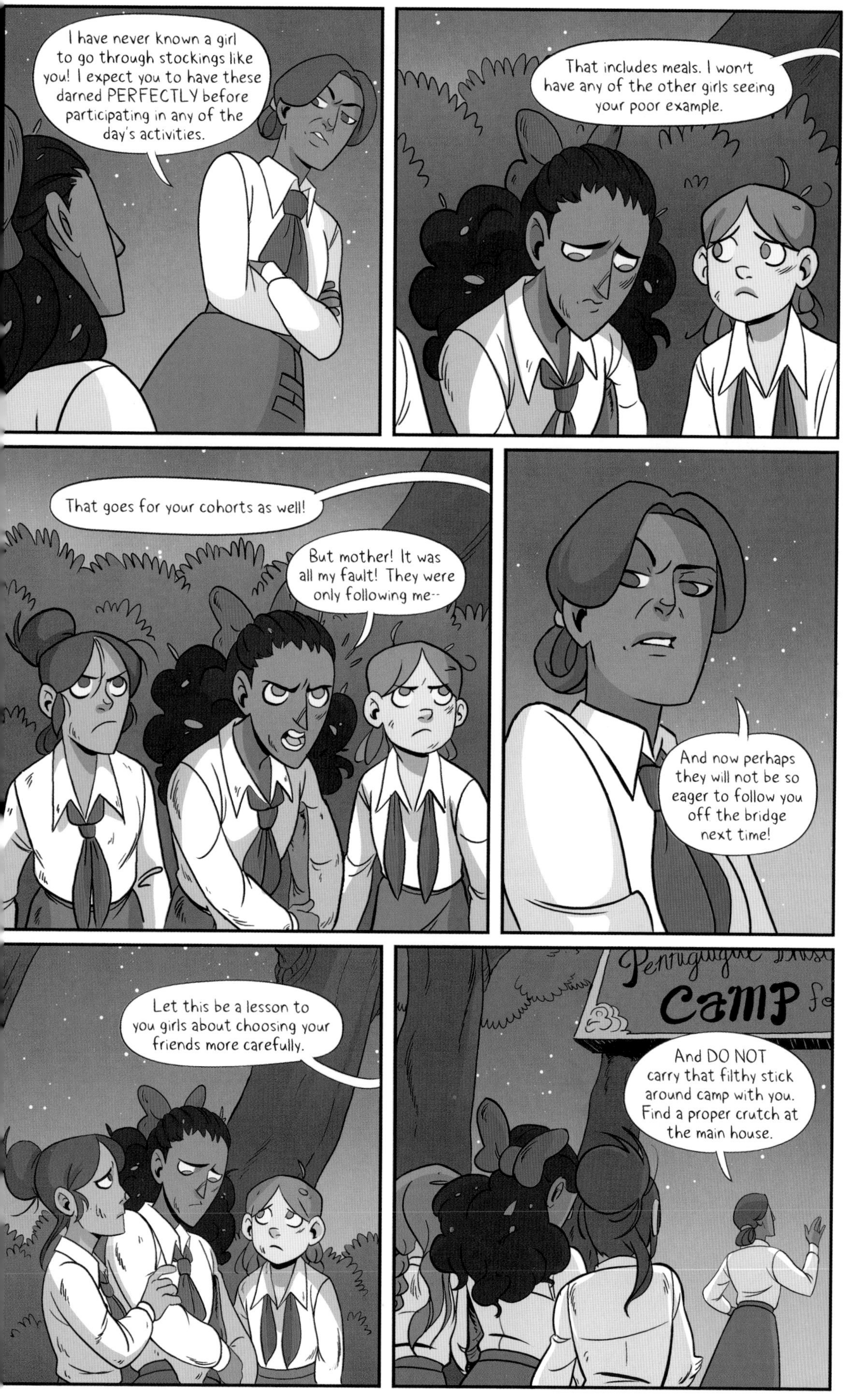
I have never known a girl to go through stockings like you! I expect you to have these darned PERFECTLY before participating in any of the day's activities.
That includes meals. I won't have any of the other girls seeing your poor example.
That goes for your cohorts as well!
But mother! It was all my fault! They were only following me--
And now perhaps they will not be so eager to follow you off the bridge next time!
Let this be a lesson to you girls about choosing your friends more carefully.
CAMP
And DO NOT carry that filthy stick around camp with you. Find a proper crutch at the main house.

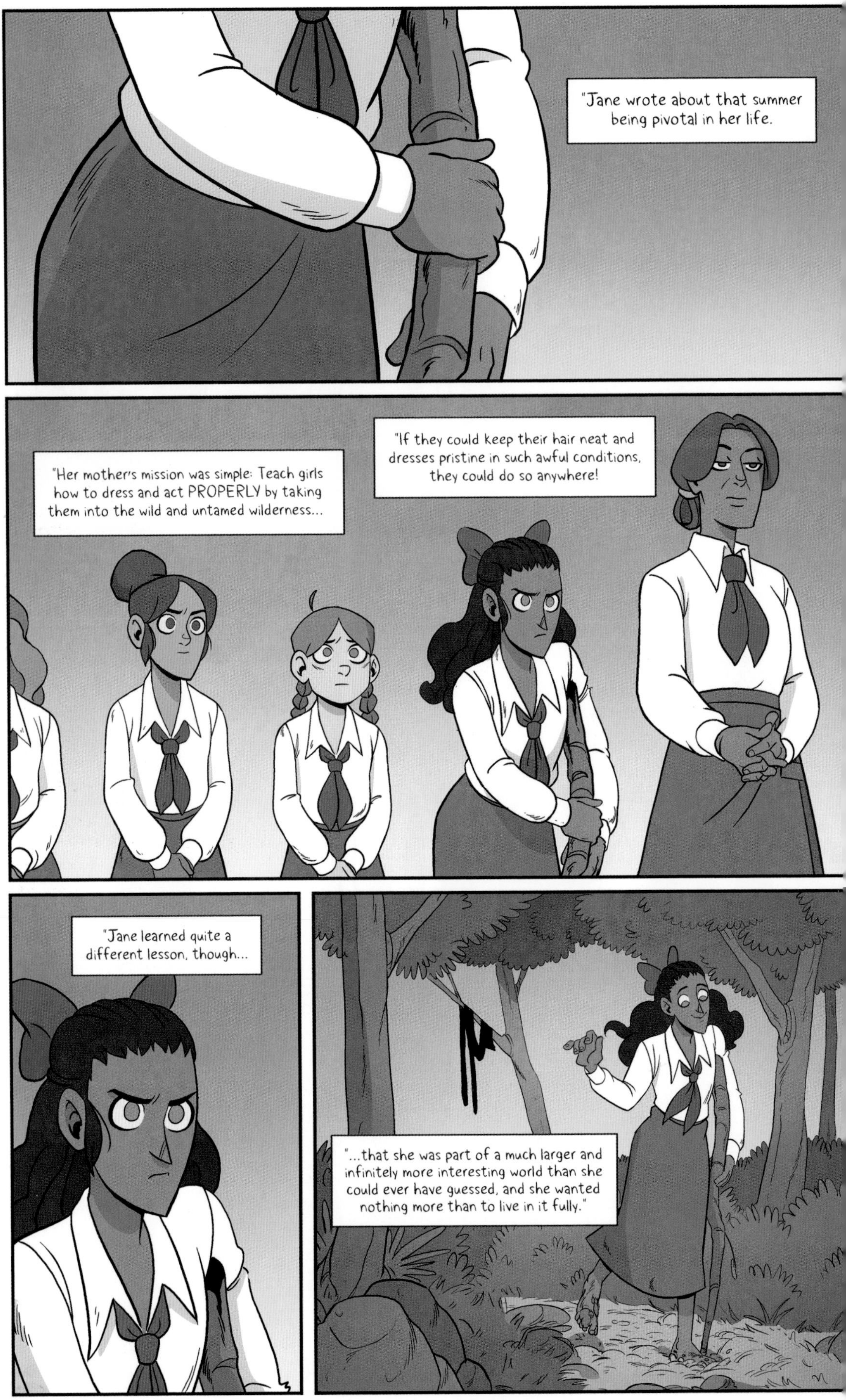
"Jane wrote about that summer being pivotal in her life.
"Her mother's mission was simple: Teach girls how to dress and act PROPERLY by taking them into the wild and untamed wilderness...
"If they could keep their hair neat and dresses pristine in such awful conditions, they could do so anywhere!
"Jane learned quite a different lesson, though...
"...that she was part of a much larger and infinitely more interesting world than she could ever have guessed, and she wanted nothing more than to live in it fully."

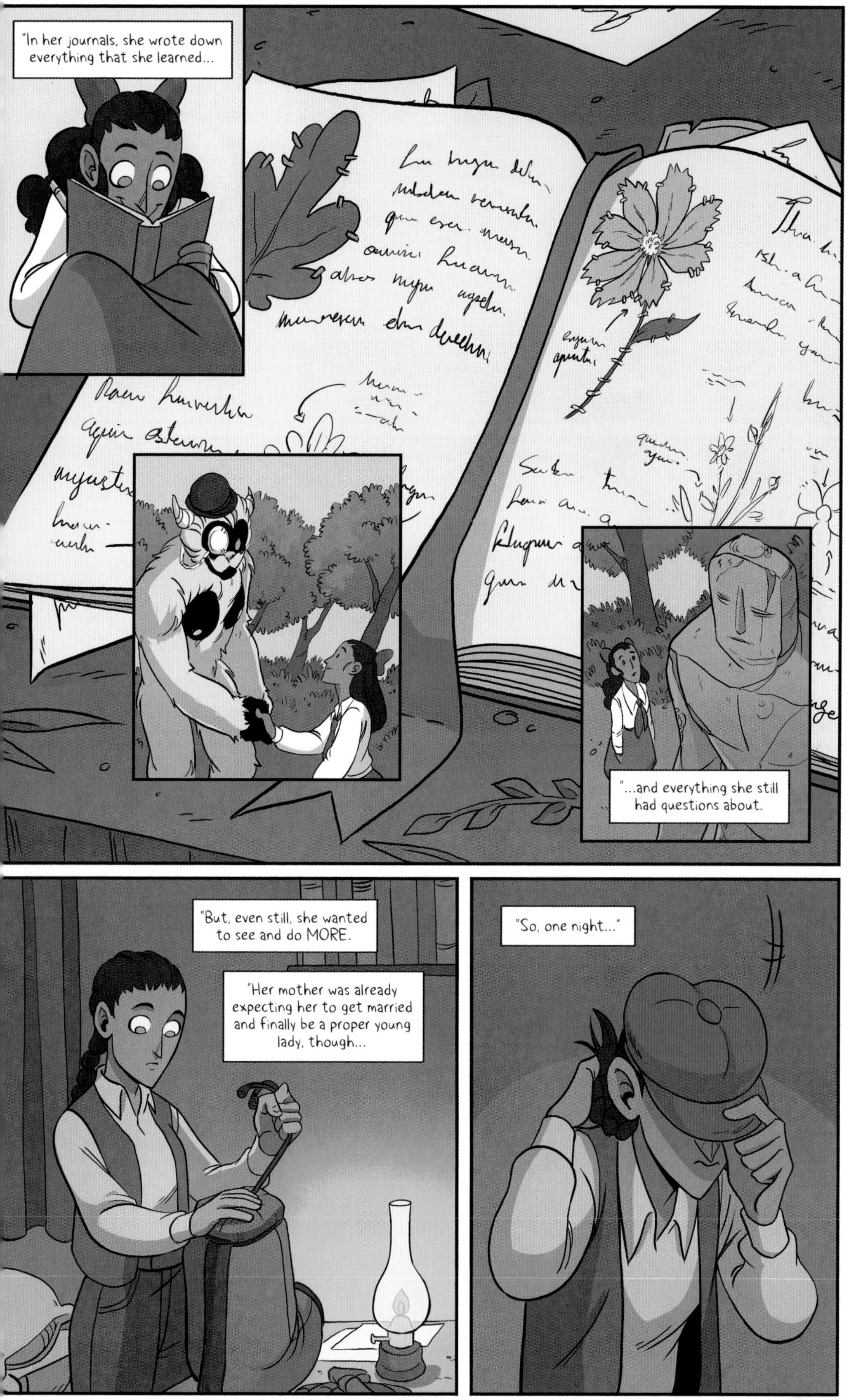
"In her journals, she wrote down everything that she learned...
"...and everything she still had questions about.
"But, even still, she wanted to see and do MORE.
"Her mother was already expecting her to get married and finally be a proper young lady, though...
"So, one night..."

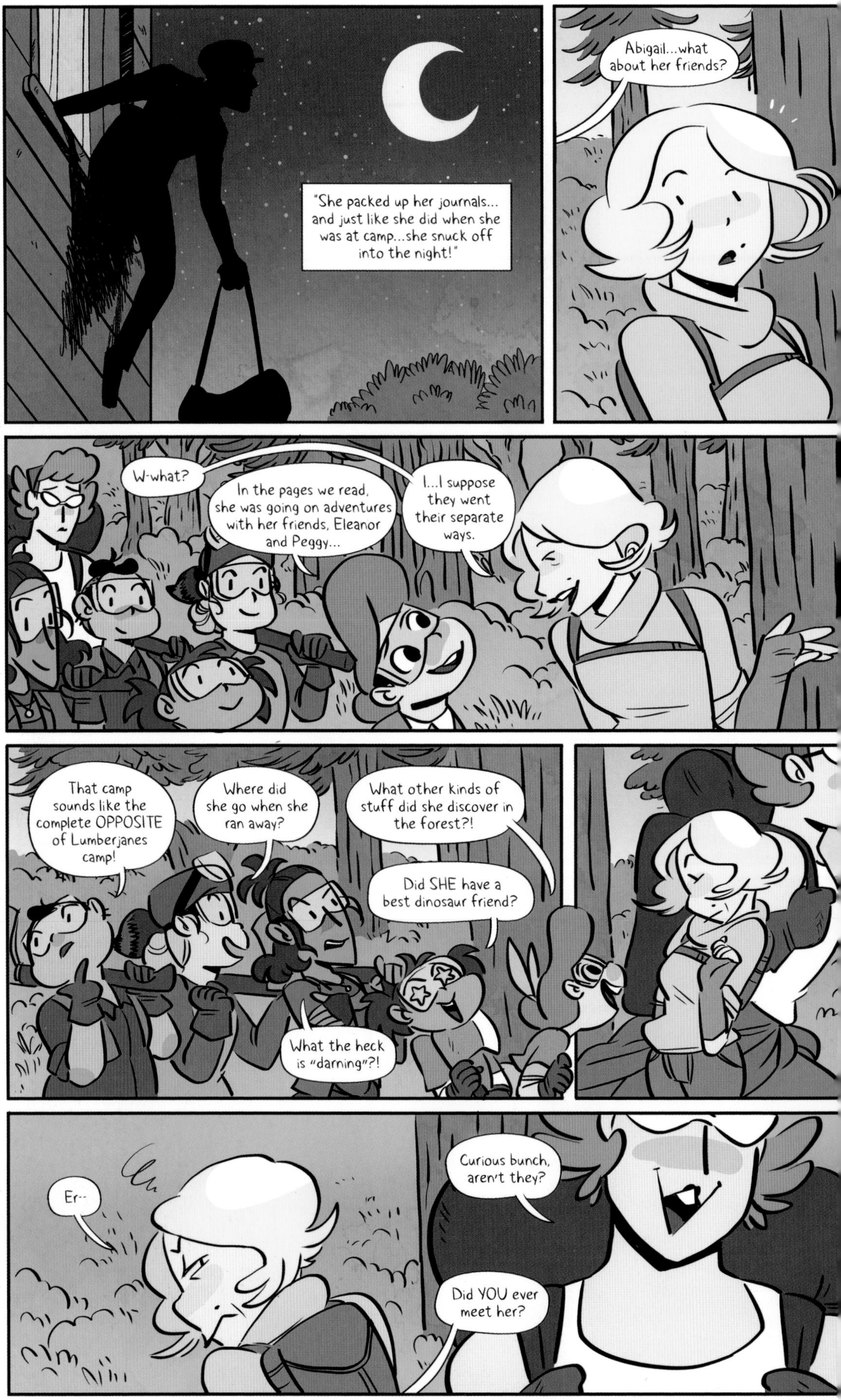
"She packed up her journals... and just like she did when she was at camp...she snuck off into the night!"
Abigail...what about her friends?
W-what?
In the pages we read, she was going on adventures with her friends, Eleanor and Peggy...
I...I suppose they went their separate ways.
That camp sounds like the complete OPPOSITE of Lumberjanes camp!
Where did she go when she ran away?
What other kinds of stuff did she discover in the forest?!
Did SHE have a best dinosaur friend?
What the heck is "darning"?!
Er--
Curious bunch, aren't they?
Did YOU ever meet her?

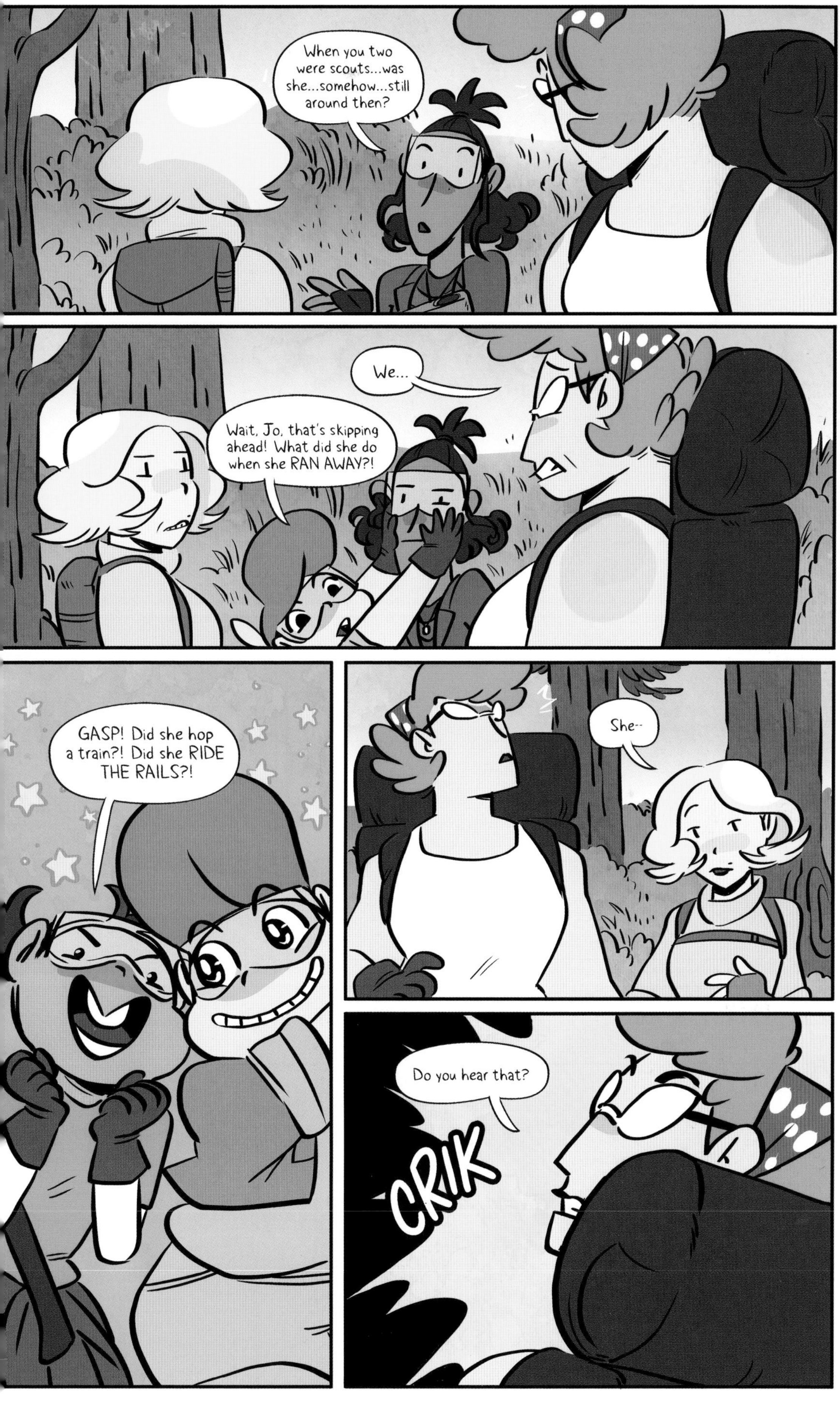
When you two were scouts...was she...somehow...still around then?
We...
Wait, Jo, that's skipping ahead! What did she do when she RAN AWAY?!
GASP! Did she hop a train?! Did she RIDE THE RAILS?!
She--
Do you hear that?
CRIK

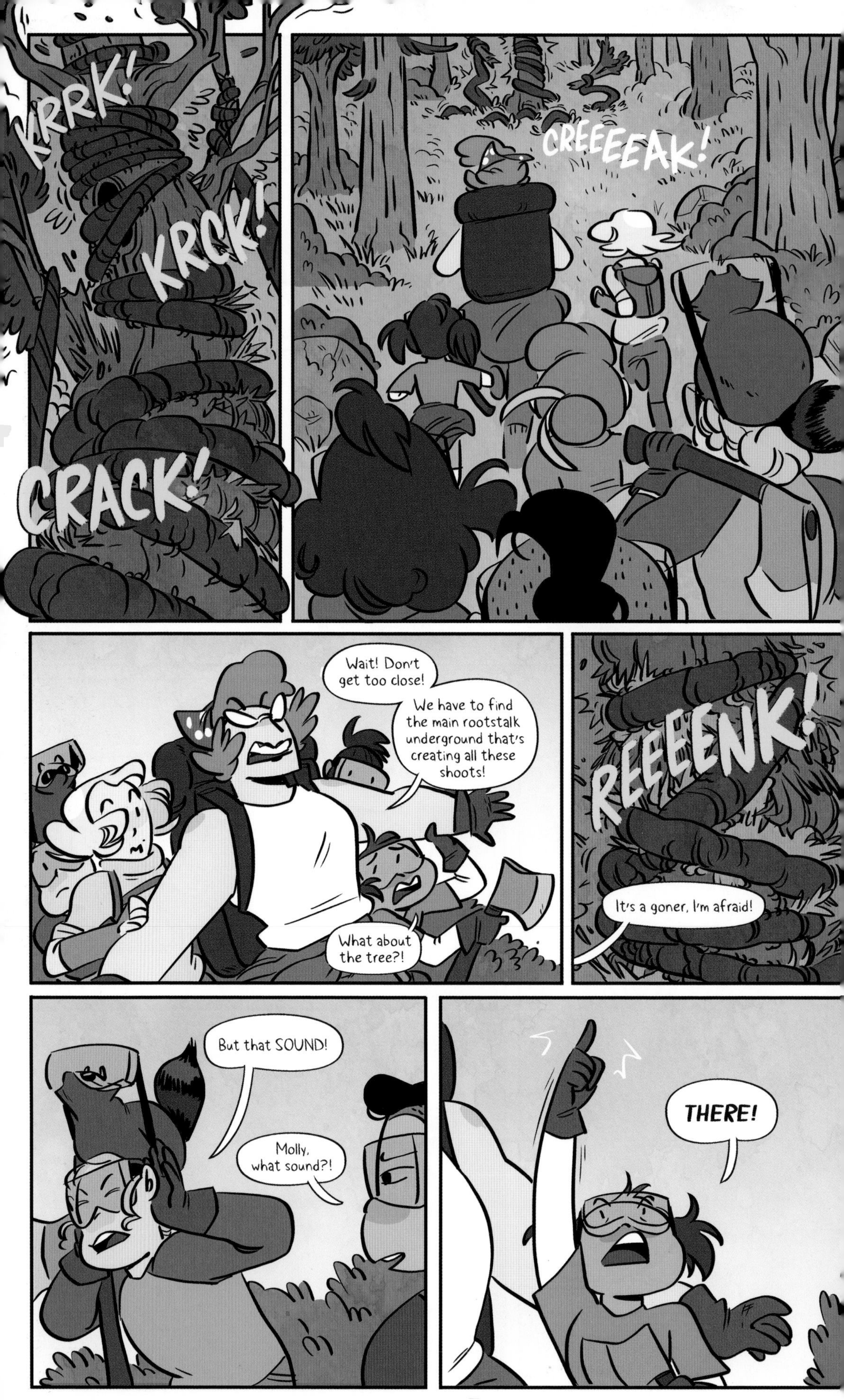
KRRK!
KRCK!
CRACK!
CREEEEAK!
Wait! Don't get too close!
We have to find the main rootstalk underground that's creating all these shoots!
What about the tree?!
REEEENK!
It's a goner, I'm afraid!
But that SOUND!
Molly, what sound?!
THERE!

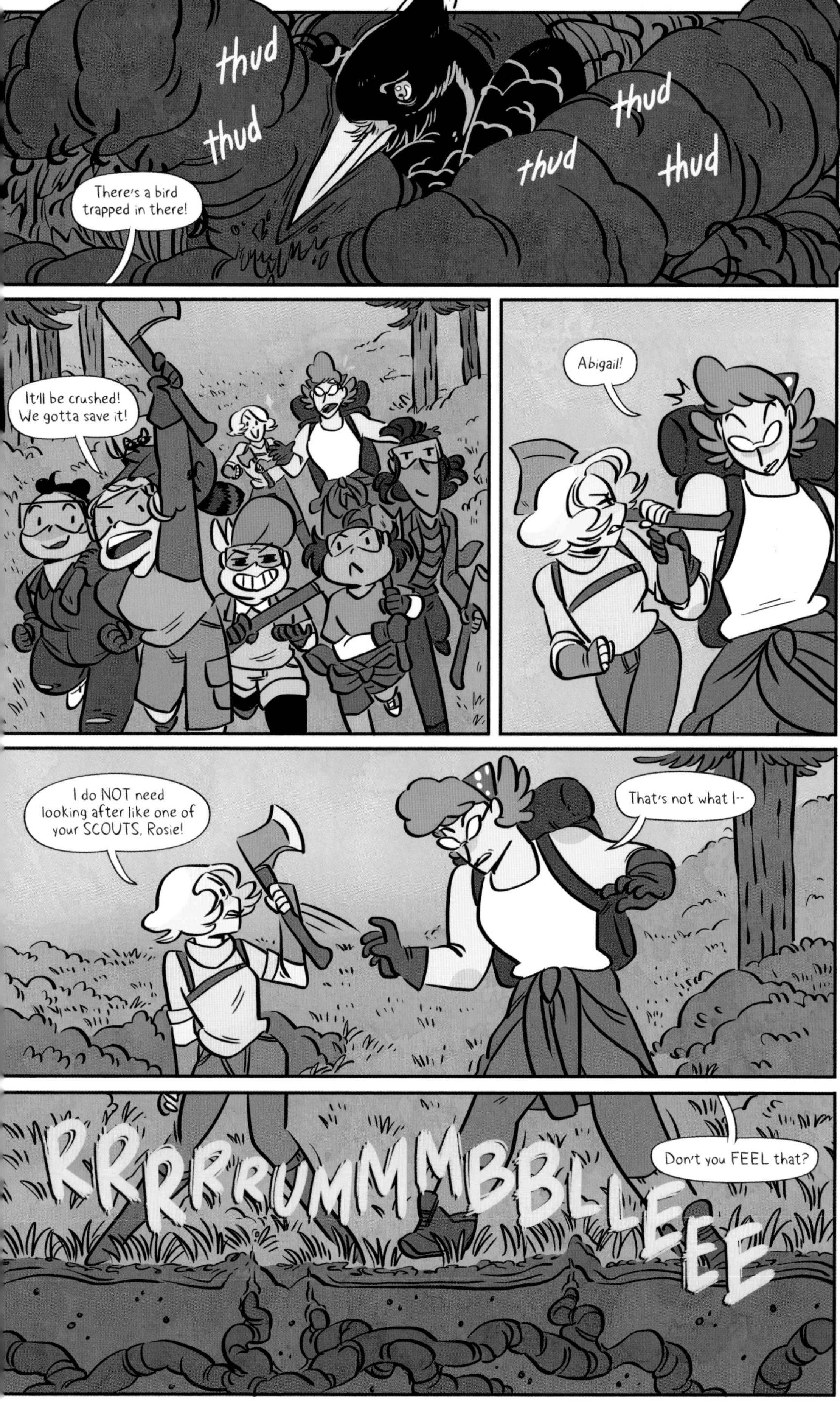
thud
thud
thud
thud
thud
There's a bird trapped in there!
It'll be crushed! We gotta save it!
Abigail!
I do NOT need looking after like one of your SCOUTS, Rosie!
That's not what I--
RRRRRUMMMBBLLEEE
Don't you FEEL that?

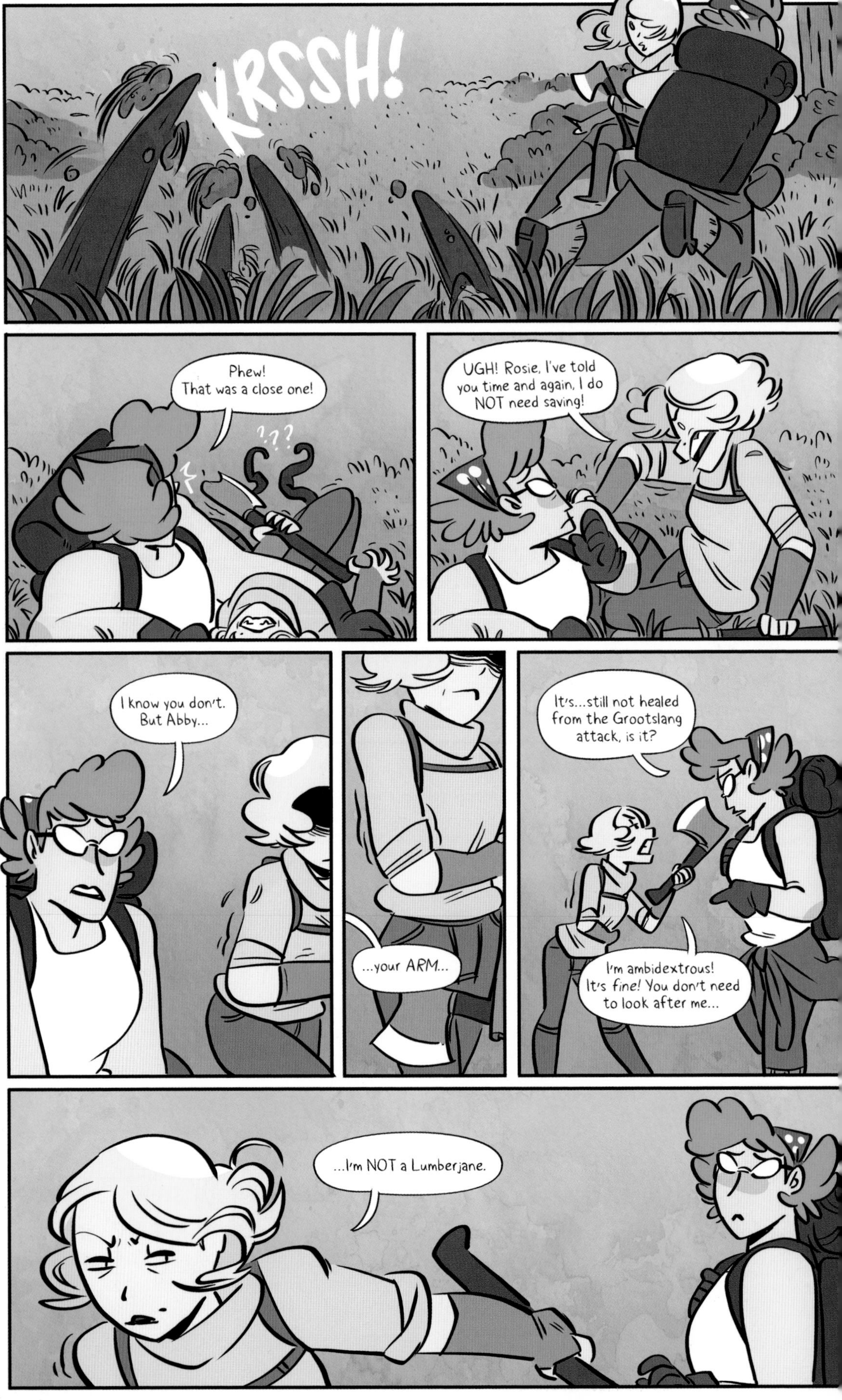
KRSSH!
Phew! That was a close one!
???
UGH! Rosie, I've told you time and again, I do NOT need saving!
I know you don't. But Abby...
...your ARM...
It's...still not healed from the Grootslang attack, is it?
I'm ambidextrous! It's fine! You don't need to look after me...
...I'm NOT a Lumberjane.

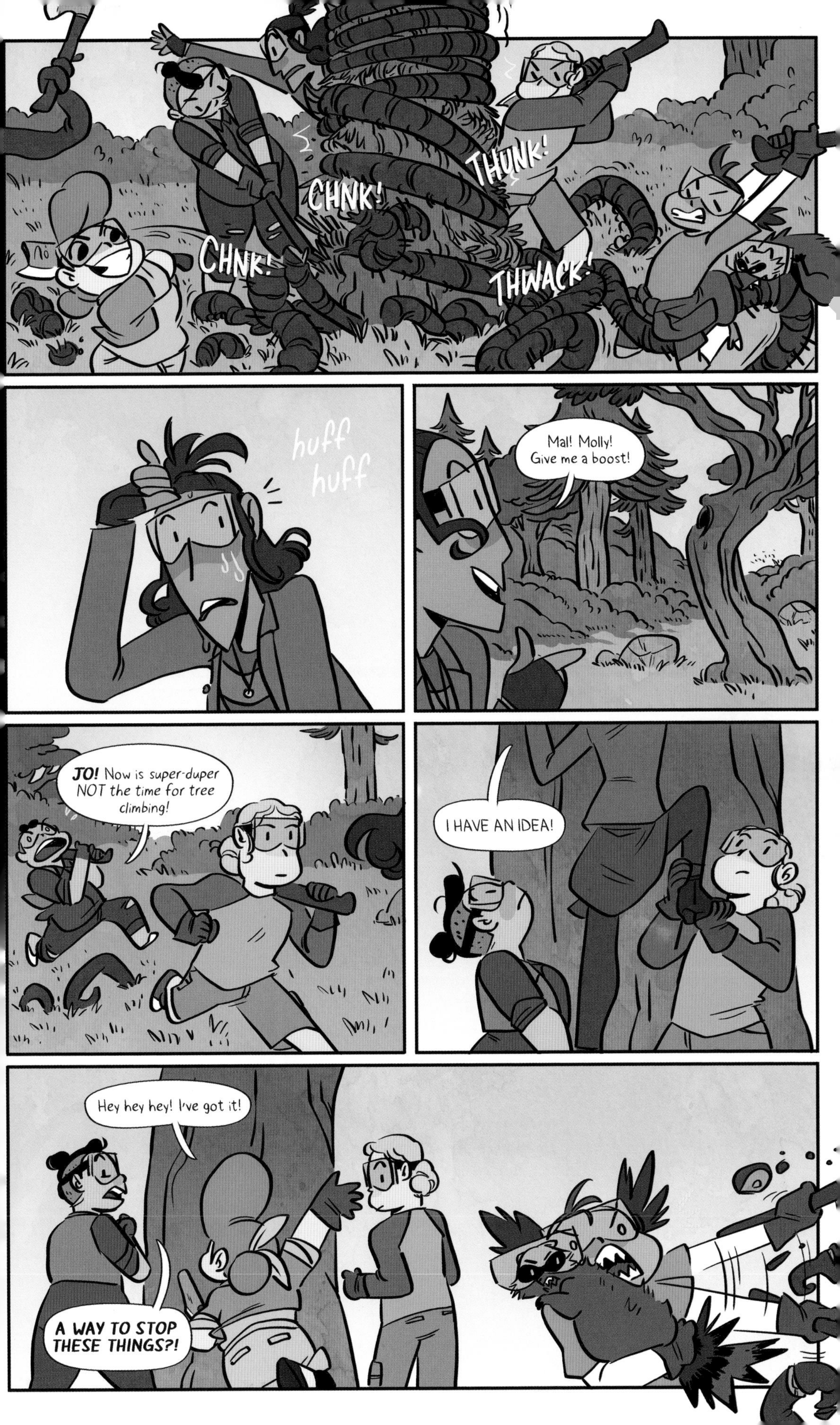
CHNK!
CHNK!
THUNK!
THWACK!
huff huff
Mal! Molly! Give me a boost!
JO! Now is super-duper NOT the time for tree climbing!
I HAVE AN IDEA!
Hey hey hey! I've got it!
A WAY TO STOP THESE THINGS?!

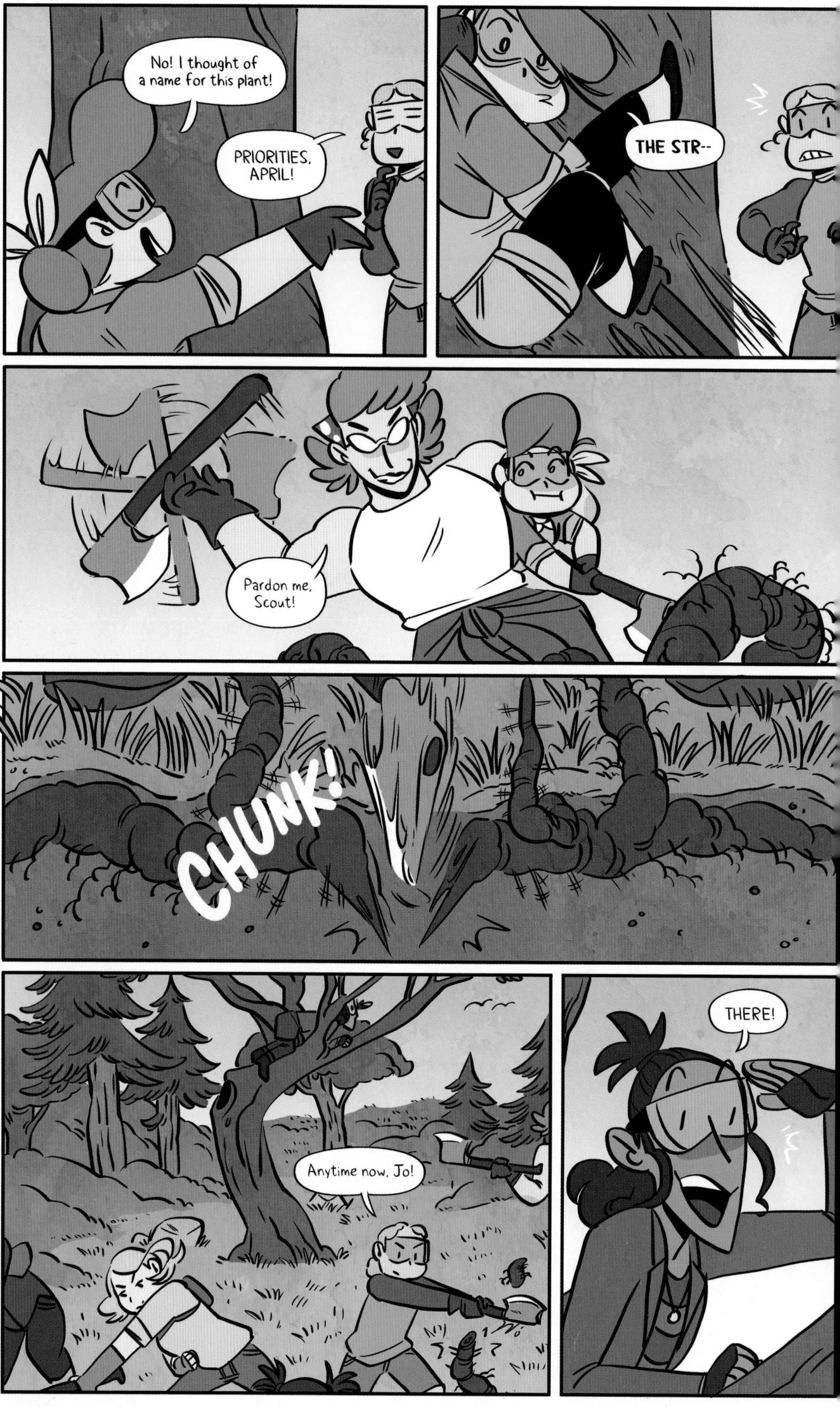
No! I thought of a name for this plant!
PRIORITIES, APRIL!
THE STR--
Pardon me, Scout!
CHUNK!
Anytime now, Jo!
THERE!

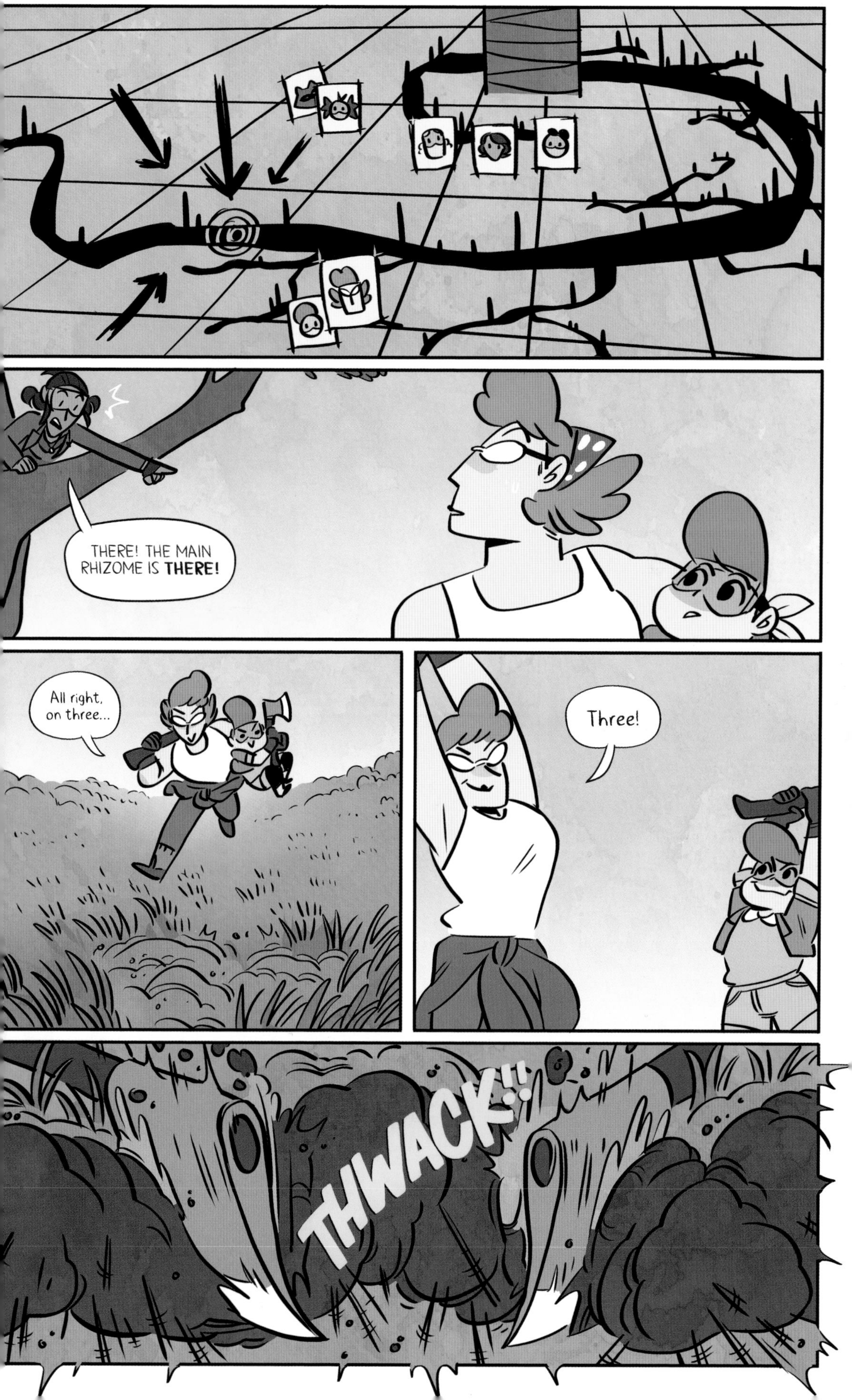
THERE! THE MAIN RHIZOME IS **THERE!**
All right, on three...
Three!
THWACK!!

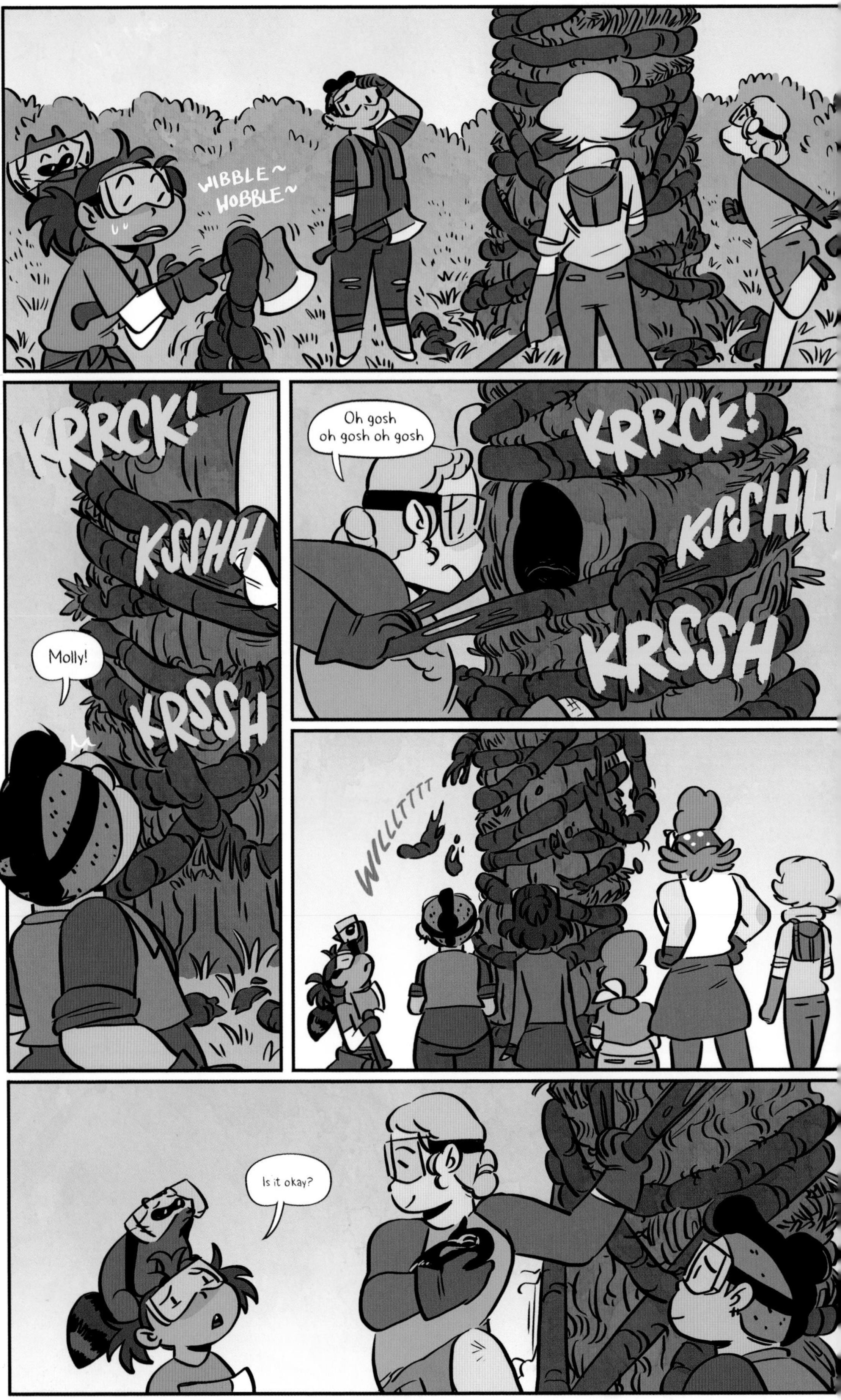
WIBBLE~
WOBBLE~
KRRCK!
KSSHH
Molly!
KRSSH
Oh gosh
oh gosh oh gosh
KRRCK!
KSSHH
KRSSH
WILLLTTTT
Is it okay?

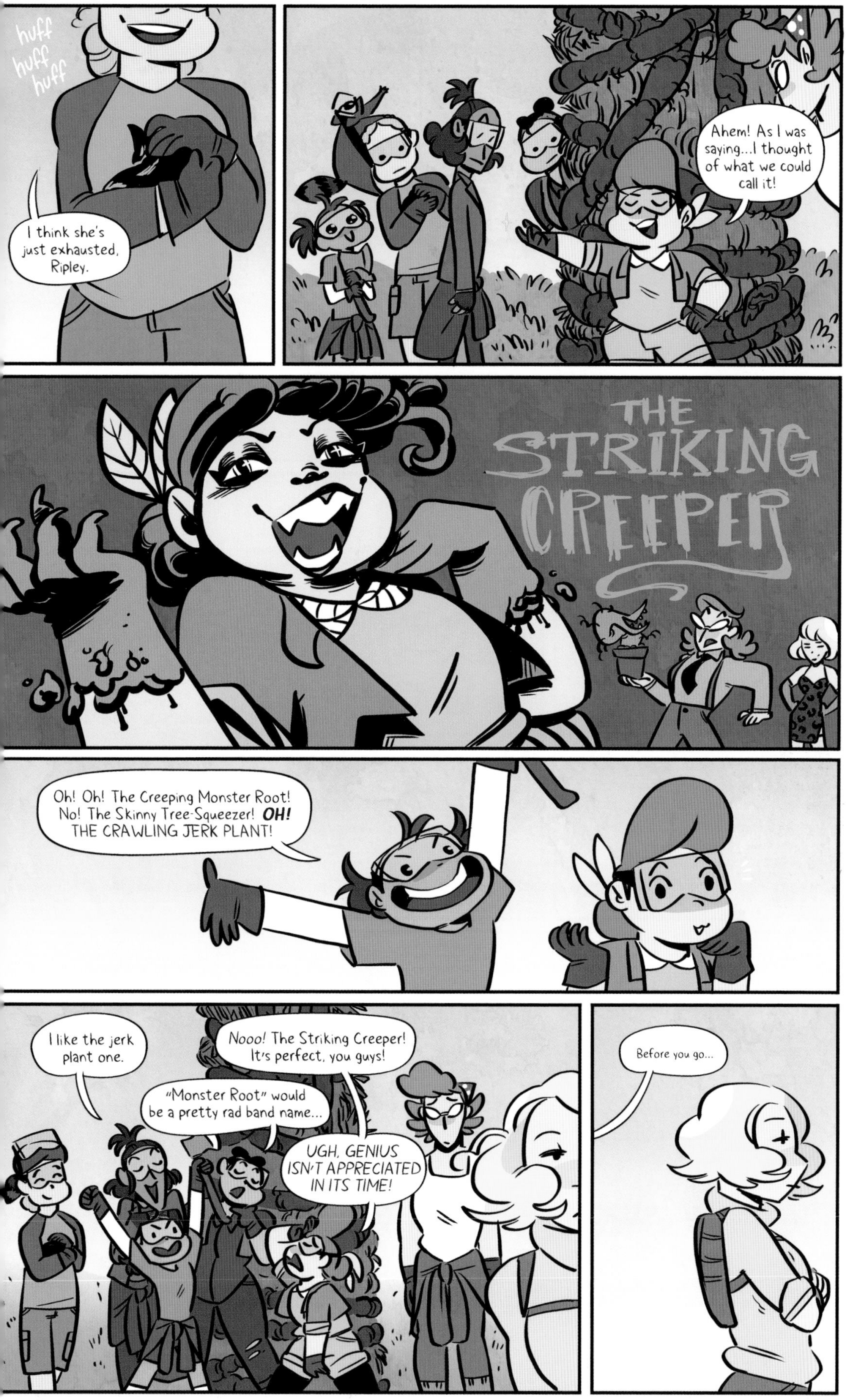
huff huff huff
I think she's just exhausted, Ripley.
Ahem! As I was saying...I thought of what we could call it!
THE STRIKING CREEPER
Oh! Oh! The Creeping Monster Root! No! The Skinny Tree-Squeezer! OH! THE CRAWLING JERK PLANT!
I like the jerk plant one.
"Monster Root" would be a pretty rad band name...
Nooo! The Striking Creeper! It's perfect, you guys!
UGH, GENIUS ISN'T APPRECIATED IN ITS TIME!
Before you go...

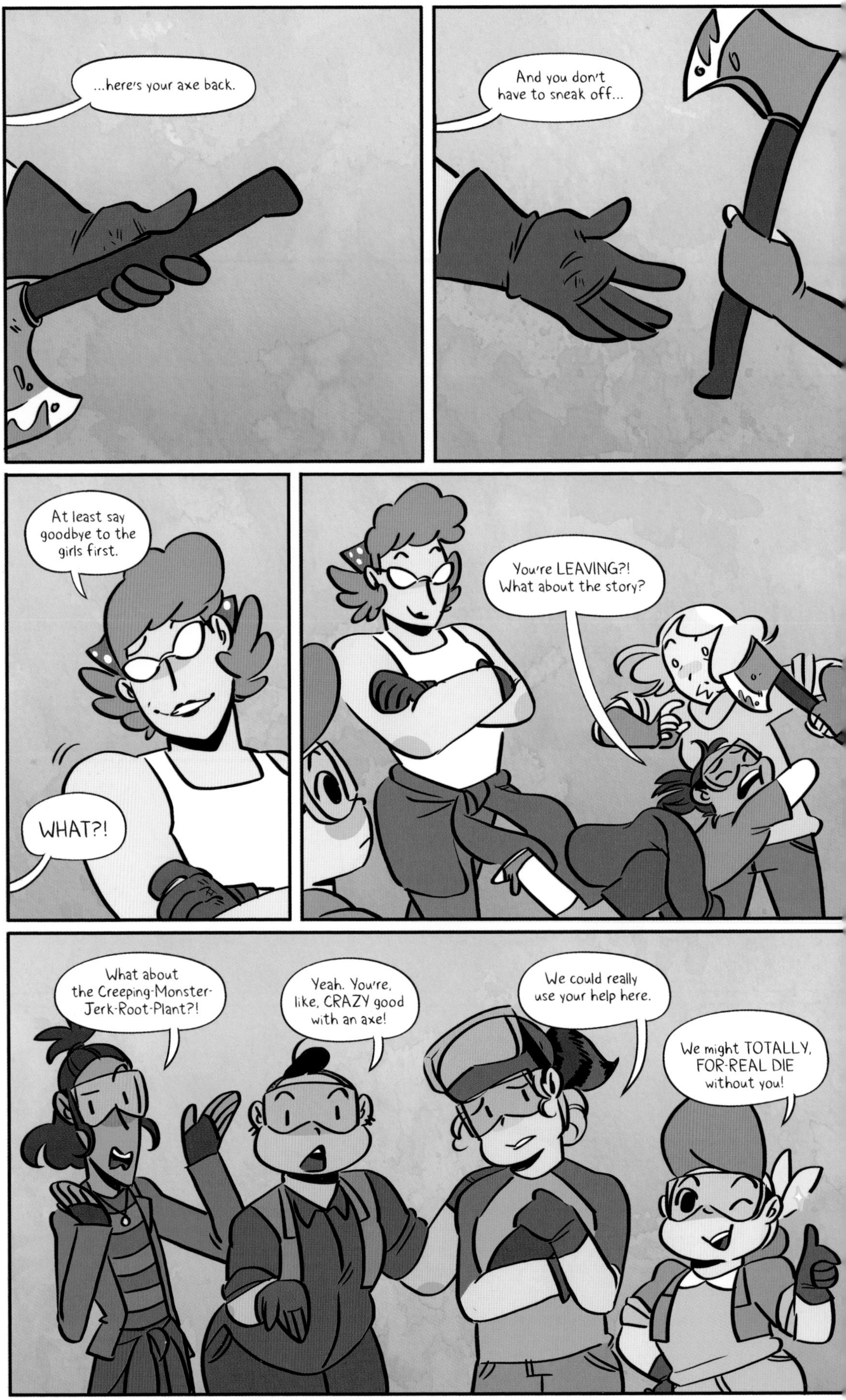
...here's your axe back.
And you don't have to sneak off...
At least say goodbye to the girls first.
WHAT?!
You're LEAVING?! What about the story?
What about the Creeping-Monster-Jerk-Root-Plant?!
Yeah. You're, like, CRAZY good with an axe!
We could really use your help here.
We might TOTALLY, FOR-REAL DIE without you!

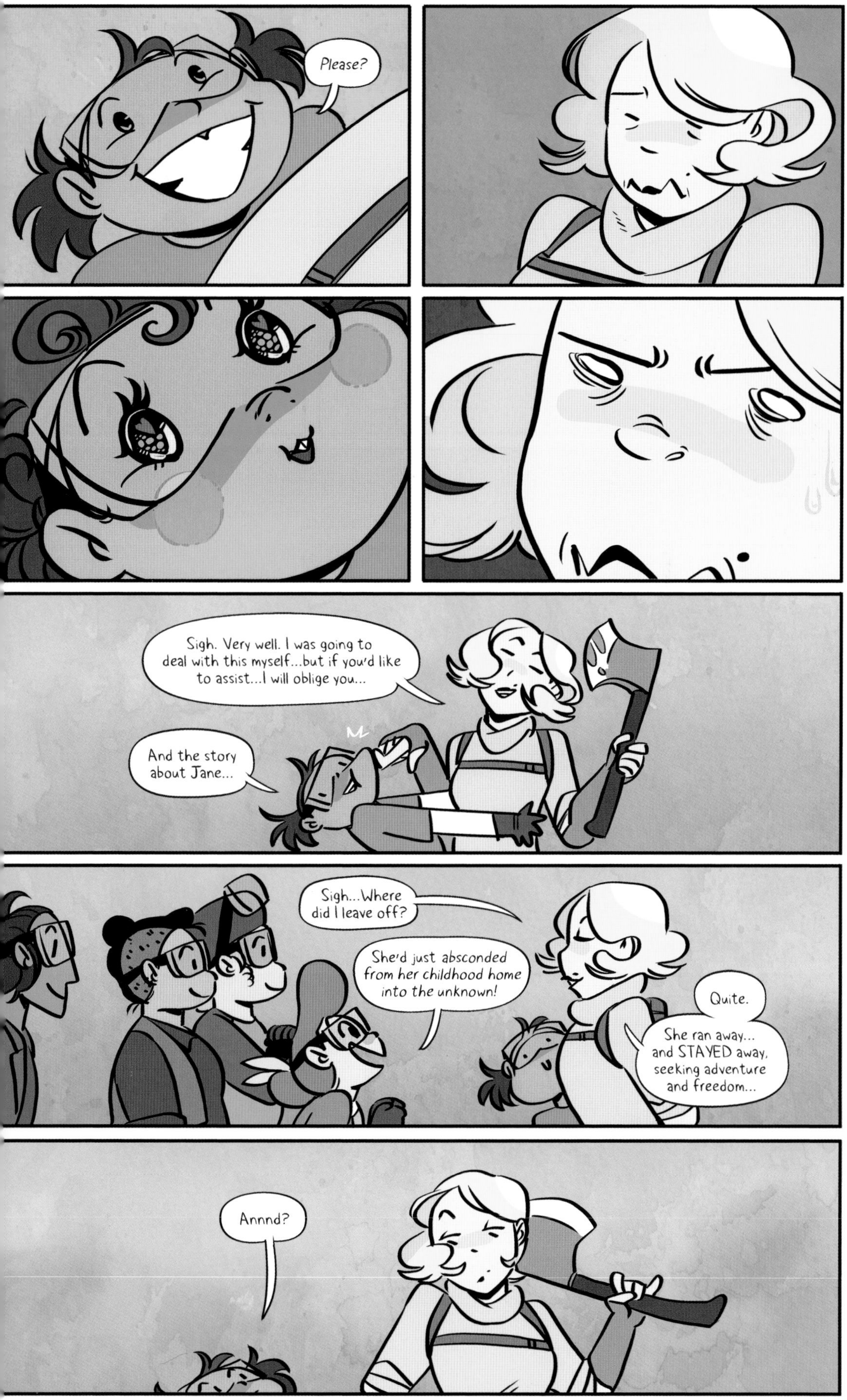
Please?
Sigh. Very well. I was going to deal with this myself...but if you'd like to assist...I will oblige you...
And the story about Jane...
Sigh...Where did I leave off?
She'd just absconded from her childhood home into the unknown!
Quite.
She ran away... and STAYED away, seeking adventure and freedom...
Annnd?

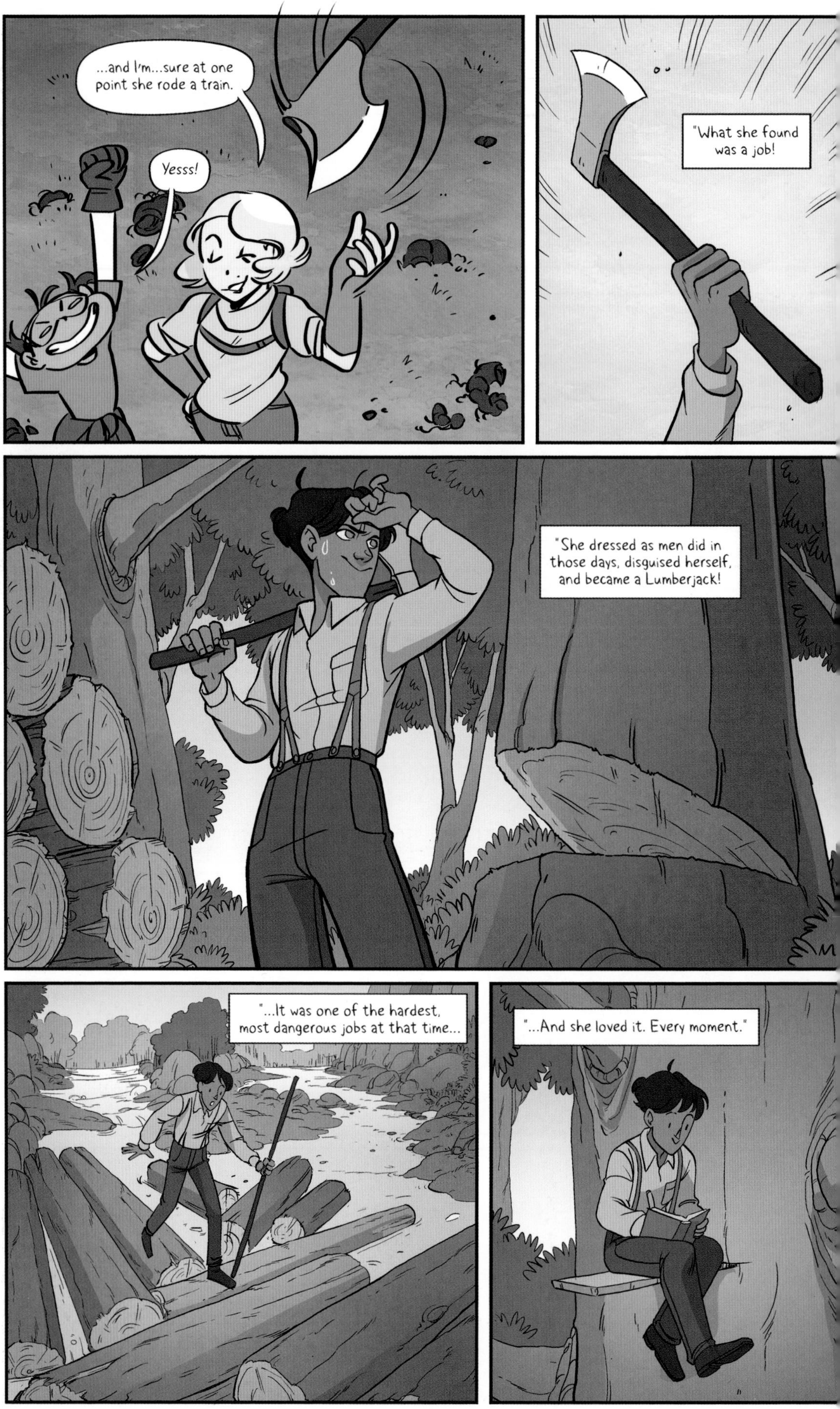

...and I'm...sure at one point she rode a train.
Yesss!
"What she found was a job!
"She dressed as men did in those days, disguised herself, and became a Lumberjack!
"...It was one of the hardest, most dangerous jobs at that time...
"...And she loved it. Every moment."

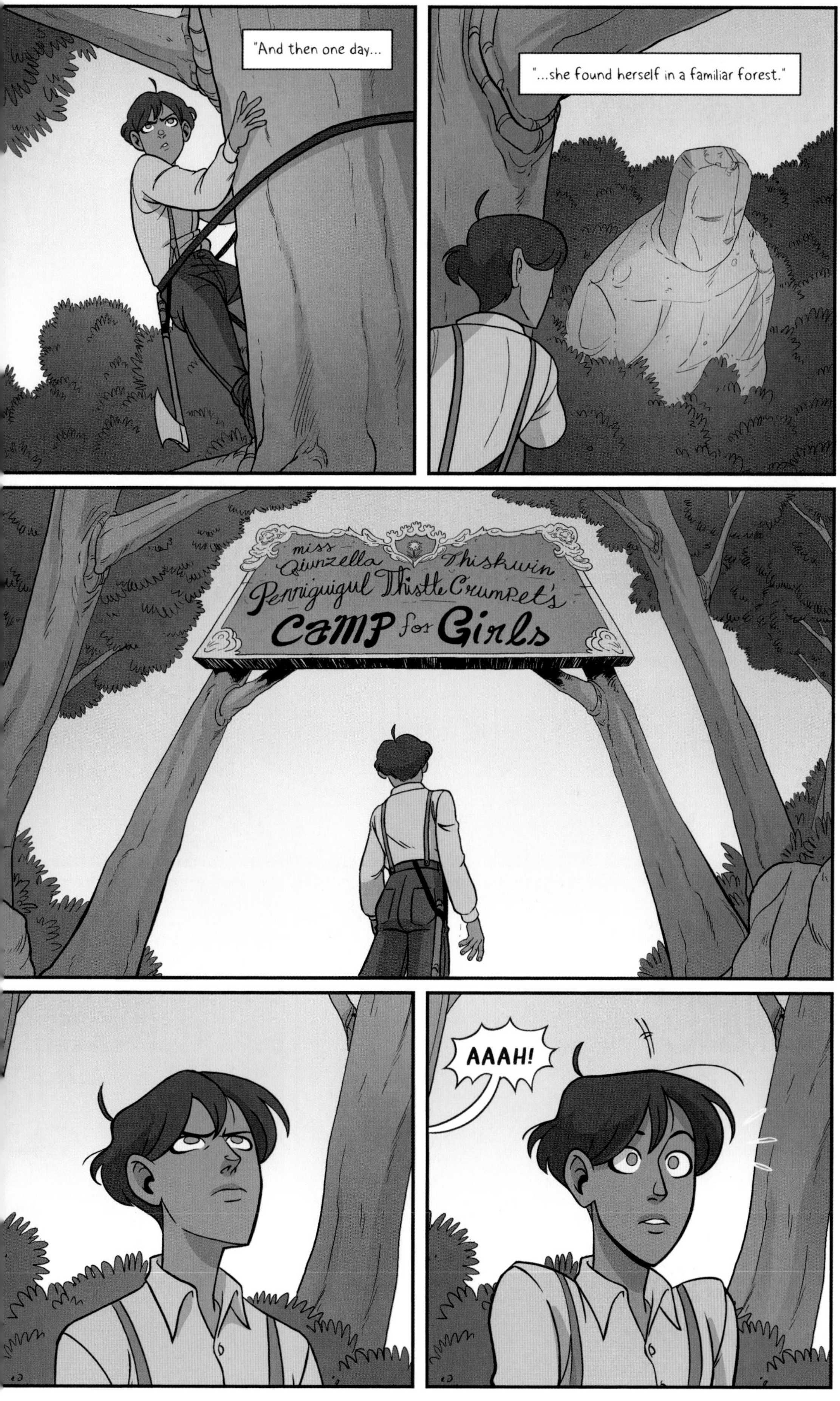
"And then one day...
"...she found herself in a familiar forest."
miss Qiunzella Thiskwin
Penniquiqul Thistle Crumpet's
CAMP for Girls
AAAH!

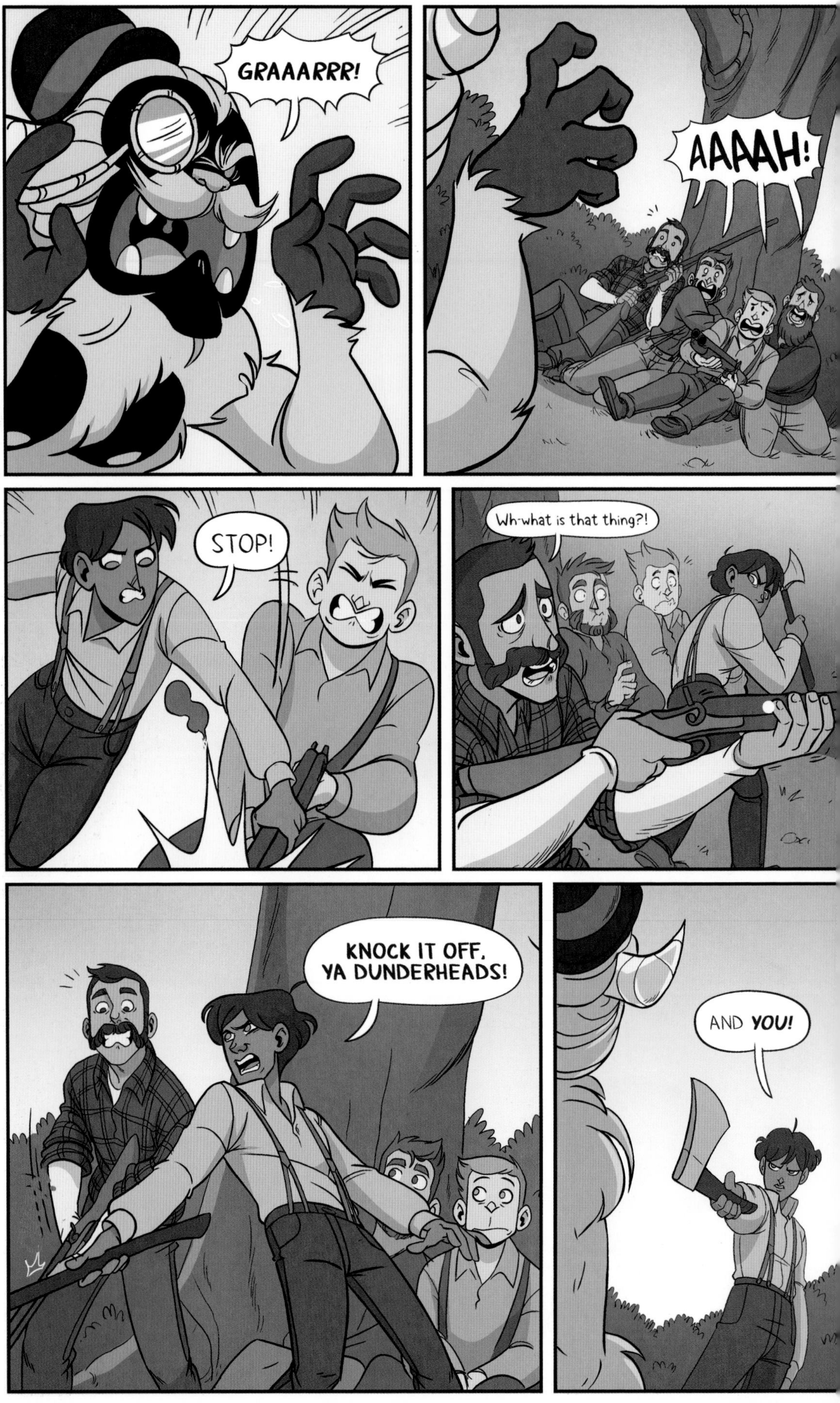
GRAAARRR!
AAAAH!
STOP!
Wh-what is that thing?!
KNOCK IT OFF, YA DUNDERHEADS!
AND YOU!

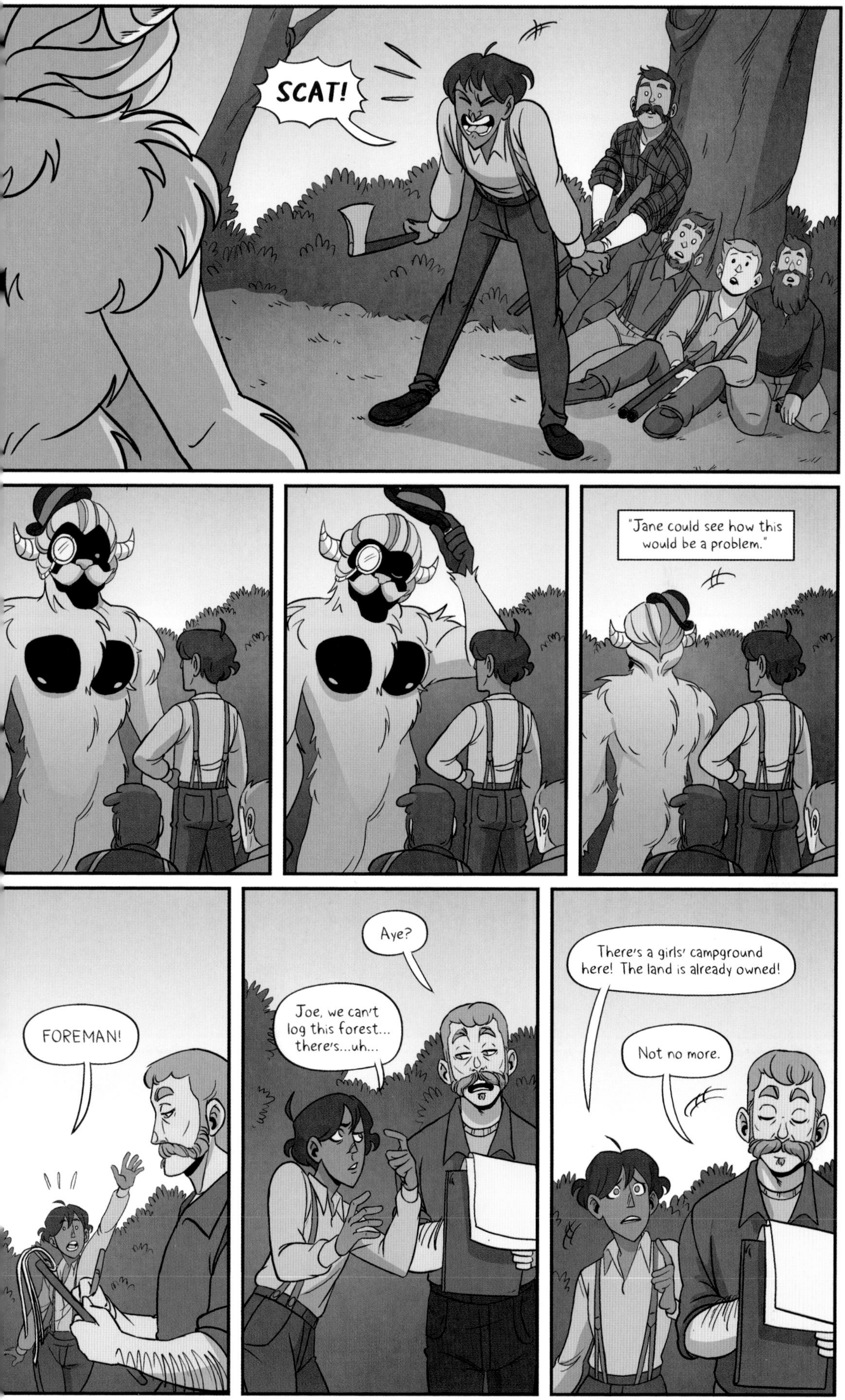
SCAT!
"Jane could see how this would be a problem."
FOREMAN!
Aye?
Joe, we can't log this forest... there's...uh...
There's a girls' campground here! The land is already owned!
Not no more.

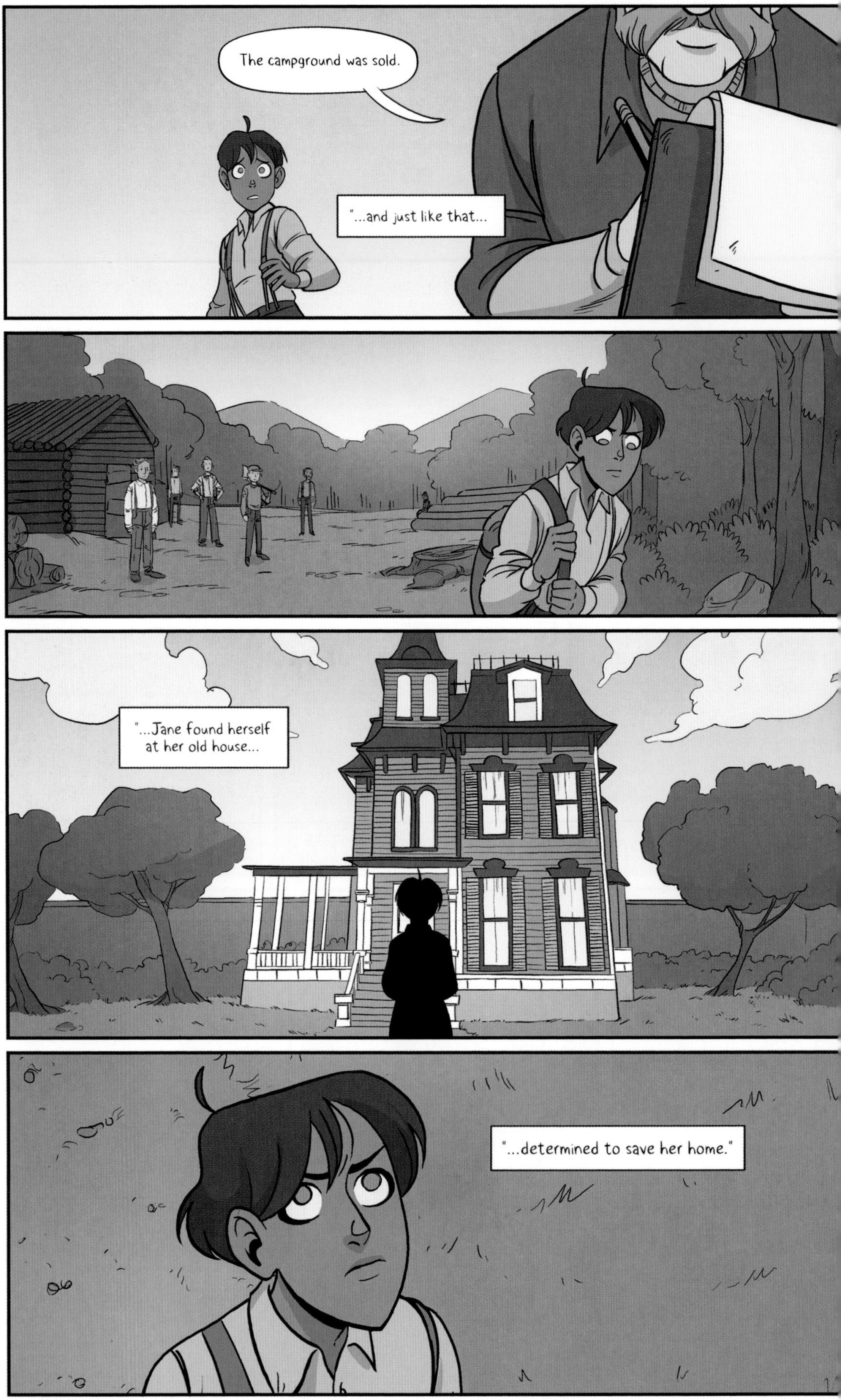
The campground was sold.
"...and just like that...
"...Jane found herself at her old house...
"...determined to save her home."

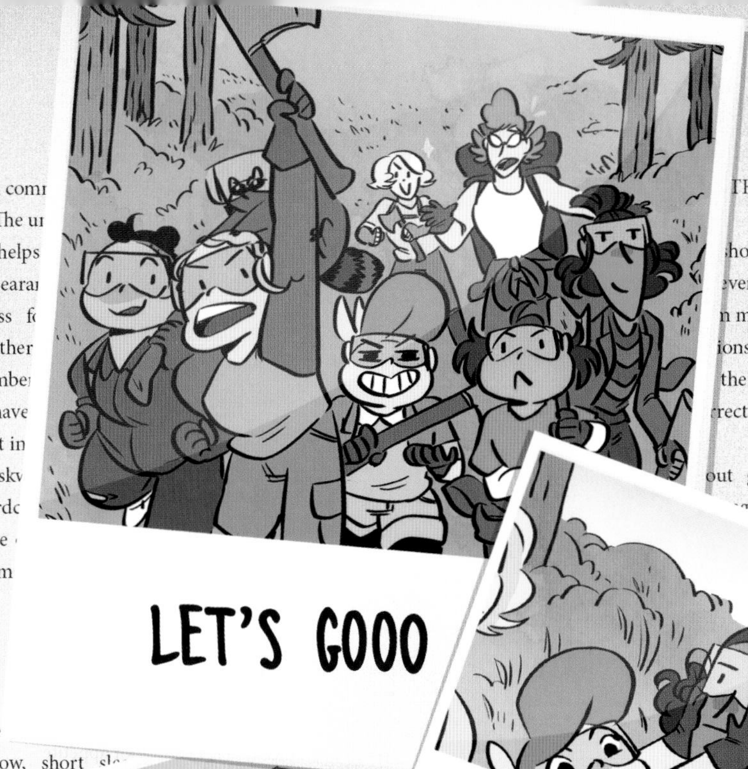
LET'S GOOO

will comr

The ur
It helps
appearar
dress fo
Further
Lumbe
to have
part in
Thiskv
Hardc
have
them

THE UNIFORM

should be worn at camp
events when Lumberjanes
n may also be worn at other
ions. It should be worn as a
the uniform dress with
rrect shoes, and stocking or

out grows her uniform or
to another Lumberjane.
insignia she has
her
her

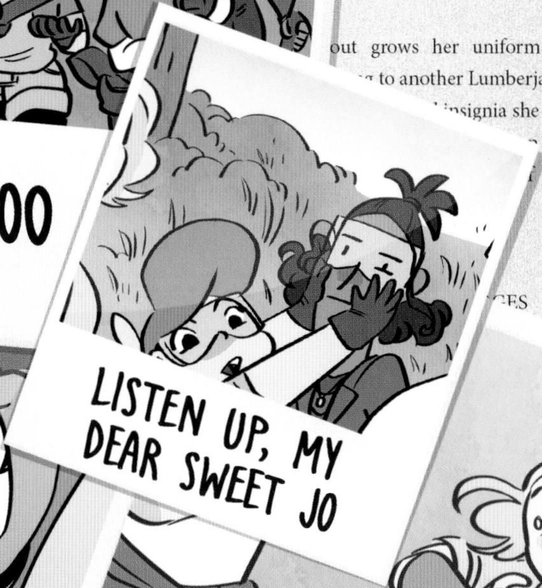
LISTEN UP, MY
DEAR SWEET JO

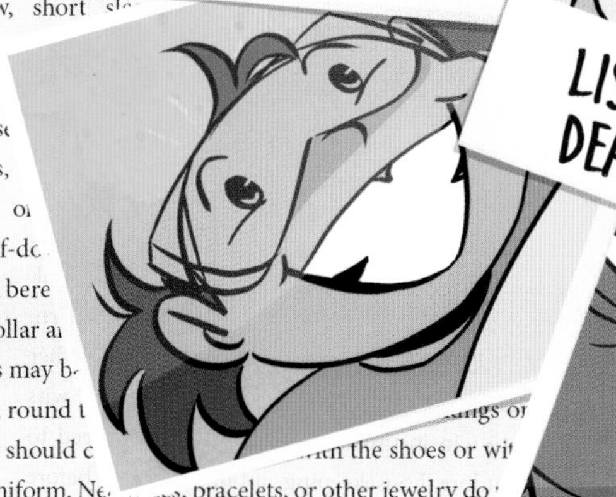

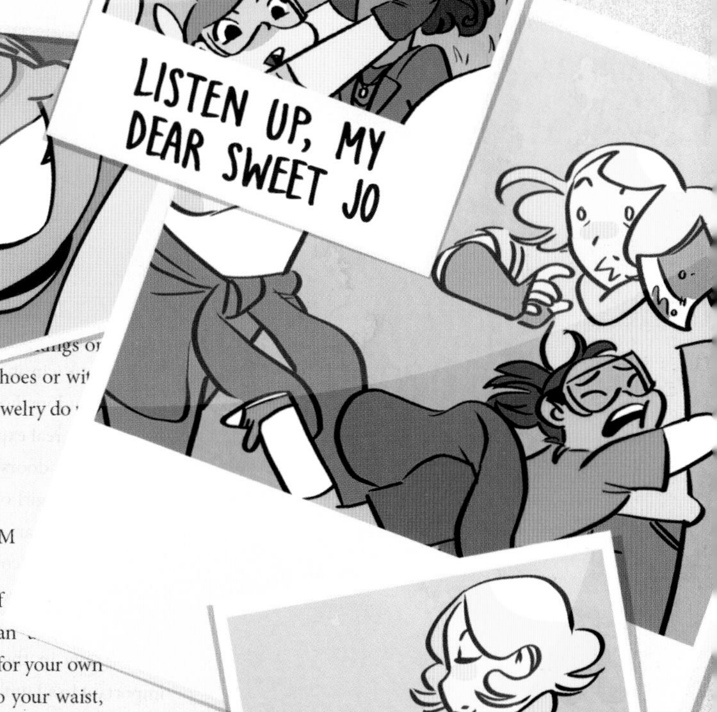

The
yellow, short sl
emb
the w
choose
slacks,
made o
out-of-do
green bere
the collar a
Shoes may b
heels, round t ... ings or
socks should c ... with the shoes or wit
the uniform. Ne... es, bracelets, or other jewelry do
belong with a Lumberjane uniform.

HOW TO WEAR THE UNIFORM

To look well in a uniform demands first of ... uniform be kept in good condition—clean ... pressed. See that the skirt is the right length for your own height and build, that the belt is adjusted to your waist, that your shoes and stockings are in keeping with the uniform, that you watch your posture and carry yourself with dignity and grace. If the beret is removed indoors, be sure that your hair is neat and kept in place with an inconspicuous clip or ribbon. When you wear a Lumberjane uniform you are identified as a member of this organization and you should be doubly careful to conduct yourself in a way that will show everyone that courtesy and thoughtfulness are part of being a Lumberjane. People are likely to judge a whole nation by the selfishness of a few individuals, to criticize a whole family because of the misconduct of one member, and to feel unkindly toward an organization because of the

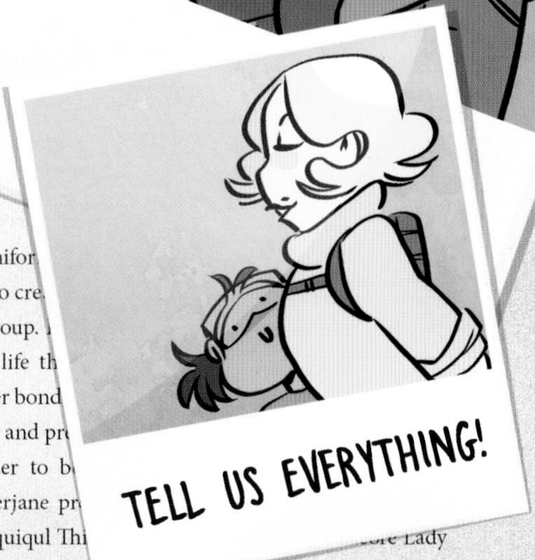
TELL US EVERYTHING!

The unifor
helps to cre
in a group.
active life th
another bond
future, and pr
in order to b
Lumberjane pr
Penniquiqul Thi ... core Lady
Types, but most ... will wish to have one. They
can either buy the uniform, or make it themselves from
materials available at the trading post.

LUMBERJANES FIELD MANUAL

CHAPTER
SEVENTY-TWO

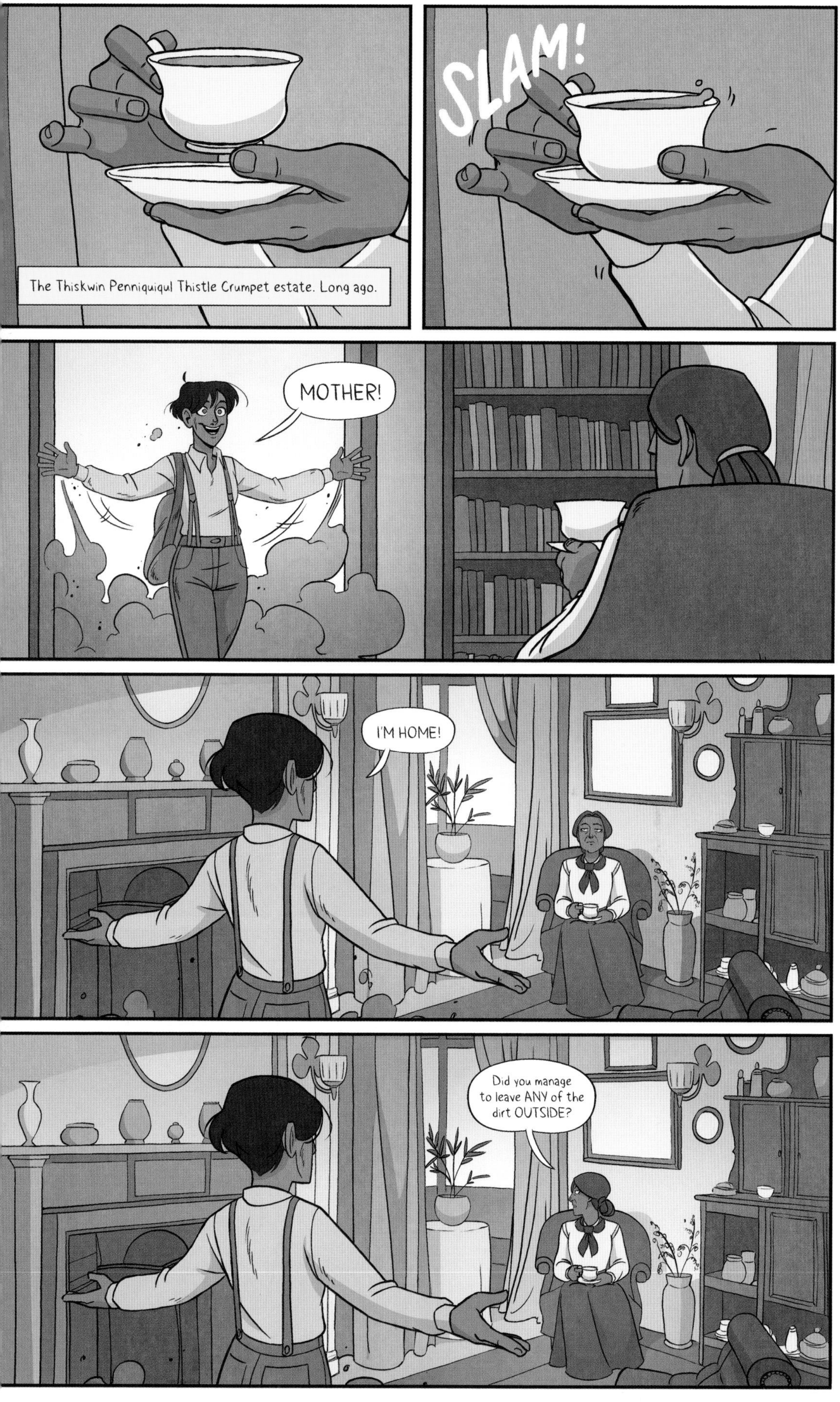

The Thiskwin Penniquiqul Thistle Crumpet estate. Long ago.
SLAM!
MOTHER!
I'M HOME!
Did you manage to leave ANY of the dirt OUTSIDE?

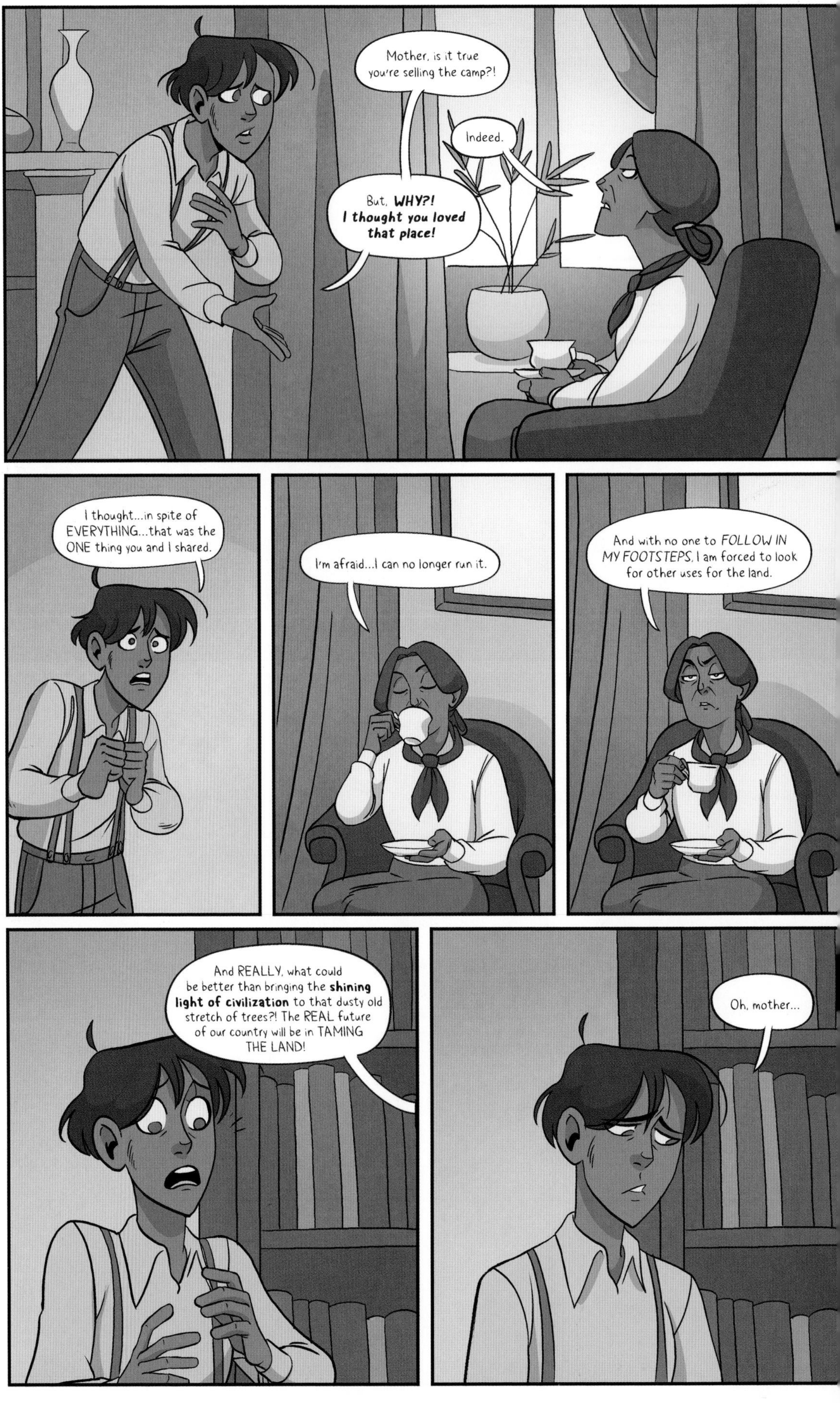

Mother, is it true you're selling the camp?!
Indeed.
But, **WHY?! I thought you loved that place!**
I thought...in spite of EVERYTHING...that was the ONE thing you and I shared.
I'm afraid...I can no longer run it.
And with no one to *FOLLOW IN MY FOOTSTEPS*, I am forced to look for other uses for the land.
And REALLY, what could be better than bringing the **shining light of civilization** to that dusty old stretch of trees?! The REAL future of our country will be in TAMING THE LAND!
Oh, mother...

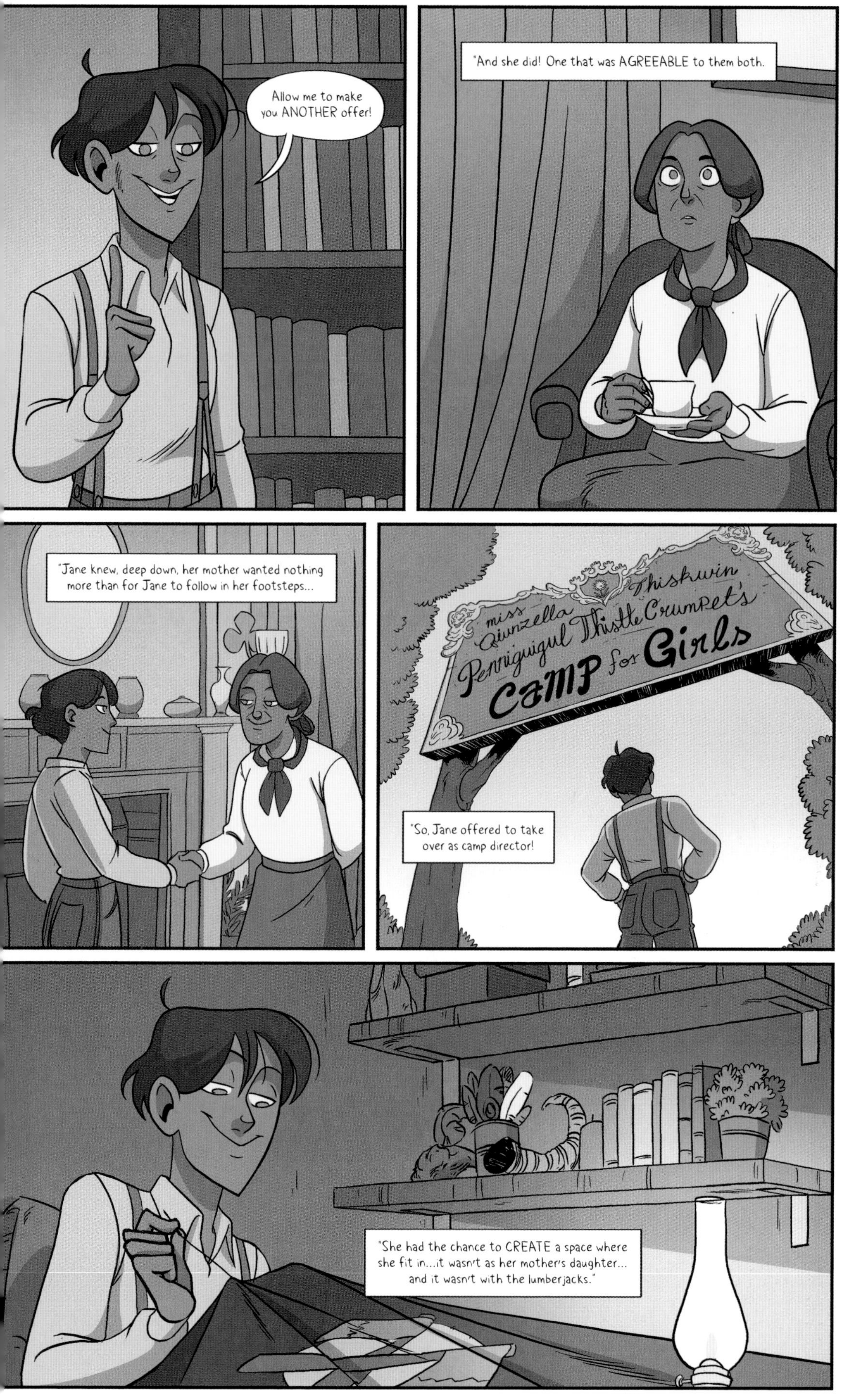
Allow me to make you ANOTHER offer!
"And she did! One that was AGREEABLE to them both.
"Jane knew, deep down, her mother wanted nothing more than for Jane to follow in her footsteps...
miss Quinzella Thiskwin Penniquiqul Thistle Crumpet's
CAMP for Girls
"So, Jane offered to take over as camp director!
"She had the chance to CREATE a space where she fit in...it wasn't as her mother's daughter... and it wasn't with the lumberjacks."

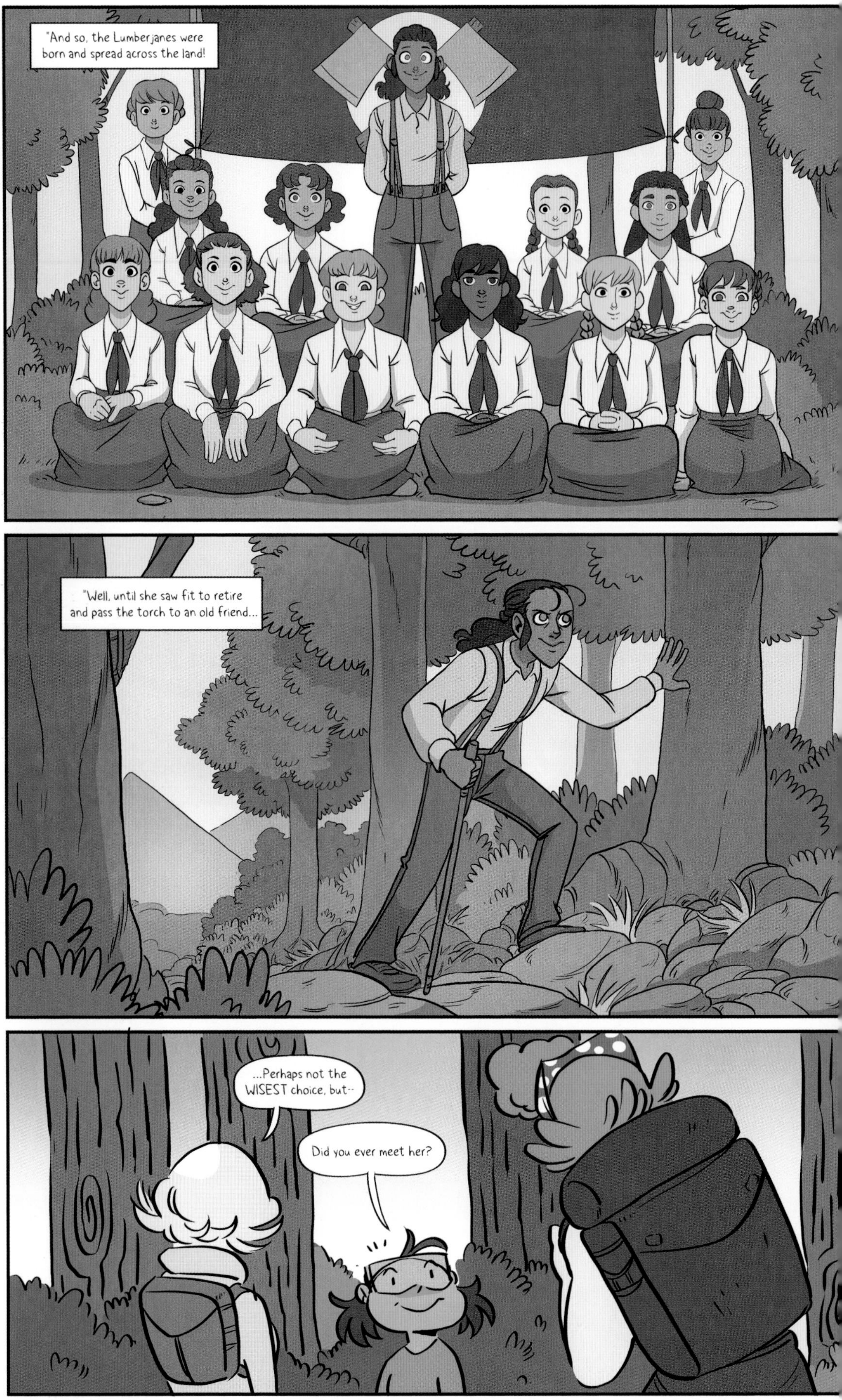
"And so, the Lumberjanes were born and spread across the land!
"Well, until she saw fit to retire and pass the torch to an old friend...
...Perhaps not the WISEST choice, but--
Did you ever meet her?

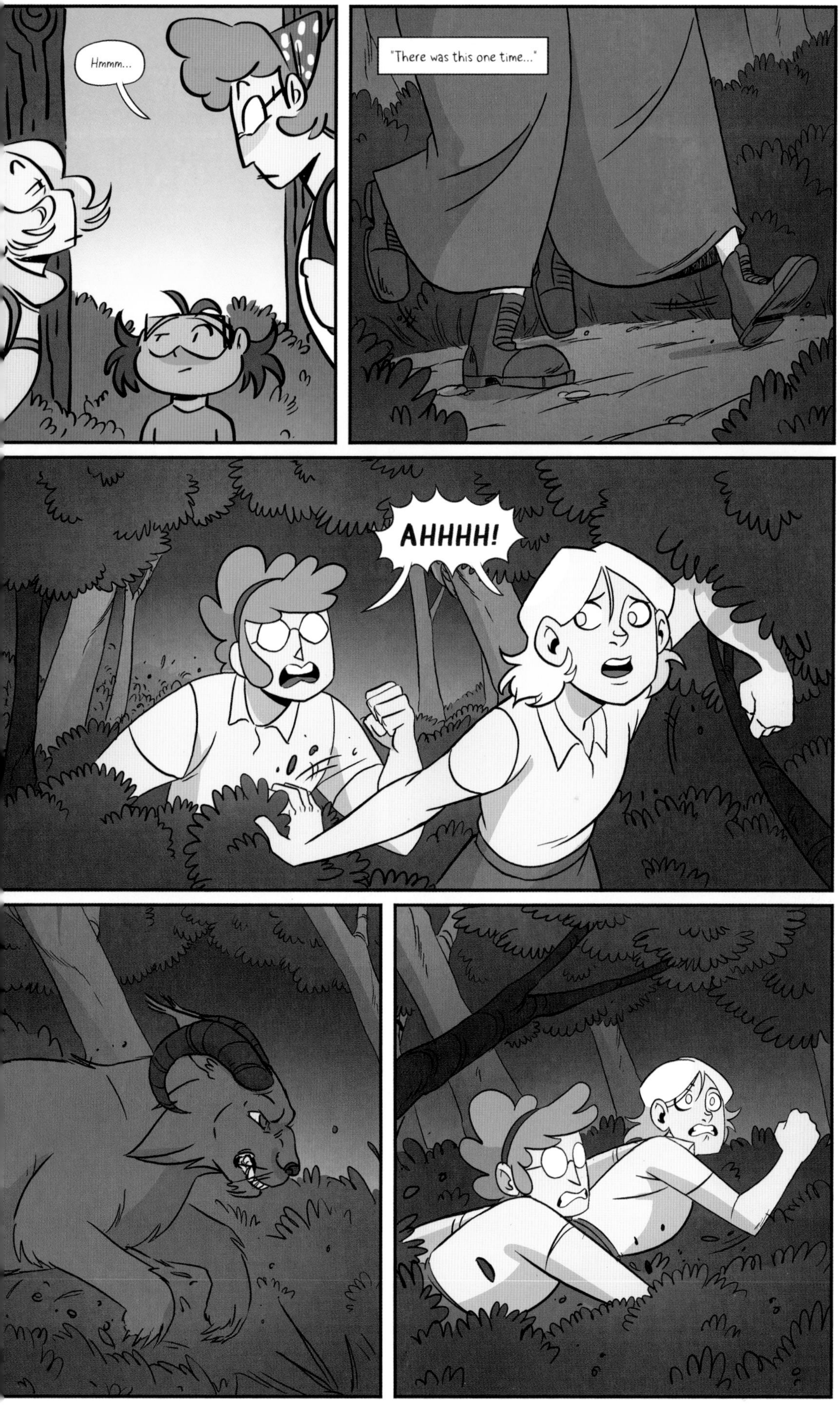
Hmmm...
"There was this one time..."
AHHHH!

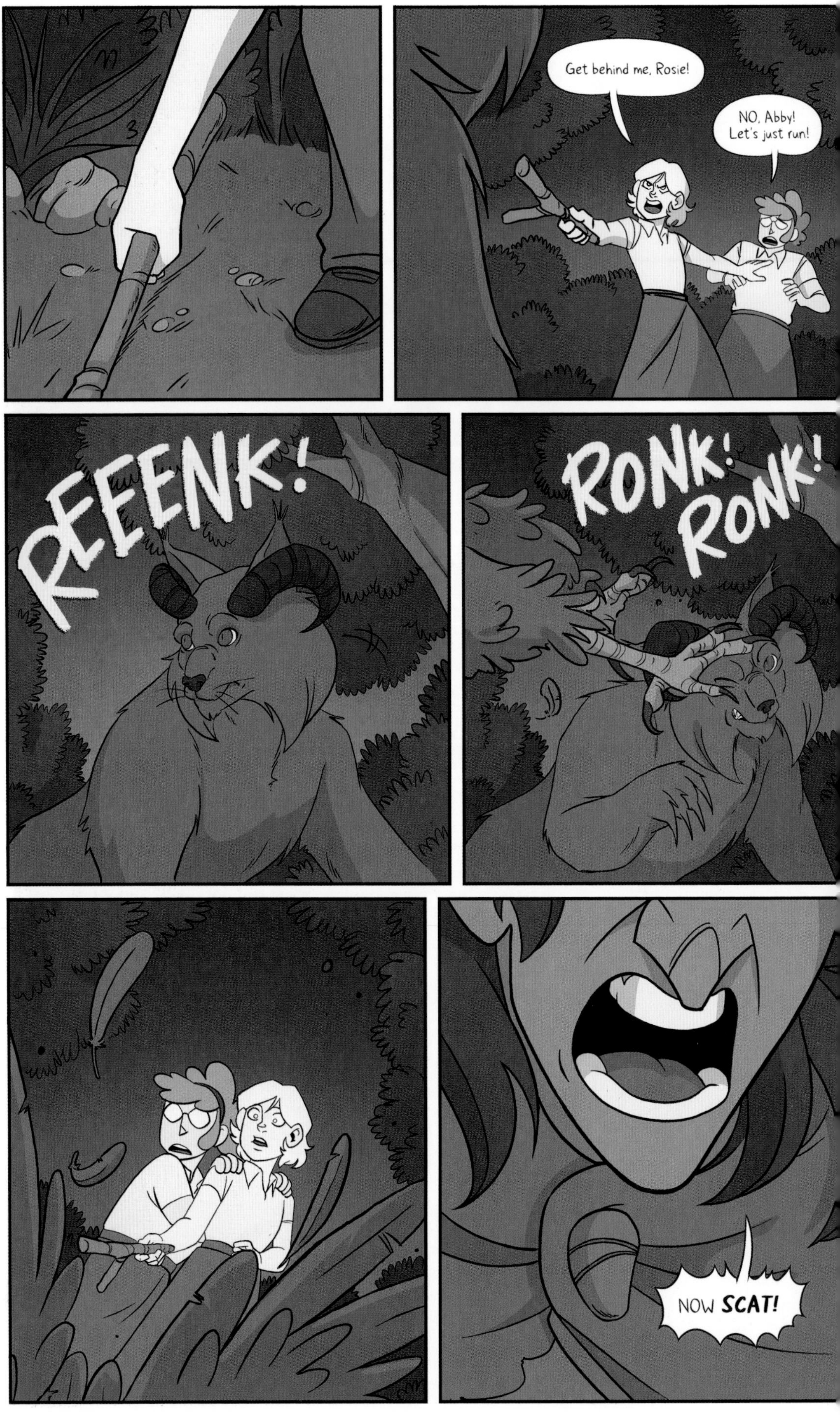
Get behind me, Rosie!
NO, Abby! Let's just run!
REEENK!
RONK! RONK!
NOW SCAT!

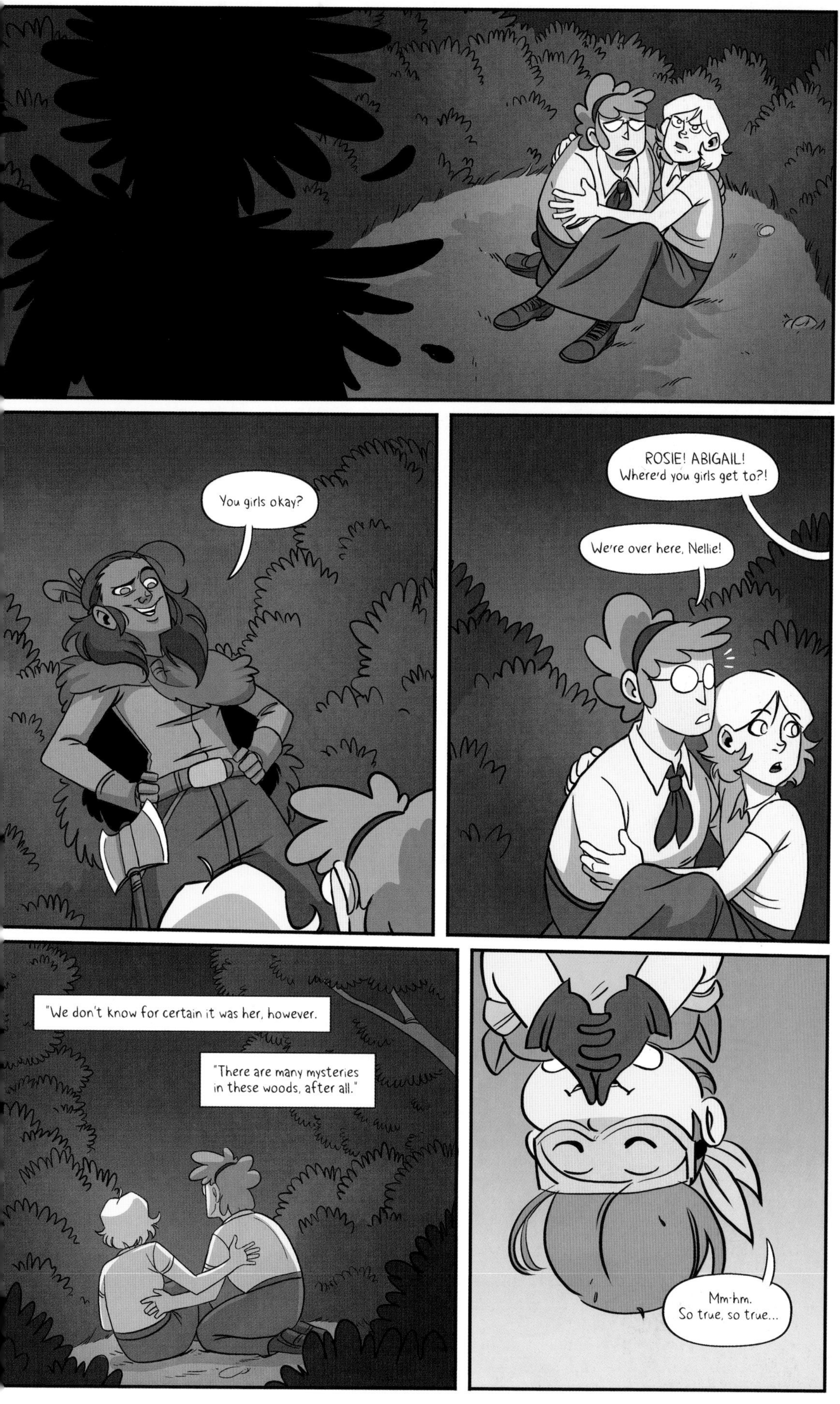
You girls okay?
ROSIE! ABIGAIL! Where'd you girls get to?!
We're over here, Nellie!
"We don't know for certain it was her, however.
"There are many mysteries in these woods, after all."
Mm-hm. So true, so true...

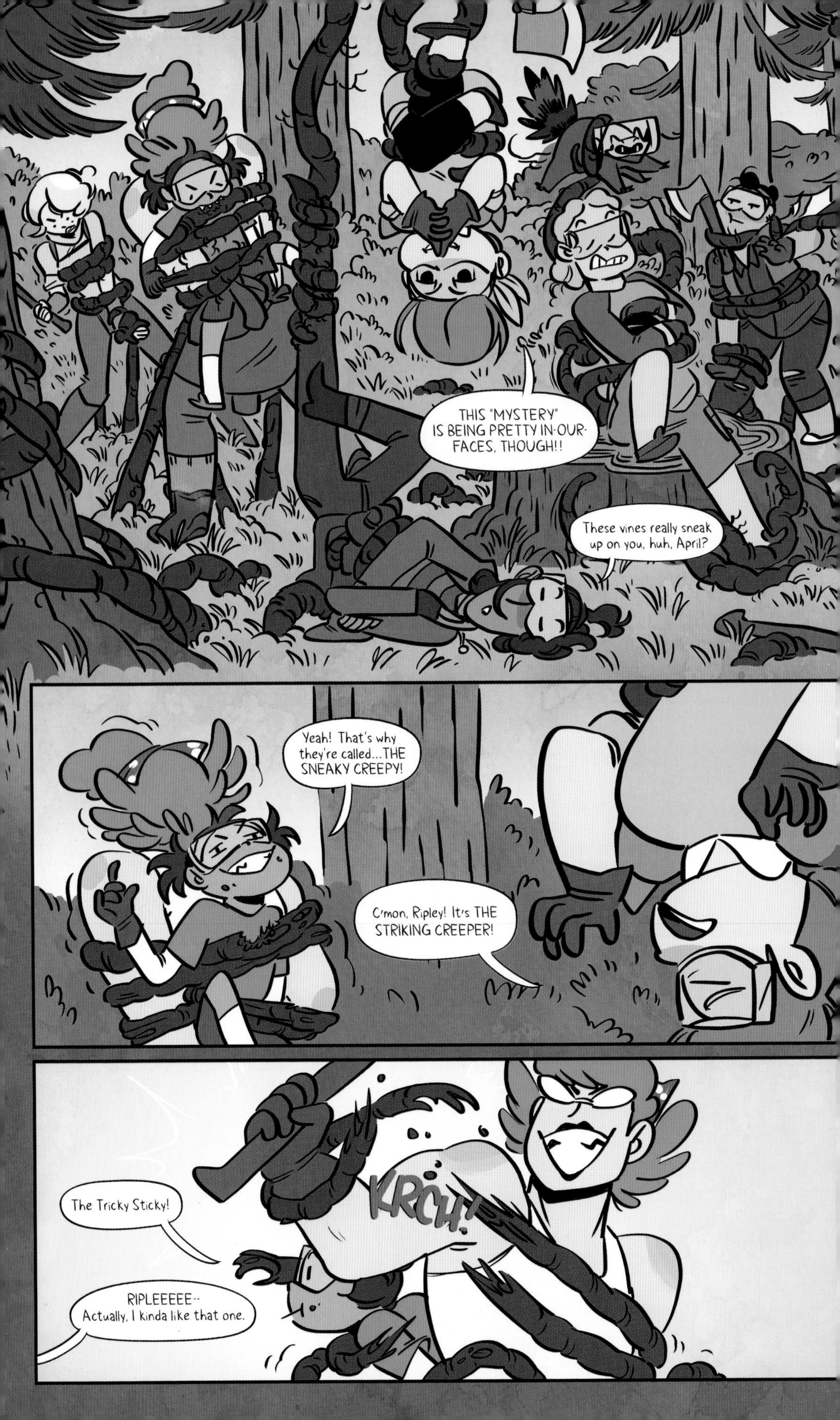

THIS "MYSTERY" IS BEING PRETTY IN-OUR-FACES, THOUGH!!
These vines really sneak up on you, huh, April?
Yeah! That's why they're called...THE SNEAKY CREEPY!
C'mon, Ripley! It's THE STRIKING CREEPER!
The Tricky Sticky!
KRCH!
RIPLEEEEE-- Actually, I kinda like that one.

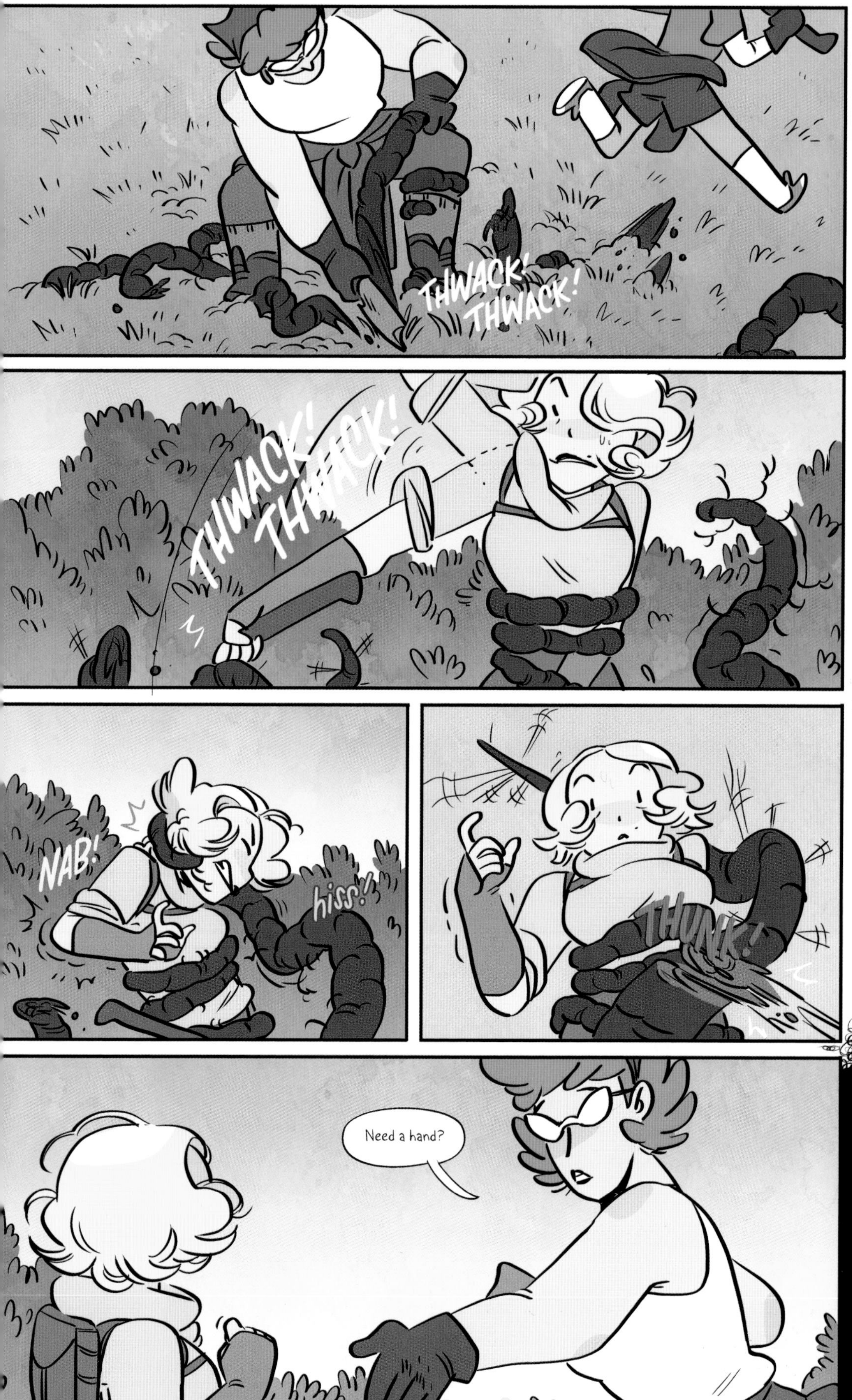
THWACK! THWACK!
THWACK! THWACK!
NAB!
hiss!
THUNK!
Need a hand?

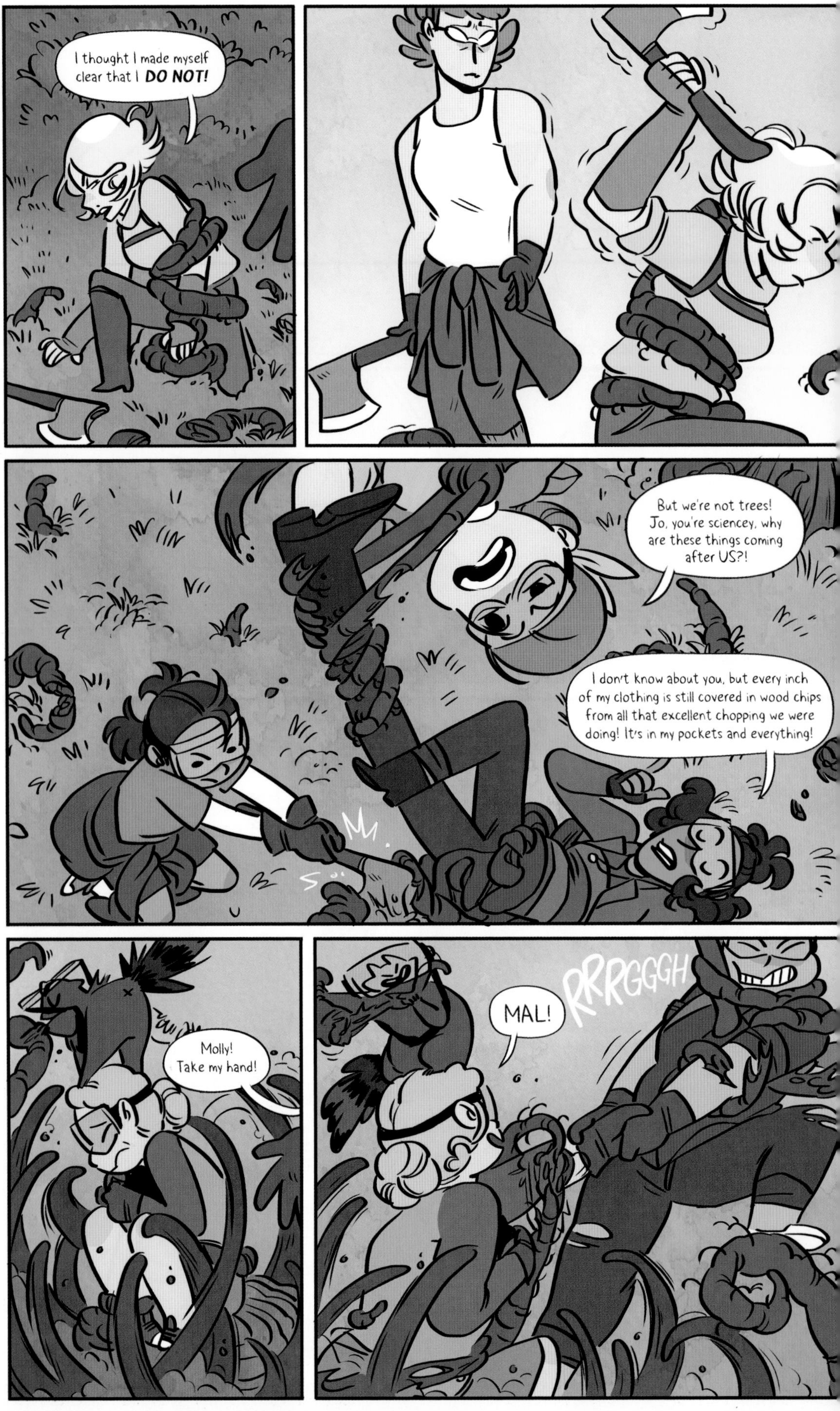
I thought I made myself clear that I **DO NOT!**
But we're not trees! Jo, you're sciencey, why are these things coming after US?!
I don't know about you, but every inch of my clothing is still covered in wood chips from all that excellent chopping we were doing! It's in my pockets and everything!
Molly! Take my hand!
MAL!
RRRGGGH

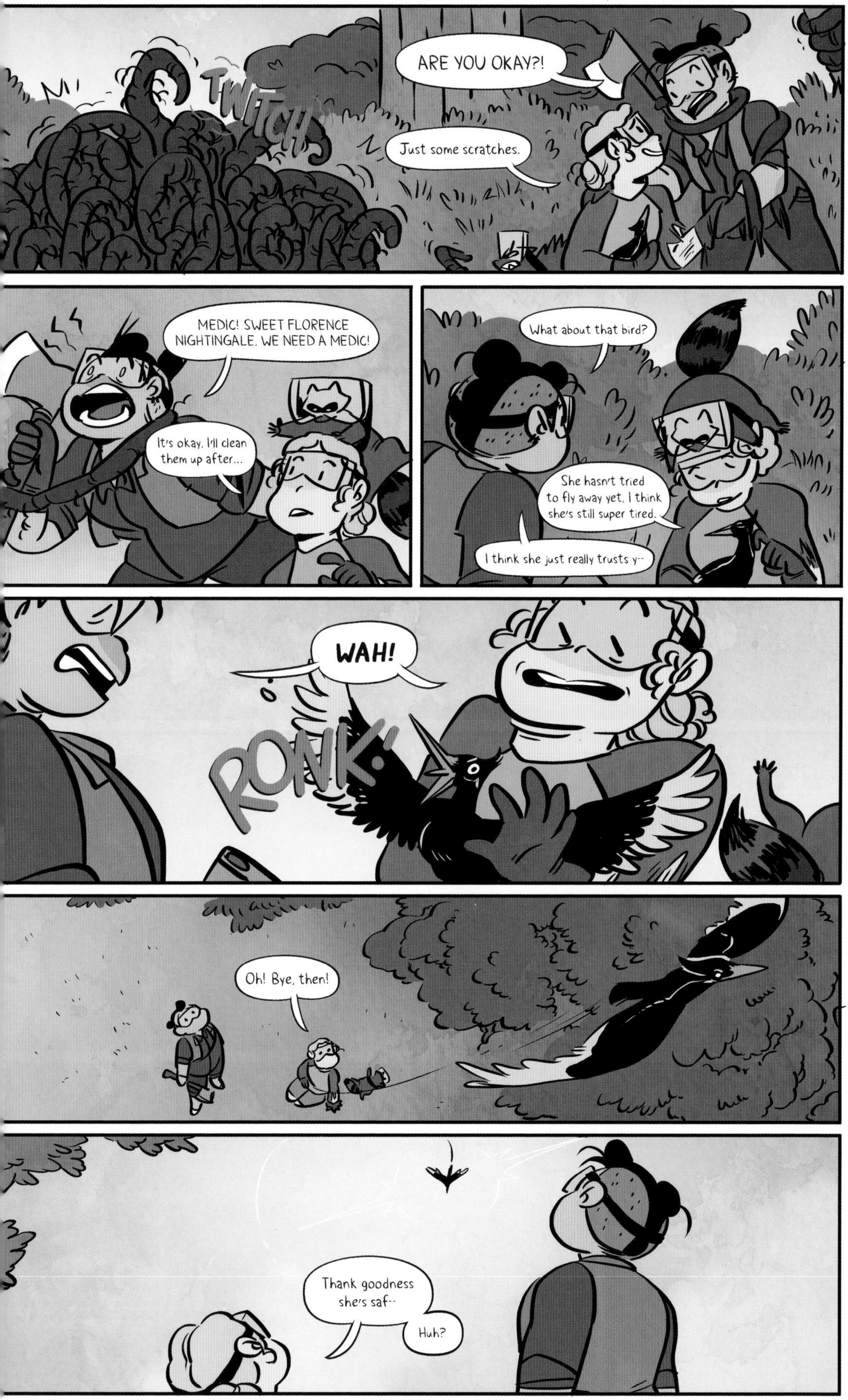
TWITCH
ARE YOU OKAY?!
Just some scratches.
MEDIC! SWEET FLORENCE NIGHTINGALE, WE NEED A MEDIC!
It's okay, I'll clean them up after...
What about that bird?
She hasn't tried to fly away yet, I think she's still super tired.
I think she just really trusts y--
WAH!
RONK!
Oh! Bye, then!
Thank goodness she's saf--
Huh?

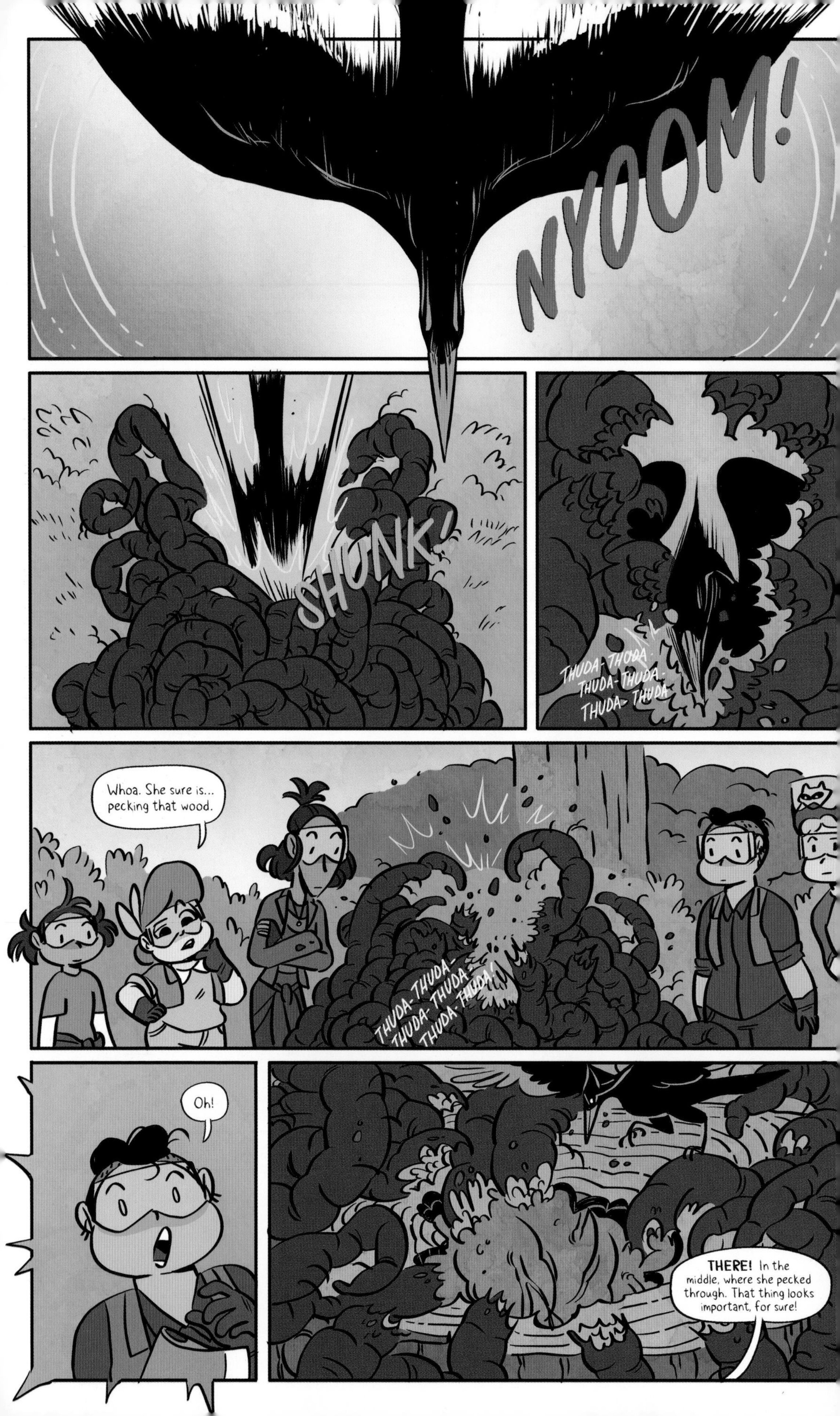
NYOOM!
SHUNK!
THUDA-THUDA-
THUDA-THUDA-
THUDA-THUDA
Whoa. She sure is... pecking that wood.
THUDA-THUDA-
THUDA-THUDA-
THUDA-THUDA!
Oh!
THERE! In the middle, where she pecked through. That thing looks important, for sure!

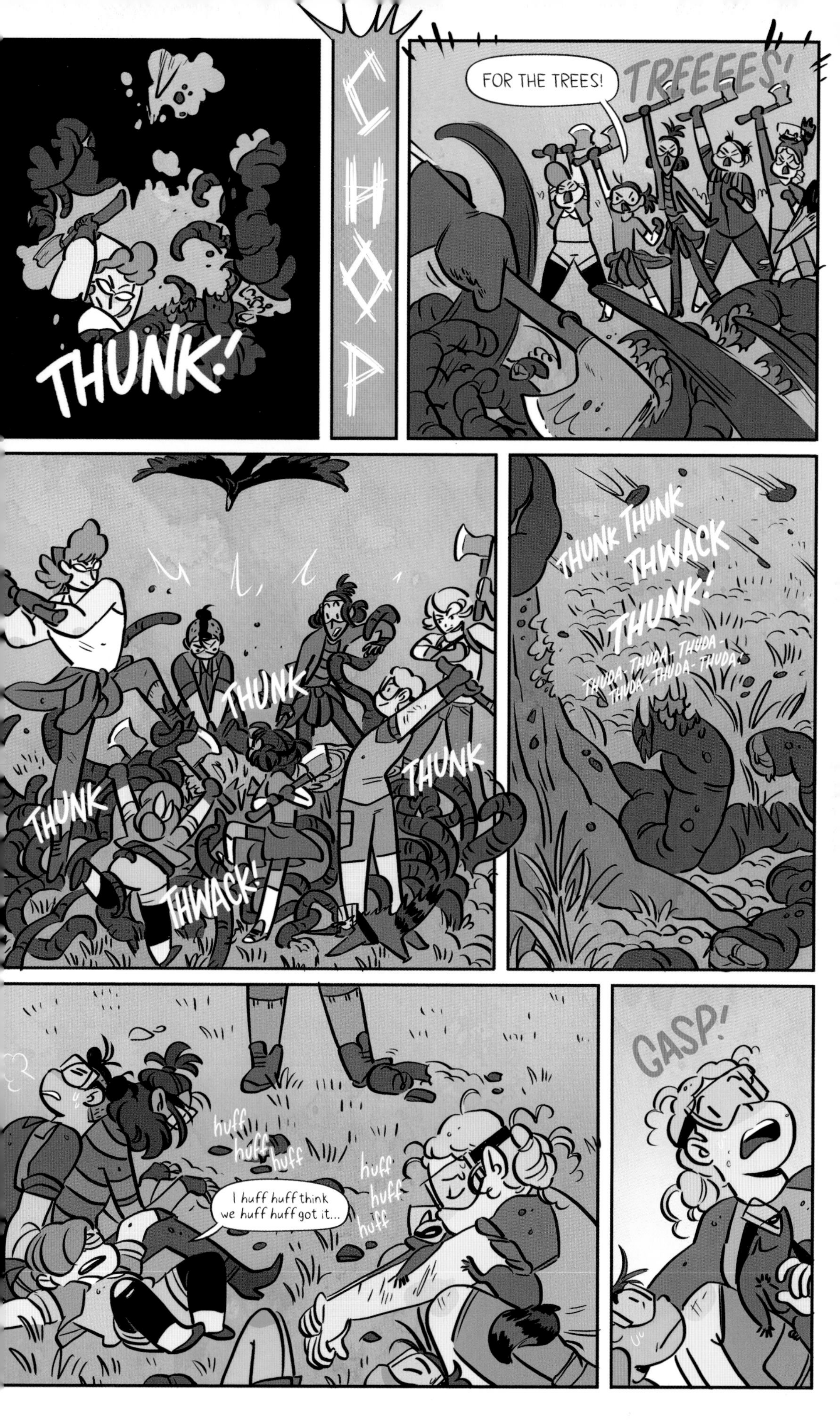
THUNK!
CHOP
FOR THE TREES!
TREEEES!
THUNK
THUNK
THUNK
THWACK!
THUNK THUNK
THWACK
THUNK!
THUDA-THUDA-THUDA-
THUDA-THUDA-THUDA!
huff
huff
huff
I huff huff think
we huff huff got it...
huff
huff
huff
GASP!

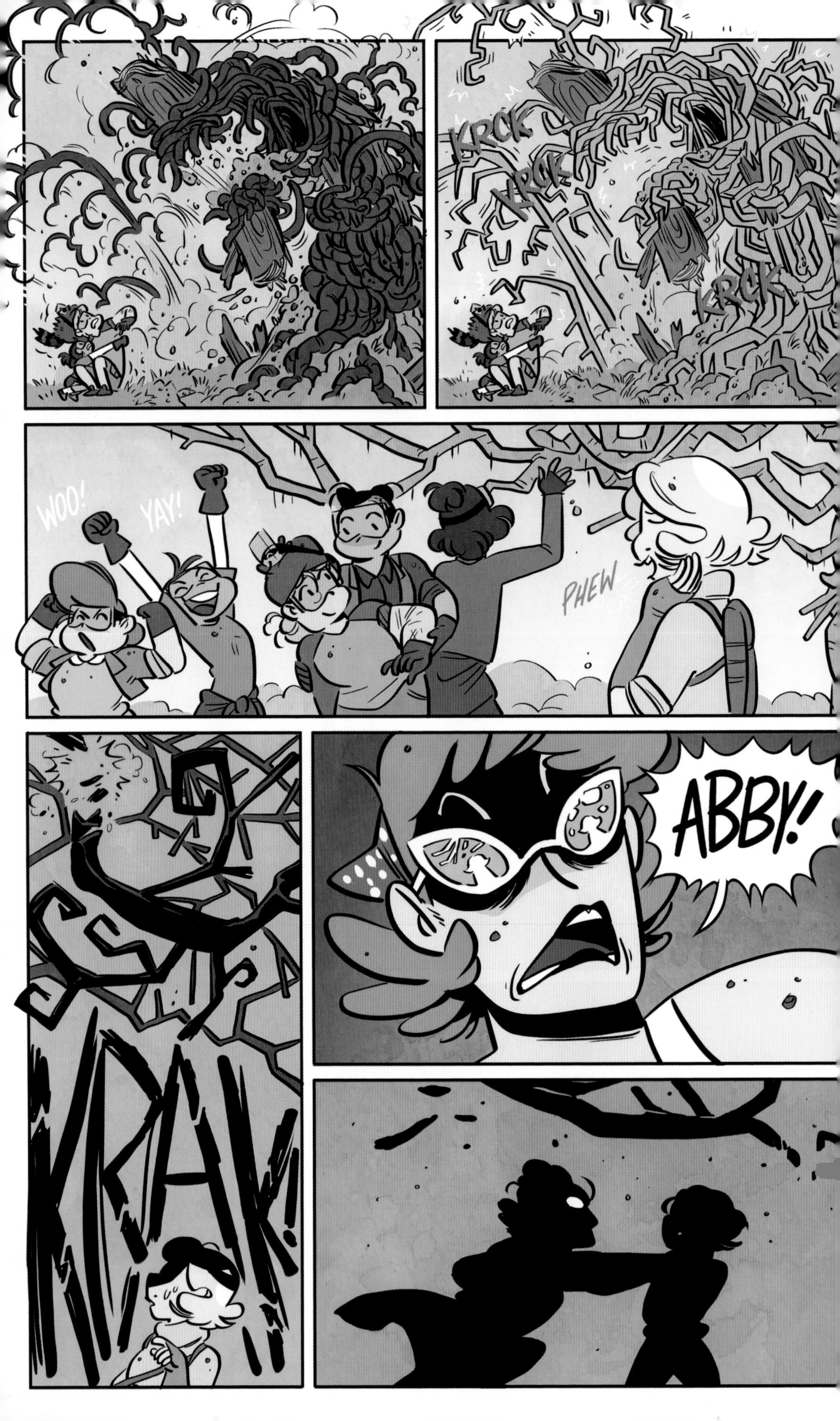
KRCK
KRCK
KRCK
WOO!
YAY!
PHEW
KRAK!
ABBY!

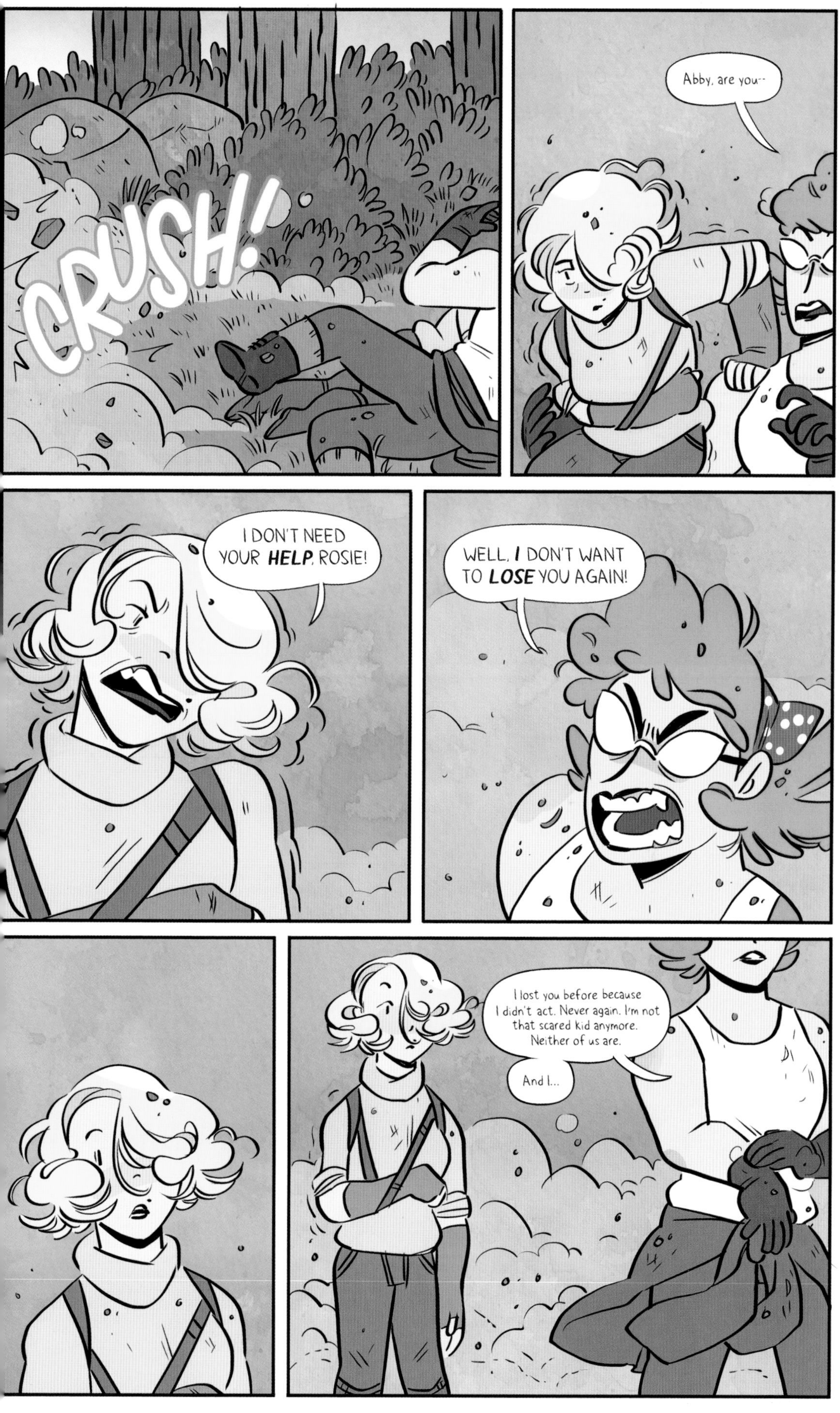
CRUSH!
Abby, are you--
I DON'T NEED YOUR HELP, ROSIE!
WELL, I DON'T WANT TO LOSE YOU AGAIN!
I lost you before because I didn't act. Never again. I'm not that scared kid anymore. Neither of us are.
And I...

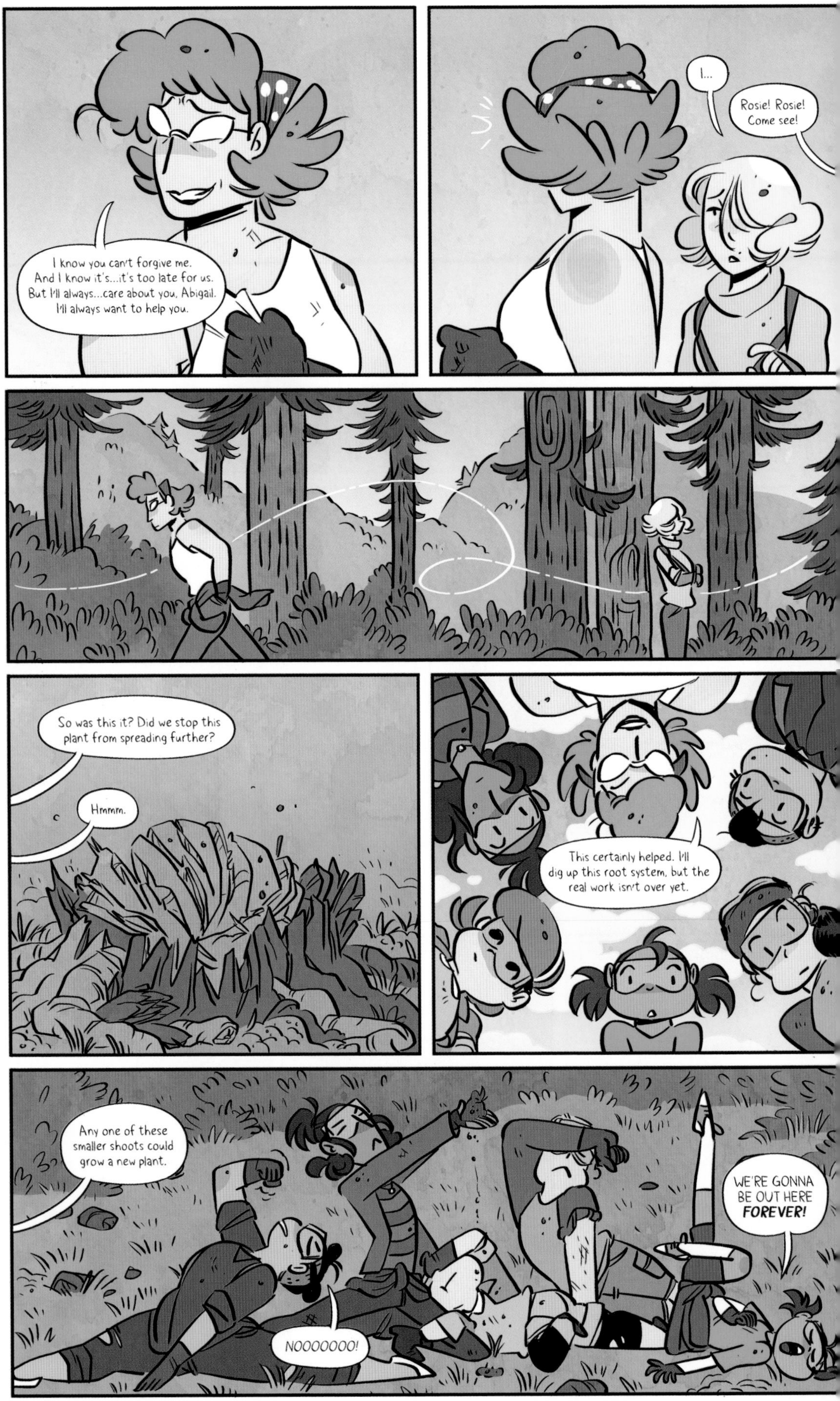
I know you can't forgive me. And I know it's...it's too late for us. But I'll always...care about you, Abigail. I'll always want to help you.
I...
Rosie! Rosie! Come see!
So was this it? Did we stop this plant from spreading further?
Hmmm.
This certainly helped. I'll dig up this root system, but the real work isn't over yet.
Any one of these smaller shoots could grow a new plant.
WE'RE GONNA BE OUT HERE FOREVER!
NOOOOOOO!

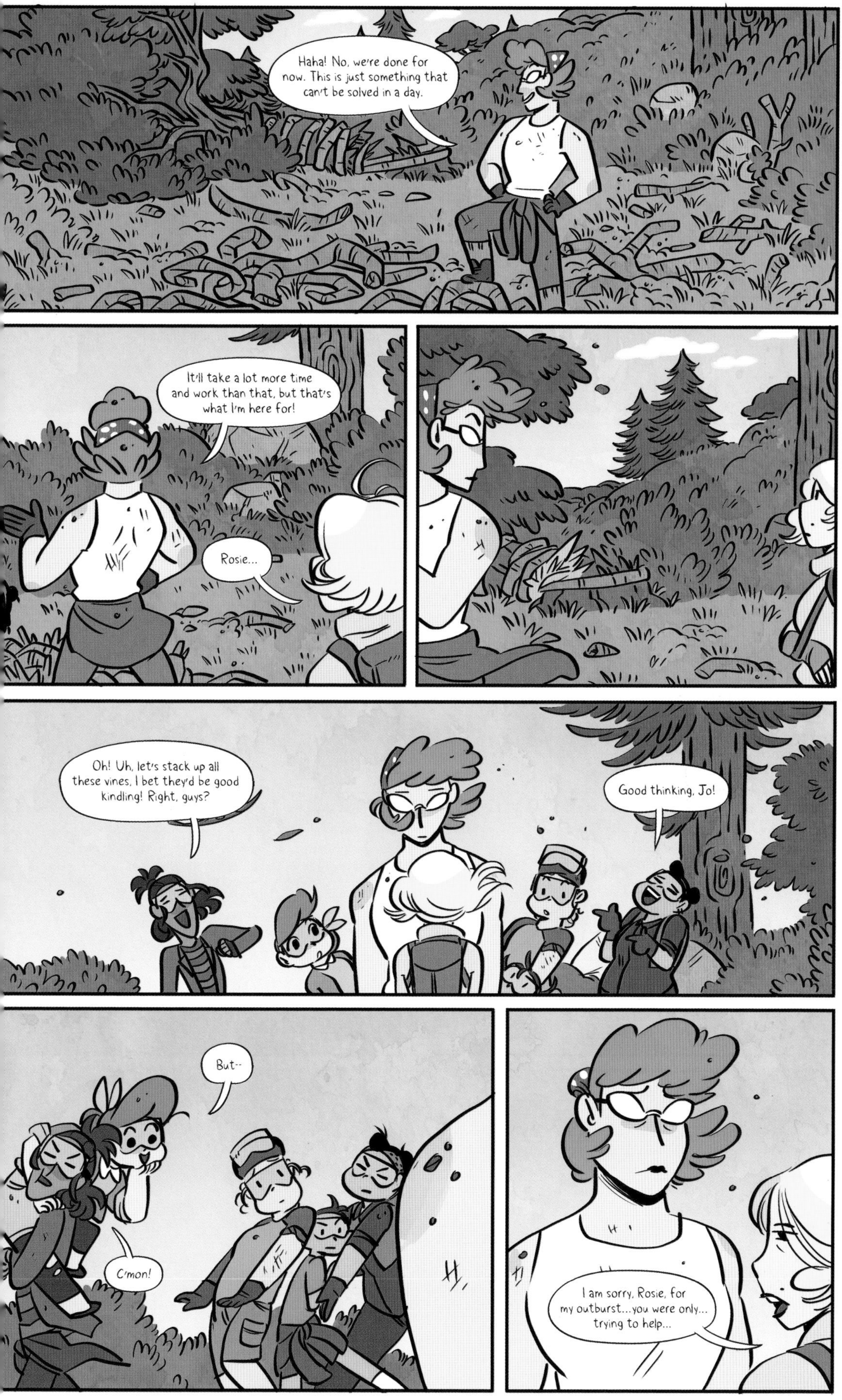

Haha! No, we're done for now. This is just something that can't be solved in a day.
It'll take a lot more time and work than that, but that's what I'm here for!
Rosie...
Oh! Uh, let's stack up all these vines, I bet they'd be good kindling! Right, guys?
Good thinking, Jo!
But--
C'mon!
I am sorry, Rosie, for my outburst...you were only... trying to help...

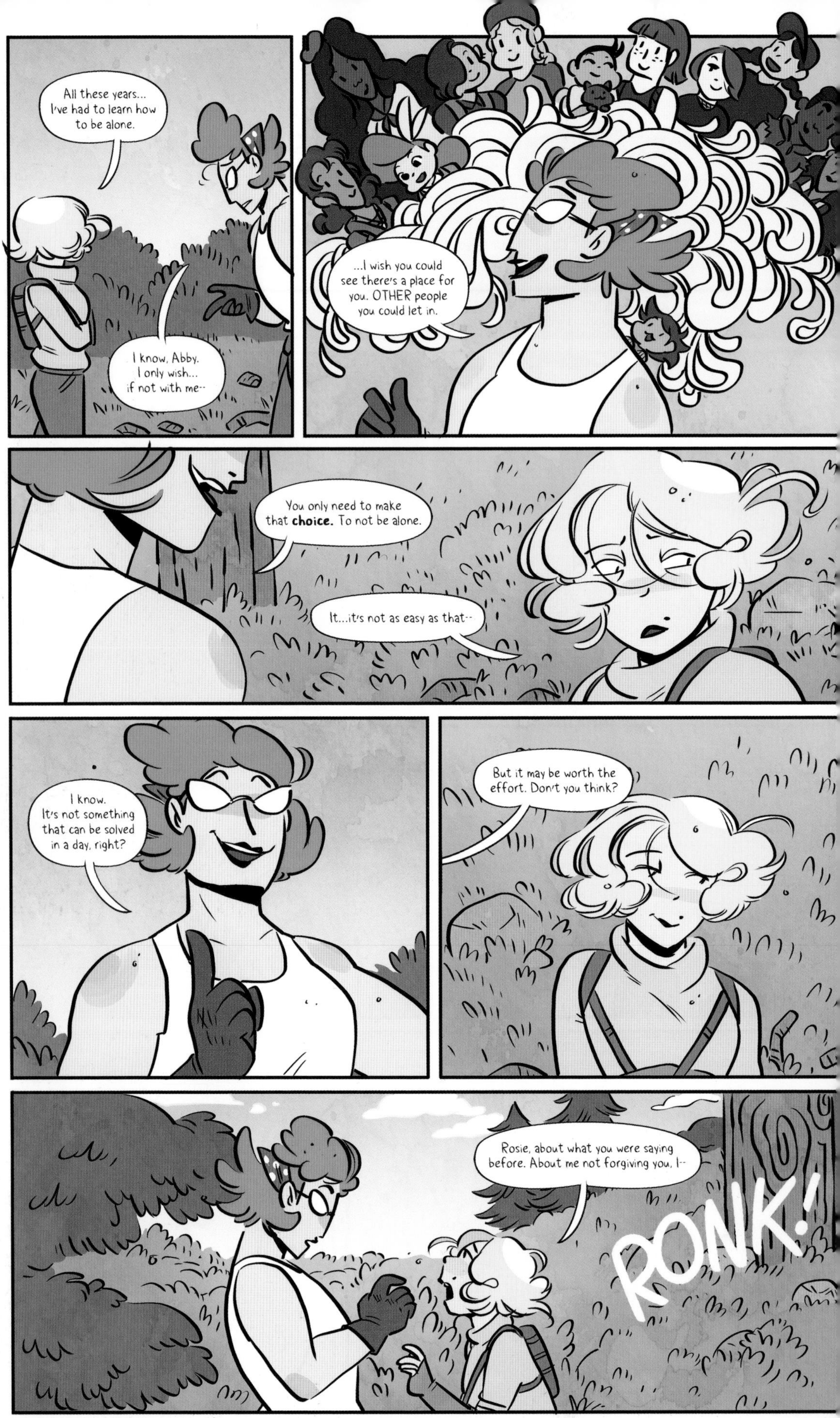
All these years... I've had to learn how to be alone.
I know, Abby. I only wish... if not with me--
...I wish you could see there's a place for you. OTHER people you could let in.
You only need to make that **choice.** To not be alone.
It...it's not as easy as that--
I know. It's not something that can be solved in a day, right?
But it may be worth the effort. Don't you think?
Rosie, about what you were saying before. About me not forgiving you, I--
RONK!

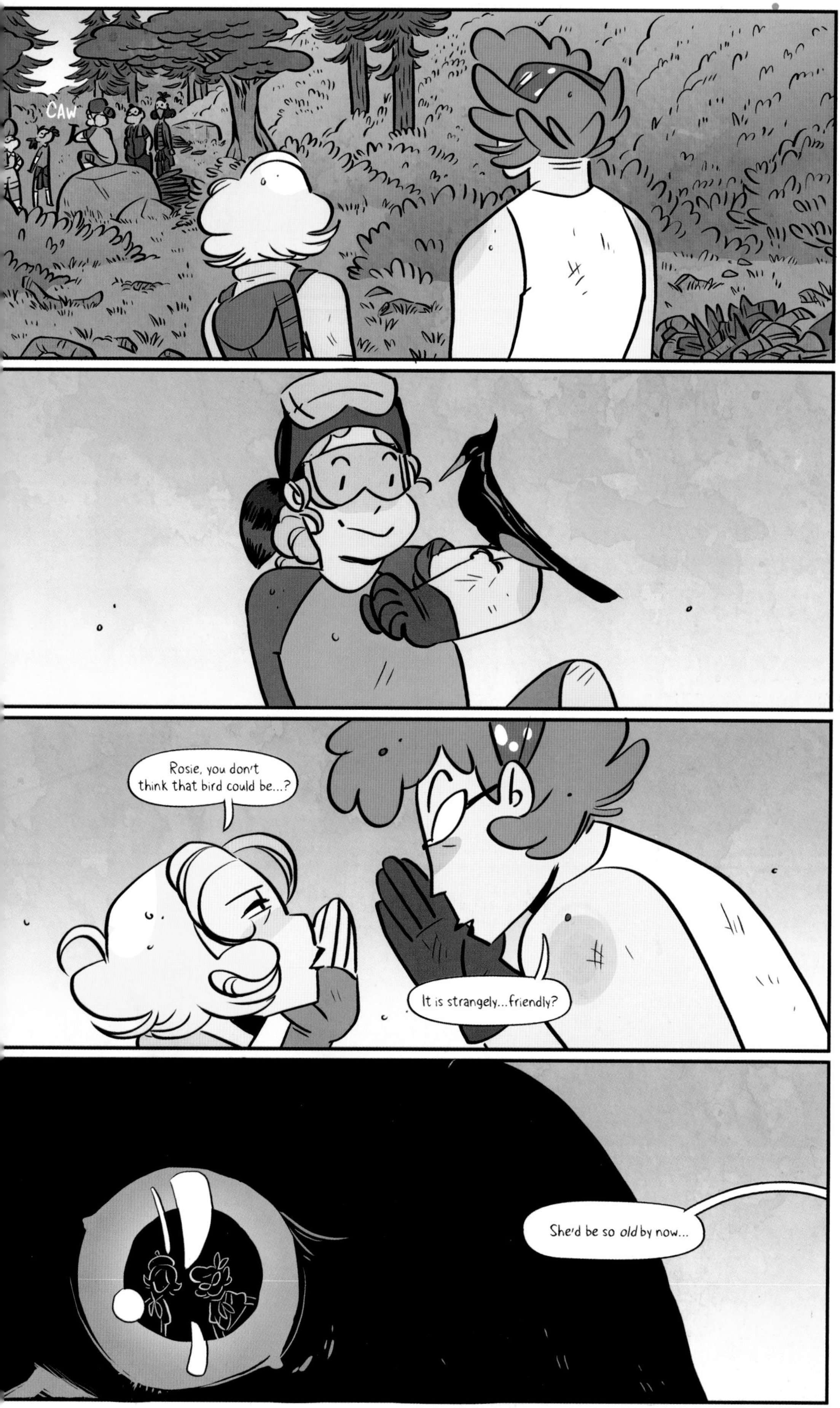
CAW
Rosie, you don't think that bird could be...?
It is strangely...friendly?
She'd be so *old* by now...

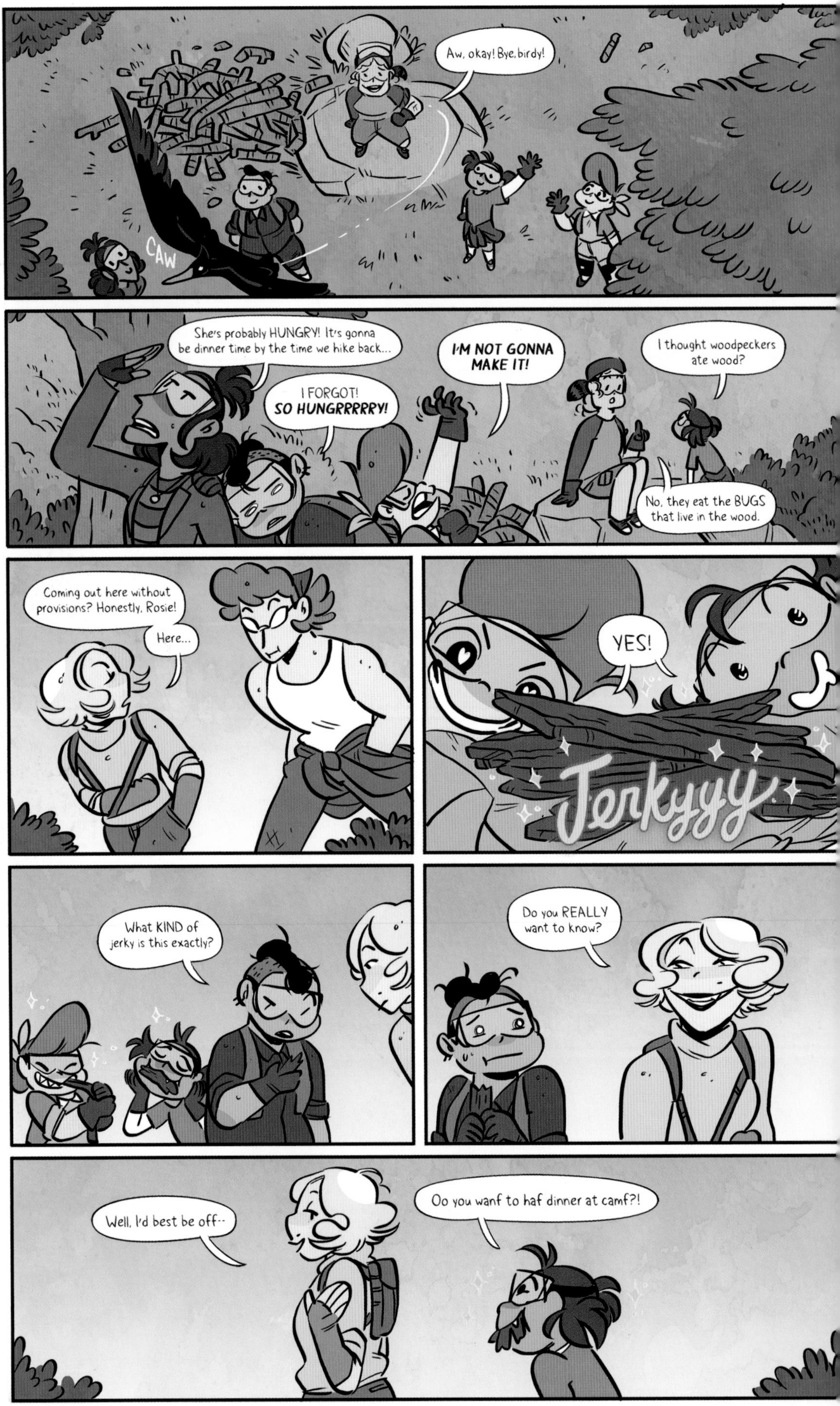
Aw, okay! Bye, birdy!
CAW
She's probably HUNGRY! It's gonna be dinner time by the time we hike back...
I FORGOT! SO HUNGRRRRRY!
I'M NOT GONNA MAKE IT!
I thought woodpeckers ate wood?
No, they eat the BUGS that live in the wood.
Coming out here without provisions? Honestly, Rosie!
Here...
YES!
Jerkyyy
What KIND of jerky is this exactly?
Do you REALLY want to know?
Well, I'd best be off--
Oo you wanf to haf dinner at camf?!

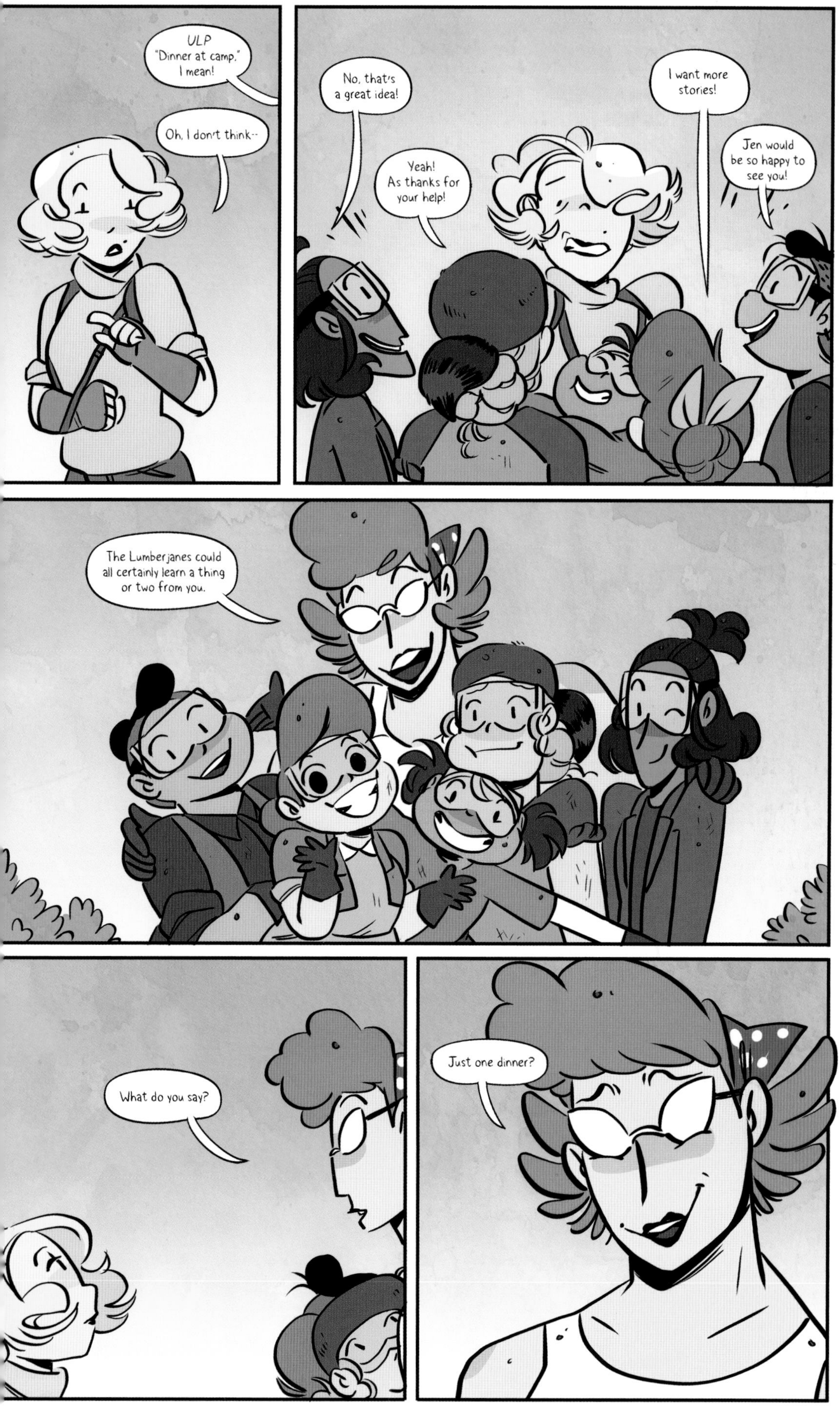
ULP
"Dinner at camp." I mean!
Oh, I don't think--
No, that's a great idea!
Yeah! As thanks for your help!
I want more stories!
Jen would be so happy to see you!
The Lumberjanes could all certainly learn a thing or two from you.
What do you say?
Just one dinner?

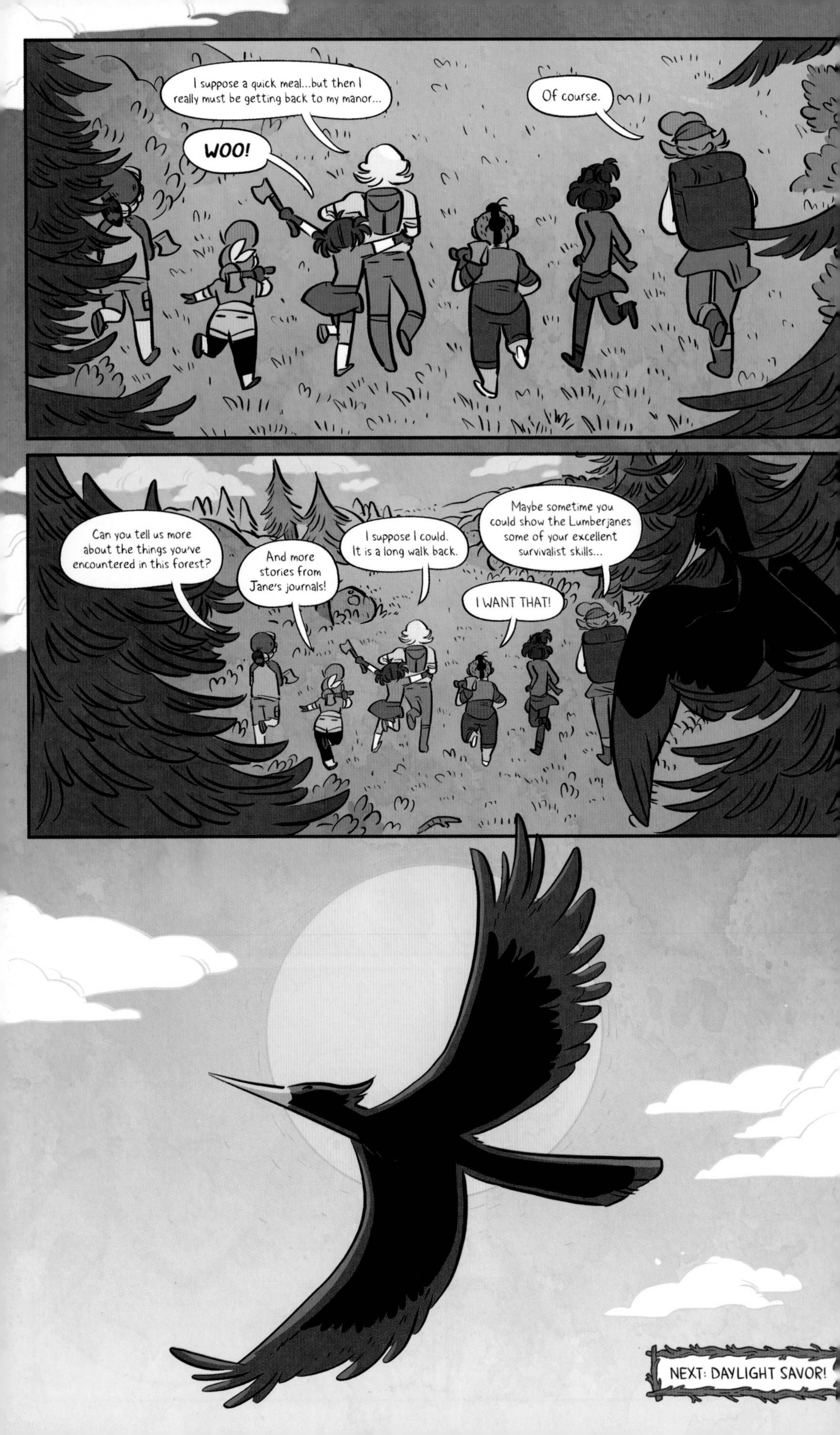
I suppose a quick meal...but then I really must be getting back to my manor...
WOO!
Of course.
Can you tell us more about the things you've encountered in this forest?
And more stories from Jane's journals!
I suppose I could. It is a long walk back.
Maybe sometime you could show the Lumberjanes some of your excellent survivalist skills...
I WANT THAT!
NEXT: DAYLIGHT SAVOR!

will co

The

It he   should be worn at camp
appearan   events when Lumberjanes
dress f   may also be worn at other
Further   ions. It should be worn as a
Lumber   the uniform dress with
to have   rect shoes, and stocking or
part in
Thiskv   out grows her uniform or
Hardc   her Lumberjane.
have   a she has
them   her
     her

The
yellow, short sl
emb
the w
choose
slacks,
made o
out-of-do
green bere
the colla
Shoes ma
heels, rou   ngs or
socks shou   th the shoes or wi
the uniform. Ne   , bracelets, or other jewelry do
belong with a Lumberjane uniform.

HOW TO WEAR THE UNIFORM

To look well in a uniform demands first of
uniform be kept in good condition—clean
pressed. See that the skirt is the right length for your own
height and build, that the belt is adjusted to your waist,
that your shoes and stockings are in keeping with the
uniform, that you watch your posture and carry yourself
with dignity and grace. If the beret is removed indoors,
be sure that your hair is neat and kept in place with an
inconspicuous clip or ribbon. When you wear a
Lumberjane uniform you are identified as a member of
this organization and you should be doubly careful to
conduct yourself in a way that will show everyone that
courtesy and thoughtfulness are part of being a
Lumberjane. People are likely to judge a whole nation by
the selfishness of a few individuals, to criticize a whole
family because of the misconduct of one member, and to
feel unkindly toward an organization because of the

The unifor
helps to cre
in a group.
active life th
another bond
future, and pr
in order to b
Lumberjane pr
Penniquiqul Thi   e Lady
Types, but m   es will wish to have one. They
can either b   , or make it themselves from
materials available at the trading post.

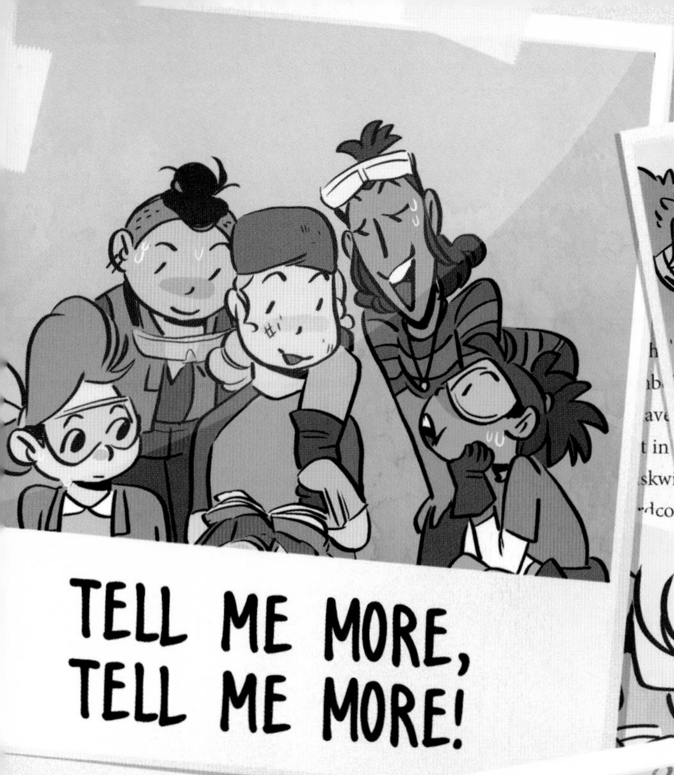
TELL ME MORE,
TELL ME MORE!

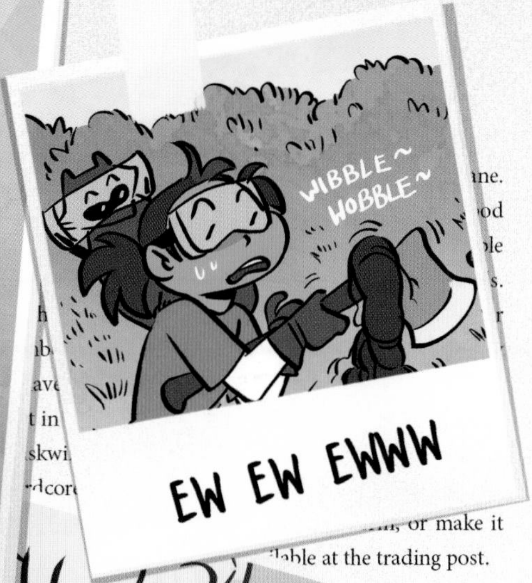
WIBBLE~
WOBBLE~
EW EW EWWW

ane.
od
ple
s.
...or make it
...lable at the trading post.

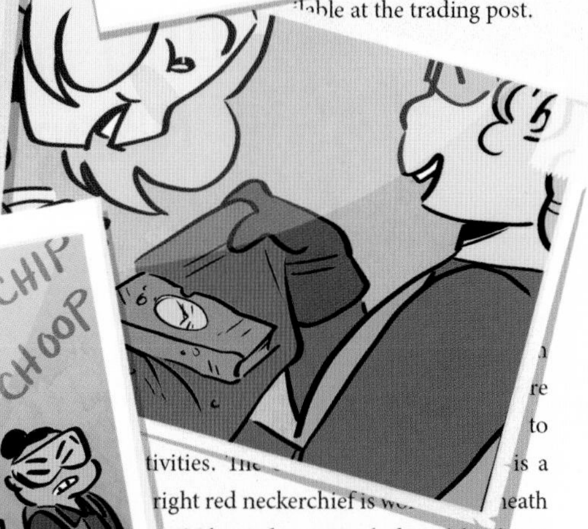

The Lumberjane uniform sh...
meeting...

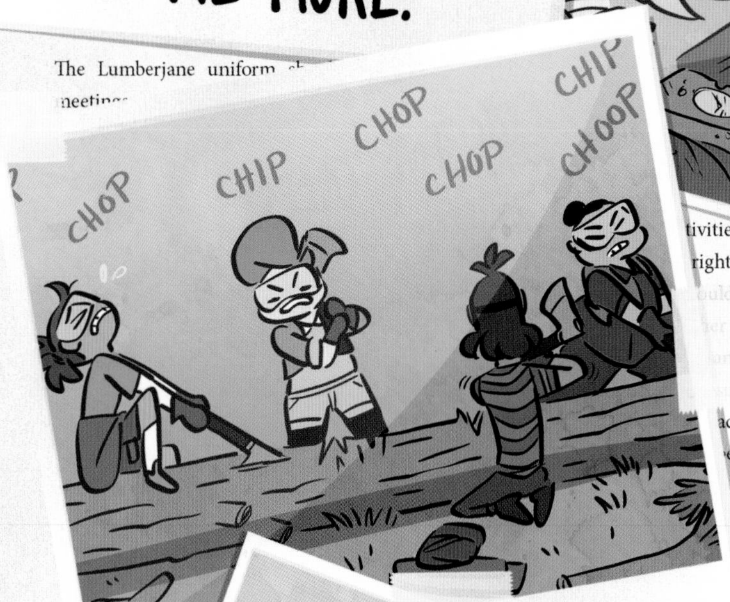
CHOP
CHIP
CHOP
CHOP
CHIP
CHOOP

...tivities. The ... is a
...right red neckerchief is wo... neath
...be tied in a simple friendship knot.
...lack or brown and should have flat
... a straight inner line. Stockings or
...nd in color with the shoes or with
...aces, bracelets, or other jewelry do not
...erjane uniform.

...WEAR THE UNIFORM

...orm demands first of all that the
...ood condition—clean and well
...t is the right length for your own
...e belt is adjusted to your waist,
...kings are in keeping with the
...our posture and carry yourself
...dignity and grace. If the beret is removed indoors, ...e sure that your hair is neat and kept in place with an inconspicuous clip or ribbon. When you wear a Lumberjane uniform you are identified as a member of this organization and you should be doubly careful to conduct yourself in a way that will show everyone that courtesy and thoughtfulness are part of being a Lumberjane. People are likely to judge a whole nation by the selfishness of a few individuals, to criticize a whole family because of the misconduct of one member, and to feel unkindly toward an organization because of the

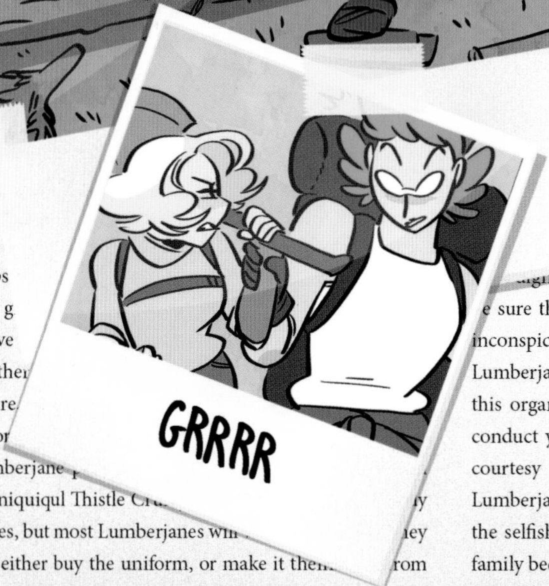
GRRRR

The ...
helps ...
in a g...
active ...
another...
future...
in or...
Lumberjane ...
Penniquiqul Thistle Cru... y
Types, but most Lumberjanes wi... ey
can either buy the uniform, or make it them... rom
materials available at the trading post.

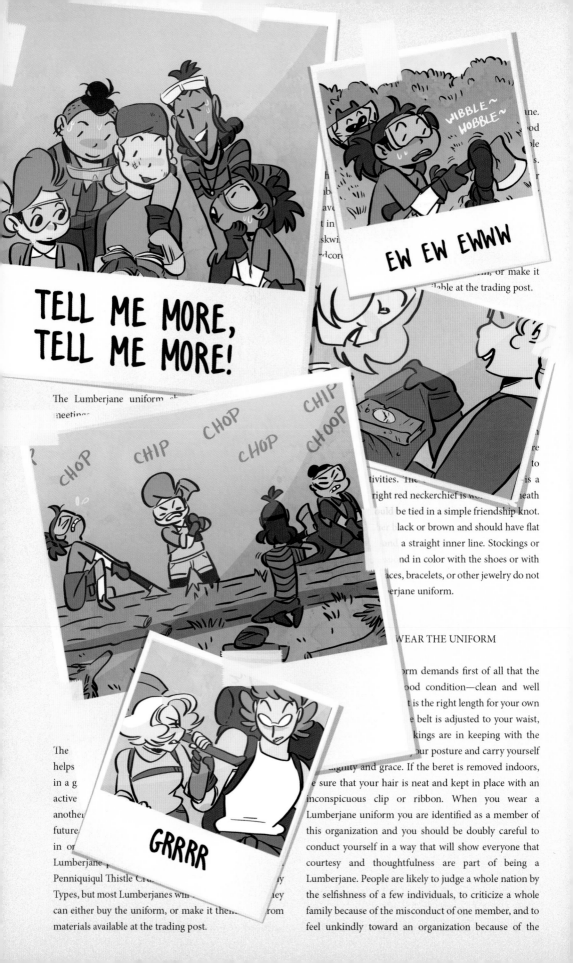

COVER GALLERY

Lumberjanes "Out-of-Doors" Program Field

FORESTRY IS THE BEST POLICY

"Go out on a limb!"

Learning to understand nature is a key aspect of the art of being a Lumberjane scout. But it is not—and never will be—simply about going out into the woods on a hike, or on a camping trip, or to a national park. The most important piece of this is not simply dabbling, or exploring an ecosystem with which you are unfamiliar. It is our hope that everything you discover and see while with the Lumberjanes or out in nature will be something that you learn and grow from—something that you carry with you, if only metaphorically. That you will hold the forests and fields in your heart wherever you go, and that you will work to protect them, both when you are with them, and when you are far away.

Forests, jungles, prairies, the tundra... these biomes support countless lives, from human beings, to birds and fish, to microbes and fungi. All ecosystems are precious, and all ecosystems deserve not just protection, but stewardship. This means learning about your local environment, and the people who manage and care for it. What work is being done to preserve and protect biodiversity, and to prevent pollution? What can you do to help on the ground level, even as a child? What policies and laws are being fought for and battled against to help to keep the woodlands, grasslands, shrublands, and swamplands healthy and thriving for generations to come? Listen to the people and communities who know these places best, and who have been doing this work for years and years. Never assume you know the whole truth, and always have your ears and heart open to learn more, and do more. It might seem that one Lumberjane wouldn't stand much chance against the threats of deforestation or pollution, but when we all work together, there is so much that we can do.

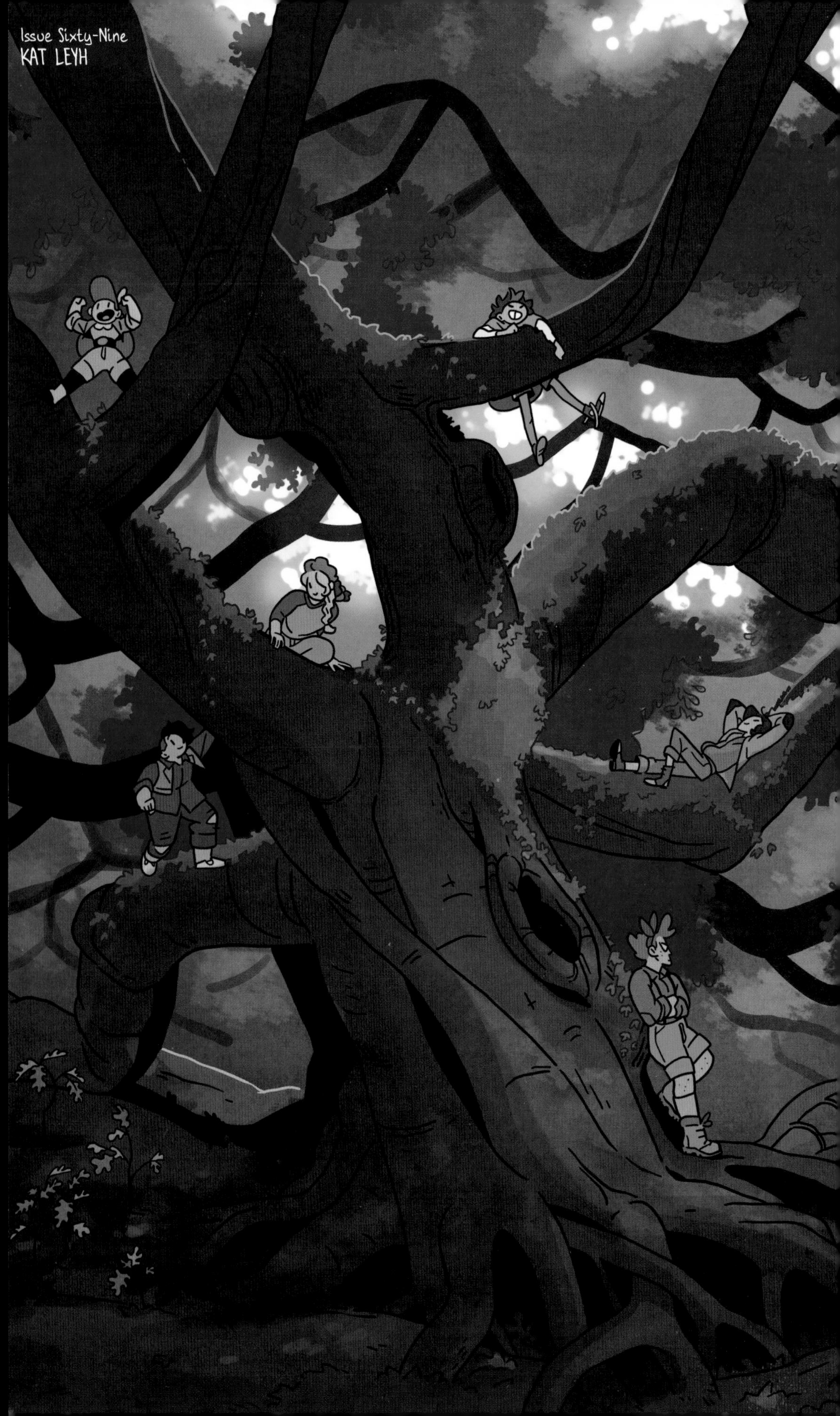
Issue Sixty-Nine
KAT LEYH

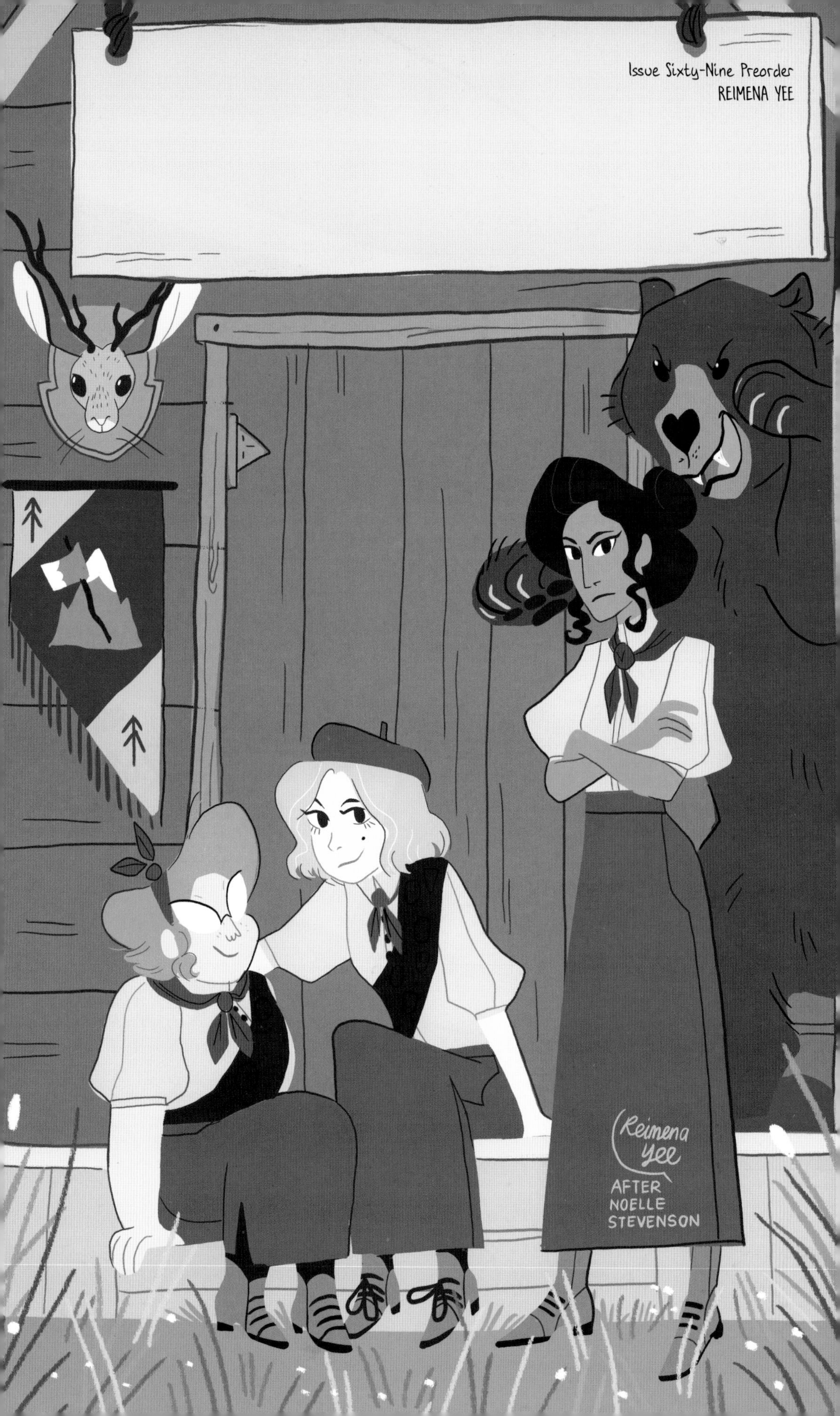
Issue Sixty-Nine Preorder
REIMENA YEE
Reimena Yee
AFTER NOELLE STEVENSON

Issue Seventy
KAT LEYH

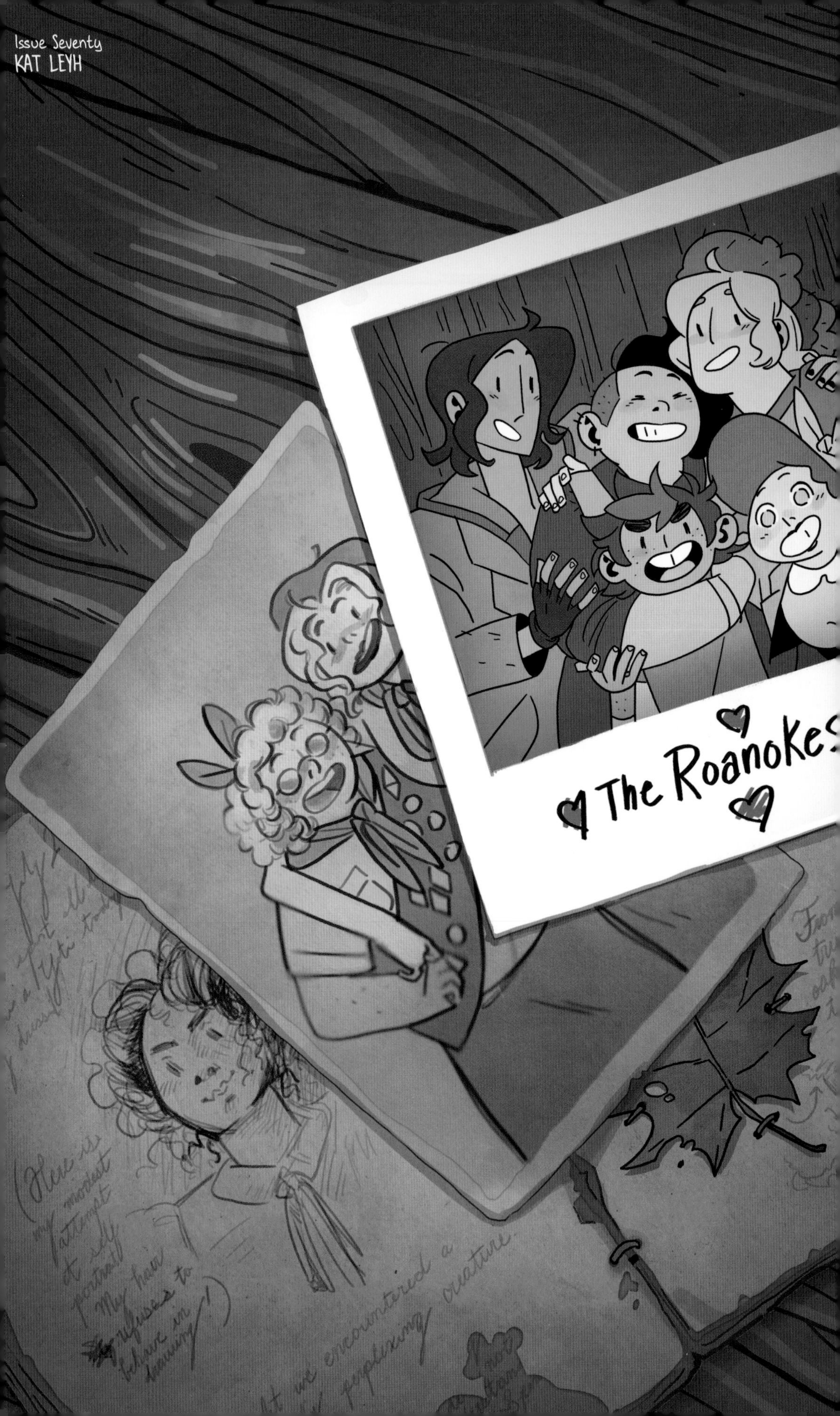
The Roanokes
(Here is my modest attempt at self portrait. My hair refuses to behave in drawing!)

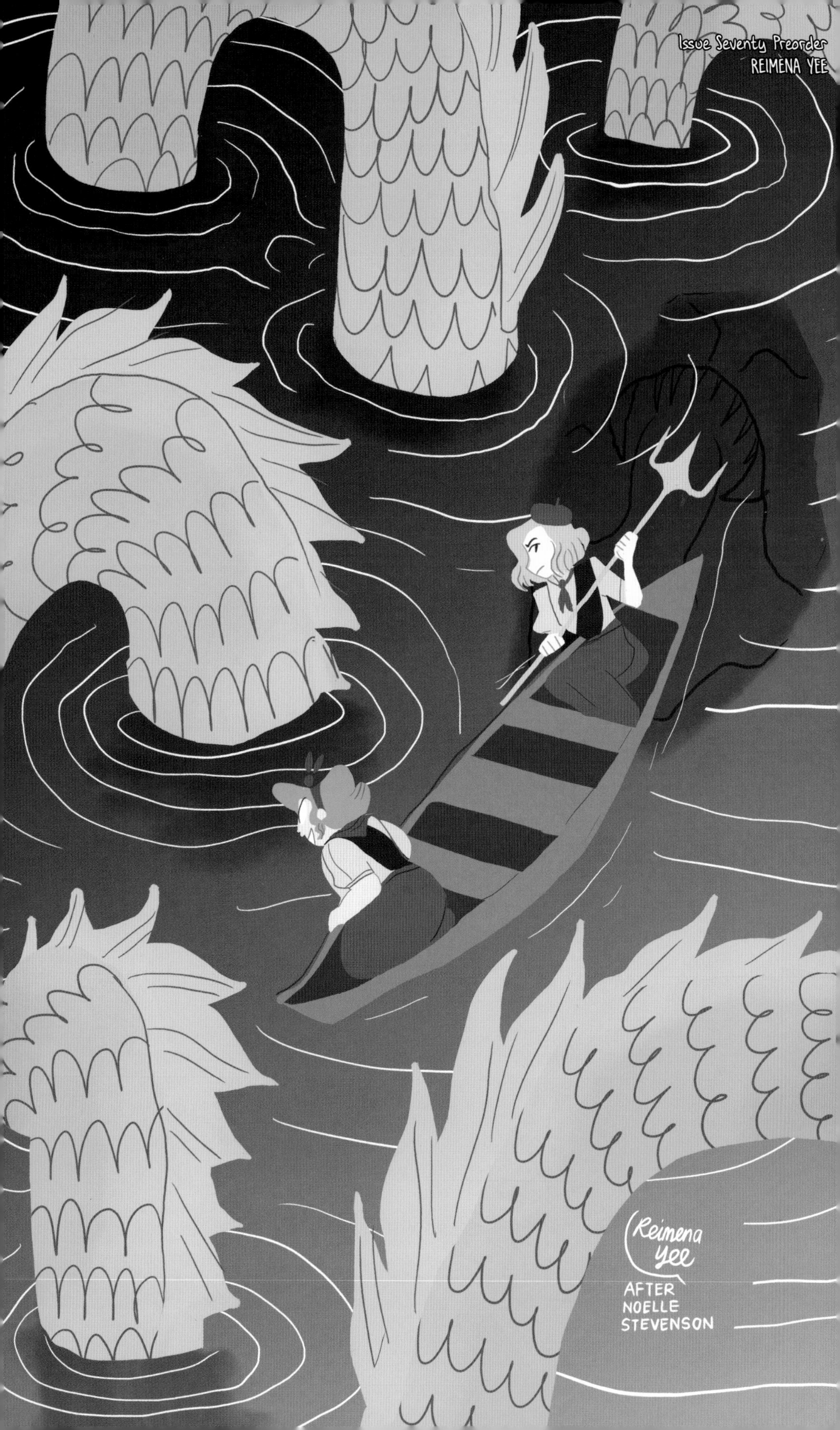
Reimena Yee
AFTER NOELLE STEVENSON

Issue Seventy Preorder
REIMENA YEE

Issue Seventy-One
KAT LEYH

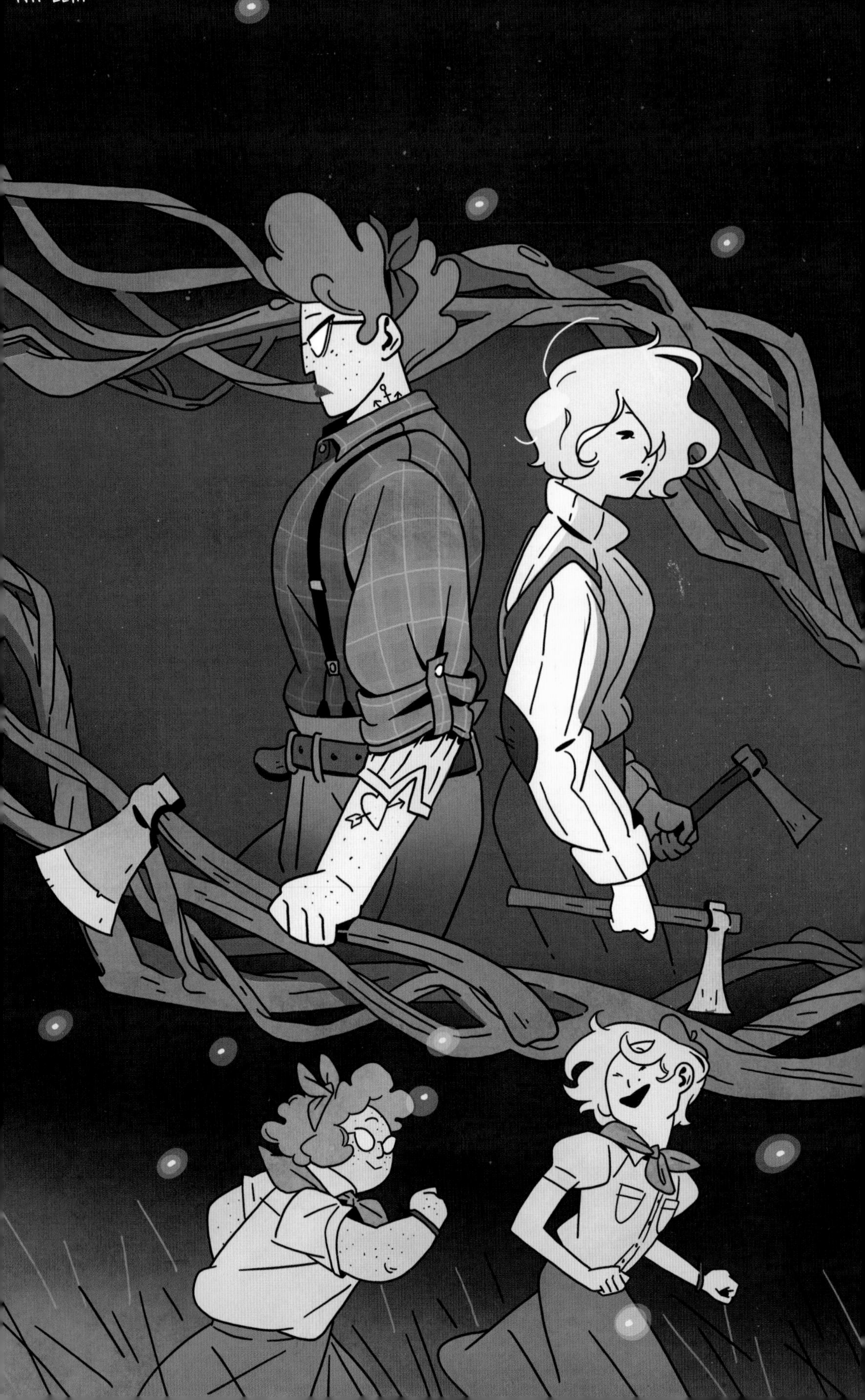

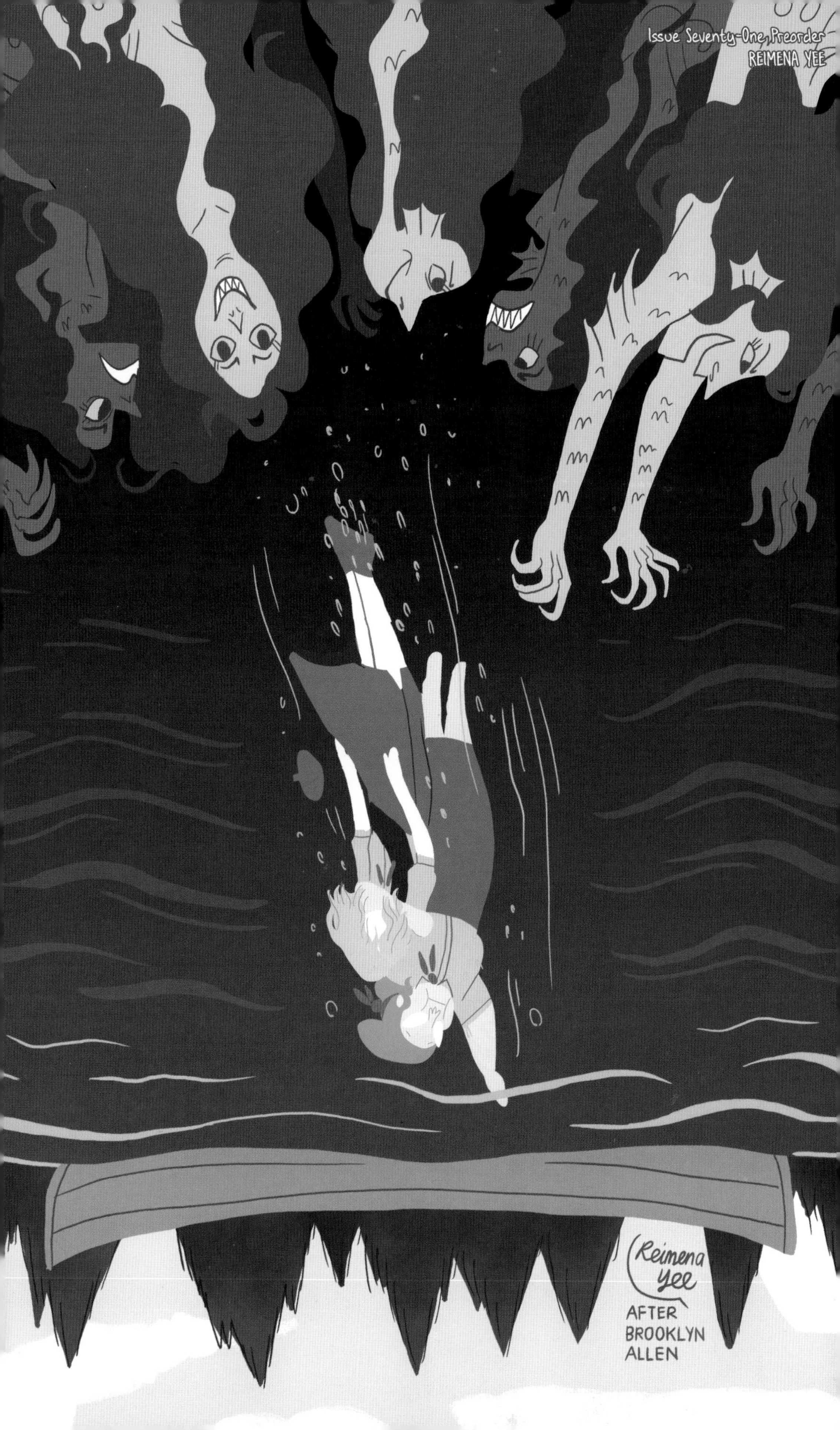
Reimena Yee
AFTER BROOKLYN ALLEN
Issue Seventy-One Preorder
REIMENA YEE

Issue Seventy-Two
KAT LEYH

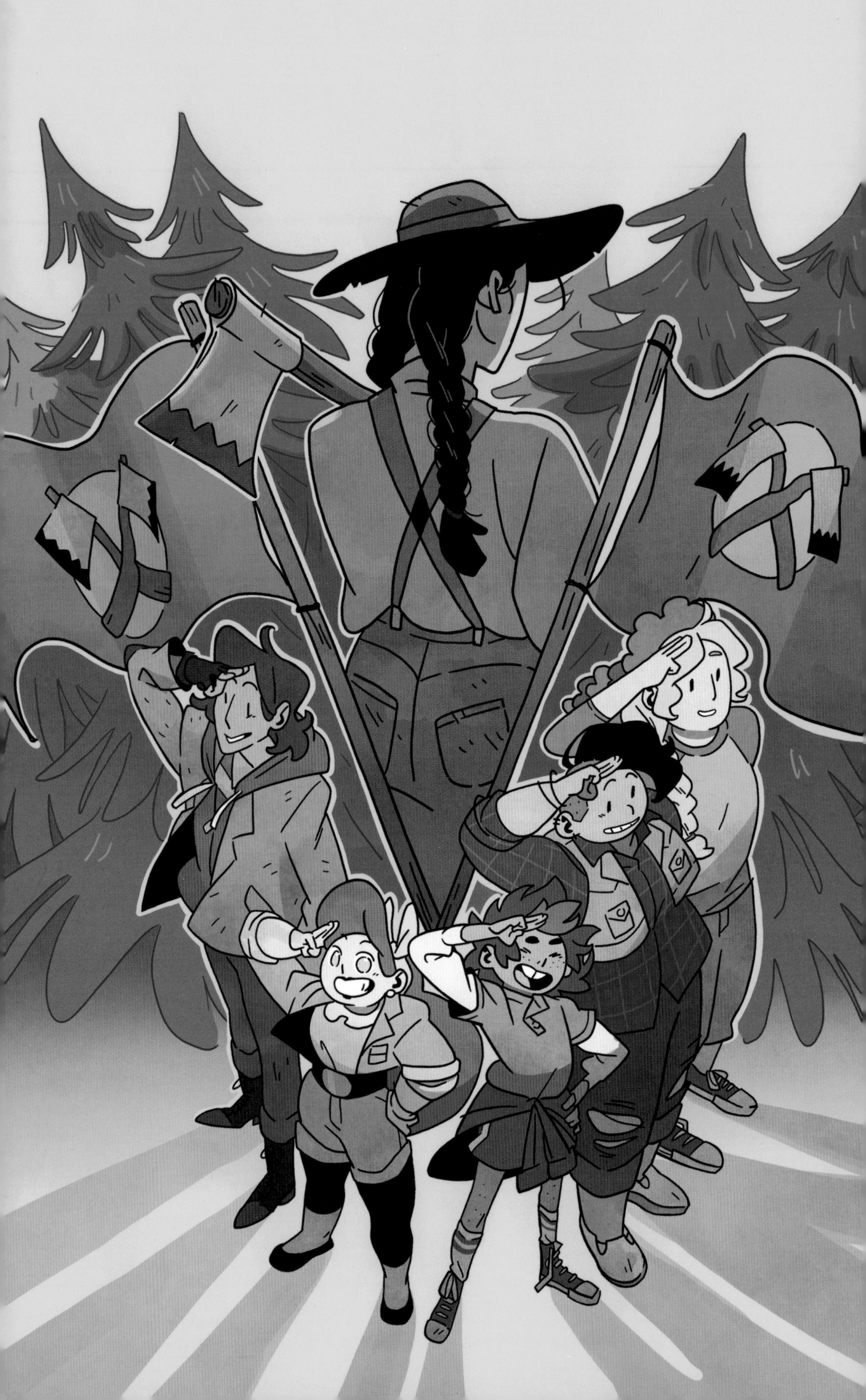

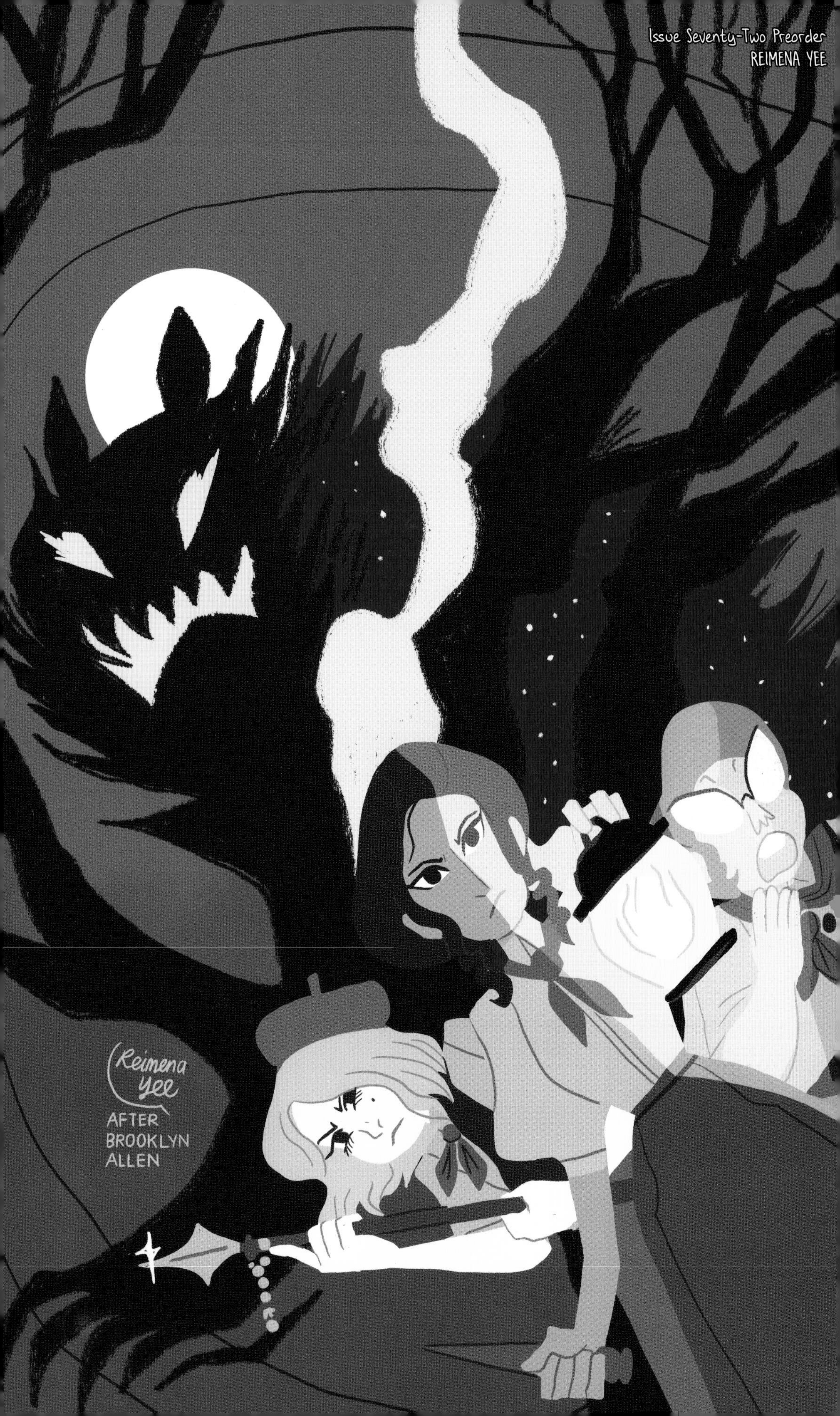
Reimena Yee
AFTER BROOKLYN ALLEN

DISCOVER
ALL THE HITS

STEVENSON · ELLIS · WATTERS · ALLEN
LUMBERJANES
BEWARE THE KITTEN HOLY
NEW YORK TIMES BESTSELLING SERIES
EISNER WINNER

Allison + Treiman + Cogar
GIANT DAYS
VOLUME ONE

From a writer of Disney's Moana
RIBON · FISH · PEER
SLAM!
VOLUME ONE

Hope Larson · Brittney Williams · Sarah Stern
GOLDIE VANCE
"Scoot over Nancy Drew..."
—Los Angeles Times
Volume One

JAMES TYNION IV · RIAN SYGH · WALTER BAIAMONTE
THE BACKSTAGERS

TYSON HESSE'S
DIESEL
IGNITION
Graphic Policy

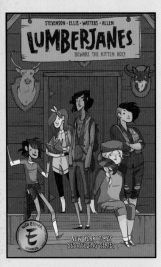

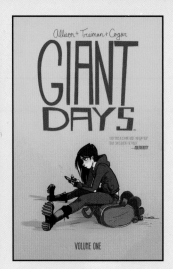

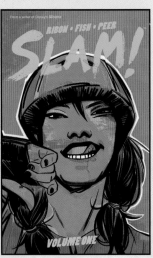

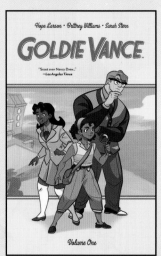

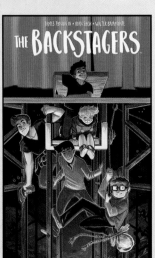

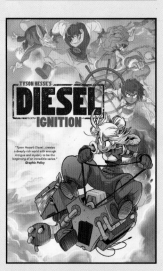

Lumberjanes
Noelle Stevenson, Shannon Watters, Grace Ellis, Brooklyn Allen, and Others
Volume 1: Beware the Kitten Holy
ISBN: 978-1-60886-687-8 | $14.99 US
Volume 2: Friendship to the Max
ISBN: 978-1-60886-737-0 | $14.99 US
Volume 3: A Terrible Plan
ISBN: 978-1-60886-803-2 | $14.99 US
Volume 4: Out of Time
ISBN: 978-1-60886-860-5 | $14.99 US
Volume 5: Band Together
ISBN: 978-1-60886-919-0 | $14.99 US

Giant Days
John Allison, Lissa Treiman, Max Sarin
Volume 1
ISBN: 978-1-60886-789-9 | $9.99 US
Volume 2
ISBN: 978-1-60886-804-9 | $14.99 US
Volume 3
ISBN: 978-1-60886-851-3 | $14.99 US

Jonesy
Sam Humphries, Caitlin Rose Boyle
Volume 1
ISBN: 978-1-60886-883-4 | $9.99 US
Volume 2
ISBN: 978-1-60886-999-2 | $14.99 US

Slam!
Pamela Ribon, Veronica Fish, Brittany Peer
Volume 1
ISBN: 978-1-68415-004-5 | $14.99 US

Goldie Vance
Hope Larson, Brittney Williams
Volume 1
ISBN: 978-1-60886-898-8 | $9.99 US
Volume 2
ISBN: 978-1-60886-974-9 | $14.99 US

The Backstagers
James Tynion IV, Rian Sygh
Volume 1
ISBN: 978-1-60886-993-0 | $14.99 US

Tyson Hesse's Diesel: Ignition
Tyson Hesse
ISBN: 978-1-60886-907-7 | $14.99 US

Coady & The Creepies
Liz Prince, Amanda Kirk, Hannah Fisher
ISBN: 978-1-68415-029-8 | $14.99 US

BOOM! BOX™

AVAILABLE AT YOUR LOCAL COMICS SHOP AND BOOKSTORE
To find a comics shop in your area, visit www.comicshoplocator.com
WWW.**BOOM-STUDIOS**.COM